D0045309

Dashiell Hammett
Man of Mystery

Also by Sally Cline

BIOGRAPHIES and BOOKS ABOUT LIFE WRITING

Life Writing: Biography Autobiography and Memoir: A Writers' and Artists' Companion (with Carole Angier)
Lillian Hellman: Memories and Myths (forthcoming)
Zelda Fitzgerald: The Tragic, Meticulously Researched Biography of the Jazz Age's High Priestess
Radclyffe Hall: A Woman Called John

LITERARY NONFICTION BOOKS

Writing Literary Nonfiction: A Writers' and Artists' Companion (with Midge Gillies)
Couples: Scene from the Inside
Lifting the Taboo: Women, Death and Dying
Women, Celibacy and Passion
Just Desserts: Women and Food
Reflecting Men at Twice their Natural Size (with Dale Spender)

EDITED BOOKS

As Series Editor:
Crime and Thriller Writing: A Writers' and Artists' Companion (Michelle Spring and Laurie King)
Writing Children's Fiction: A Writers' and Artists' Companion (Yvonne Coppard and Linda Newbery)
Writing Historical Fiction: A Writers' and Artists' Companion (Celia Brayfield and Duncan Sprott)

As Editor:
Memoirs of Emma Courtney (Mary Hays)

FICTION

One of Us Is Lying

Dashiell Hammett
Man of Mystery

A Biography by
Sally Cline

ARCADE PUBLISHING
NEW YORK

Arcade Publishing books may be purchased in bulk at special discounts for sales promotion, corporate gifts, fund-raising, or educational purposes. Special editions can also be created to specifications. For details, contact the Special Sales Department, Arcade Publishing, 307 West 36th Street, 11th Floor, New York, NY 10018 or arcade@skyhorsepublishing.com.

Arcade Publishing® is a registered trademark of Skyhorse Publishing, Inc.®, a Delaware corporation.

Visit our website at www.arcadepub.com.

10 9 8 7 6 5 4 3 2 1

Library of Congress Cataloging-in-Publication Data

Cline, Sally.
  Dashiell Hammett : Man of Mystery / Sally Cline.
    pages cm
  ISBN 978-1-61145-784-1 (hardback)
  1. Hammett, Dashiell, 1894–1961. 2. Authors, American—20th century—Biography. 3. Detective and mystery stories, American—History and criticism. I. Title.
  PS3515.A4347Z59 2014
  813'.52—dc23
  [B]
                                        2013041870

Printed in the United States of America

To

BA SHEPPARD *with great love*

*"It's raining here but only on the streets where
they don't know you are coming"*
(Dash to Lily)

Many hugs to

Theo, Marmoset, Arran,

and

Esme, Vic, Soren

CONTENTS

ACKNOWLEDGMENTS

My most important acknowledgments are to Jo Hammett Marshall, Dashiell Hammett's daughter; Julie Rivett, his granddaughter; and Peter Feibleman, Lillian Hellman's heir and companion.

Jo and Julie in Los Angeles and Peter in Barcelona and New York fed me, drove me, talked for hours to provide me with crucial information. Together with Susan Feibleman and Rita Wade, Hellman's secretary, they facilitated my access to Hammett and Hellman's wide network of friends and relations with unstinting generosity.

In grounding my Hammett material, I have had invaluable help from biographer Richard Layman and gained illuminating insights from writers Carl Rollyson, Mark Estrin, Deborah Martinson, Joan Mellen, Tenneti Nagamani, Alice Griffin, Geraldine Thornsten.

Biographer Alice Kessler-Harris warmly invited me to join her on a Thelma-and-Louise road trip to Hardscrabble Farm and Katonah, where Kathy and George Piccorelli painstakingly showed us around Hammett's last home.

I am immensely grateful to the eminent Hammett biographer, novelist Diane Johnson, and her assistant, Ashley Ratcliffe. Diane turned my Paris trip into a triumph, spending hours in reflective talk, then phoning and emailing me.

I have received several significant awards for which I am indebted: the Society of Authors Foundation Award; an International Hawthornden Fellowship (thanks to Drue Heinz and the Board); an Andrew Mellon Fellowship at the Harry Ransom Humanities Research Center, followed subsequently by university archive privileges for three further years; a three-year Arts Council, England, Research Bursary (special thanks to Lucy Sheerman) to travel and work in Europe and the United States; Royal Literary Fund Writers Fellowships and Advisory Fellowships (great thanks to Steve Cook, Eileen Gunn, David Swinnerton), which meant I could write without financial insecurity.

Many archives and institutions have supported me, but five were outstanding: the Harry Ransom Center, Texas University, Princeton University, Stanford University, Wisconsin Historical Society, and Tulane University.

For several years' support at the Harry Ransom Center I thank Thomas Staley, Richard Oram, Cathy Henderson, Debbie Armstrong, Bridget Gayle Ground, Richard Workman, Helen Adair, Jill Morena, Kurt Heinzelman, Tara Wenger, Lisa Talen, Pete Smith, Tom Best, Lynn Maphies, Debbie Smith, Bob Fuentes, Lauren Gurgulio, Gil Hartman, Linda Briscoe Myers, the patient archivist Bob Taylor, and especially my close friends Pat Fox and Margi Tenney, who helped with texts, photos, and university materials and shared food, drink, and heartening talks.

In Austin, I thank Martha Campbell for thirteen years' accommodation and bountiful breakfasts; the Compuzone team for computer help; my friends Susan and Larry Gilg for stimulating discussions, computer loans, and two years' elegant accommodation.

At Princeton University (Rare Books Department), I thank Charles Greene and AnnaLee Pauls for research help, illustrations, and photocopying and my friend Meg Rich, former Reference Librarian/Archivist, who, together with Stuart Rich, shared expertise, homegrown food, and accommodation. In Princeton, I am indebted to Kathleen Petersen and Peter Hahn for the tour around Hammett's house, offered on the day they were moving out!

At Stanford University (Special Collections Department), I thank Robert Trujillo, Maggie Kimball, and particularly Polly Armstrong. Peter Stansky's knowledge about the William Abrahams collection was invaluable, as was his comradeship. I was appreciative of support from Sally and Michael Stillman in Palo Alto, David Fechheimer, the City Lights Bookstore in San Francisco, and Don Herron for his walking tour of every Hammett site.

In Madison, Wisconsin I am indebted to Harry Miller at the Historical Society and to Susan Bernstein for feeding me!

In New Orleans at Tulane University, I thank Susan Tucker, Leon Miller, and the staff of Sophie Newcomb College and Research Center, the archivists at the New Orleans Official City Archives and New Orleans Notarial Archives, journalists on the *Picayune State Item* and the *New Orleans Times*, and Wayne Everard in the Public Library for his unfailing helpfulness and taped materials. I thank Christina Hernandez at Newcomb College Center for Research on Women, Susan Lawson, Kenneth Holdrich, and writer Curtis Wilkie for afternoon tea and talks. My guide-informant, Pattie Elliott, and my researcher, Helena Shoh, were invaluable.

I was accompanied on my research trips to New Orleans, Cleveland, Ohio, Charleston, South Carolina, Savannah,

Georgia, and Austin, Texas, by my knowledgeable and indefatigable travel companion, art historian Anne Helmreich, who hosted me through libraries, archives, and photo collections and offered food and accommodation. In Cleveland, I was helped by Jean Piety and Elmer Turner at the Cleveland Public Library; Donald Burdick at the Cleveland Research Center, the Cleveland Western Reserve Historical Society; William C. Barrow in Special Collections, Cleveland State University Library; Jo Ellen Corrigan of the *Plain Dealer*; and the late Walter Leedy, founder of America's most amazing postcard collection.

In New York, for interviews and information, I thank the late Barbara Hersey, the late Milton Wexler, the late Robbie Lantz, Denis Asplend, Joy Harris, Mike Nicholls, Richard Poirier, and for several years' accommodation and support, Anne Gurnett and Jonathan Bander. In Canada, I thank Alisa Weyman, Cheryl Lean, Graham Metson. In Demopolis and Birmingham, for information on the Hellman Wyler Festival, I thank Cathy Wyler and William Gantt.

As the former writer in residence at Anglia Ruskin University, Cambridge, I thank RLF Fellows Anne Rooney, Francis Spufford, Caron Freeborn; colleagues Colette Paul, Rowlie Wymer, John Gardener, Val Purton, Holly Clover, Rod McDonald (for a nearly impossible cassette tape repair); and former colleagues John Davies and Rebecca Stott. I thank Arbury Court Library, Cambridge Central Library, and Cambridge University Library.

For UK writing retreats in Sennen Cove, Cornwall, I thank Richard and especially Tracy Baker for reading drafts and for their kindness at the Atlantic Lodge.

For support of many kinds, I thank the Cambridge Women Readers, the late Jean Adams at Sunset Heights, Davina Belling, Sally Lawrence, Raymond Cormier, Alan French, Jane

Jaffey, Christina Johnson, Stella King, Josie McConnell, Judy Jefford, Alison West, Olga Foottit, Mary Milne, Richard Nunan, and Andrew Lownie.

Most especially, I thank the late Joel Jaffey, Dr. Kate Grimshaw, Dr. Tom Alderson, Dr. Leonard Shapiro, Dr. Paul Flynn, Professor Peter Weissberg, Professor Morris Brown, and Professor Martin Bennett.

For audio transcriptions, textual permissions, and secretarial help, I thank Stephanie Croxton Blake, Angela North, Rachel Senior, Rebecca North, and Miranda Landgraf. For tape editing, I thank the BBC's Amanda Goodman. For an immaculate bibliography, I thank Sally and Chris Peters. For skilled editing, reading the whole book, and wise words, I thank Chris Carling. For thirty-five years' encouragement and counsel, I thank Kathy Bowles. For reviewing twenty chapters of a messy first draft, I thank former editor and friend Sheila McIlwraith.

Huge gratitude to biographers Millicent Dillon, chapter one's first reader, and Marion Elizabeth Rodgers, who turned around a difficult chapter, and for boosts and backing, I thank writer friends Frankie Borzello, Katharine McMahon, Midge Gillies, Carole Angier, Neil McKenna, Michelle Spring, Yvonne Coppard, Hilary Spurling, and Cliff McNish.

Thank you, Barbara Levy, former literary agent and friend, who supported this book's early stage challenges for six years.

Thank you, Rachel Calder, my good friend and literary agent, who has given her talents in creative planning of this biography. Thank you, Cal Barksdale, my editor at Arcade (Skyhorse), who has given the manuscript his detailed attention. Illustrative help beyond any call of duty goes to Sally Nicholls, my photo researcher.

Without the unstinting professional and personal help of Angie North and Rosemary Smith, this biography could not have been properly accomplished. As always, Angie has organized and cared for my house, cat, finance, and post and dealt calmly with every emergency in my frequent research absences. She has also sorted, transcribed, and retyped hundreds of Hammett's penciled notes. I have relied again on the intellectual understanding and prodigious talents of my researcher Rosemary Smith, who organized endnotes, proofread, cut, and reformatted the entire book twice.

That IT wizard Glenn Jobson offered constant imaginative meticulousness to a nontechnical author.

My family and extended family have again backed me affectionately. First and most appreciated, my daughter Marmoset Adler, who has provided ideas, cuttings, photocopies, good listening ears, and constant encouragement. My stepdaughter Carole Adler van Wieck spent hours in New York sharing memories of her friend Cathy Kober, Arthur Kober, and Lillian Hellman. My late stepdaughter Wendy Adler Sonnenberg offered me witty Hammett/Hellman anecdotes. The late Larry Adler's reminiscences of Hellman and Kober were invaluable, as were his powerful memories of Hammett and the McCarthy blacklisting. Vic Smith and Rick Wilson and my late daughter-in-law Laura Williams offered consistent support. My beloved Aunt Het (the late Harriet Shackman) enlightened every day. I wrote the last chapter the night before her funeral, as my gift to her. I thank cousins Jane, Paul, and Kathy Shackman for their loving support; and cousins Jonathan, Joan, Noam, and Danya Harris, who again fed me throughout the project. The young are amazingly helpful . . . thank you Esme and Soren, and, of course, my grandsons Theo and Arran.

My closest writer friend, novelist Jill (Ruby) Dawson, has inspired, stimulated, and propped me up.

I have been sustained for thirty-five years by Ba Sheppard, who, for this book, traveled with me to Barcelona for research, then read every word of the final draft before helping cut and edit. In Hellman's words to Hammett, thank you for the short cord that the years of love and support make into a rope.

***

The author and publisher would like to thank the following for their kind permission to reproduce quotations:

The Harry Ransom Center, The University at Austin, for permission to publish quotations from manuscripts in their Dashiell Hammett Collection, including various Hammett/ Knopf correspondence, and from their Lillian Hellman Collection.

Penguin Random House, for permission to quote from the following:

Dashiell Hammett, *The Maltese Falcon*, Orion Books, London, 2002, first published by Alfred A. Knopf, New York, 1930.
Dashiell Hammett, *The Thin Man*, Knopf, New York, 1934; Penguin, Harmondsworth, 1935.
Dashiell Hammett, *The Big Knockover*, ed. with introduction by Lillian Hellman, Vintage, New York, 1989.

Excerpt from *Dashiell Hammett: A Life* by Diane Johnson, copyright © 1983 by Diane Johnson. Used by permission of Random House, an imprint of The Random House Publishing Group, a division of Random House LLC. All rights reserved.

The Estate of Dashiell Hammett for permission to quote from the following works by Dashiell Hammett: unpublished manuscripts; *The Maltese Falcon; The Thin Man; The Big Knockover;*

from *Selected Letters of Dashiell Hammett 1921–1960*, ed. Richard Layman with Julie M. Rivett.

The Estate of Dashiell Hammett and Jo Hammett, for permission to quote from Jo Hammett Marshall, *Dashiell Hammett: A Daughter Remembers*, ed. Richard Layman and Julie M. Rivett.

The author would like to thank Sherri Feldman and Jennifer Rowley at Random House for their very hard work, Jane Gelfman of Gelfman Schneider Literary Agents, Joy Harris of the Joy Harris Literary Agency, and most especially Adam Reed at the Joy Harris Literary Agency for enormous help in securing textual permissions.

Every effort has been made to contact copyright holders, but if any have been inadvertently overlooked, the author would be glad to hear from them.

INTRODUCTION

In five groundbreaking novels published in five years, one novella, and more than sixty short stories, Dashiell Hammett (1894–1961) singlehandedly changed the face of detective fiction. He influenced Raymond Chandler and Ross MacDonald and other writers, but more significantly, he transformed and subverted the detective novel form by his moral vision, propelling the mystery genre into literature.

He altered the method by which crime fiction worked, removed most of the detecting, and changed his few clues from dropped gloves to lies told.

Hammett's books, which attempt to get at the truth behind crimes only to find there isn't any one "truth," offer the view that the world is ruled by meaningless, blind chance. Mysteries did not usually traffic in philosophy, but Hammett's near nihilism resulted in crime stories that came to be viewed as literary classics.

Yet, there is an irony in a writer whose creed is one of moral ambiguity and random results choosing to write detective fiction, which is usually predicated on linear clues and an orderly progression of facts.

Similarly paradoxical is the fact that the places where Hammett was happiest were Pinkerton's, where rules were preeminent; the army (in which he enlisted for the second time when far too old), with its military regimentation; and prison, with its punishing discipline. This may be related to Hammett's gender preferences.

Though he seduced women, used whores, and was committed to Hellman as a social and occasionally sexual companion, he liked men. He favored male society. He sought male company, understood male loyalty, wrote about male betrayal. When men betrayed women, it was trivial; when men betrayed men, it was treachery.

A former private eye with Pinkerton's National Detective Agency, Hammett was the inventor of the hard-boiled detective, first the short, fat Continental Op, then the lean, tall Sam Spade, immortalized by Humphrey Bogart in the screen version of *The Maltese Falcon*, the best-known American crime novel of all time. His final invention, the glamorous figure of the Thin Man, was also made iconic with the aid of Hollywood.

Often identified with his hard-boiled heroes, Hammett, in fact, was an invalid most of his life, stricken early with tuberculosis from which he never recovered. He denied and refused to discuss this lifelong disease, which dramatically affected his masculine role. His status as a sick man occurred during a period when masculinity was defined by his peers Hemingway and Fitzgerald as tough and healthy. Men could be drunks. Men could be mentally disturbed. Men could be angry and violent. But constant sickness was not part of the masculine brief. Male invalids were seen as literally invalid. In this biography, I consider the consequences of Hammett's struggle with sickness and the violation of his masculine identity.

A complex and mysterious man, Hammett published no novels after 1934 until his death in 1961. For twenty-seven years, he suffered from a writer's block that maimed and shamed him. As he produced less, he drank more, partly to deny his inability to write, partly to mask his tubercular image.

What was behind that silence? Did he want to write a different kind of book from his characteristic brand of crime, and did he find himself unable to do so? Or was he content to mentor Hellman in her playwriting, or even write parts of them, as some critics believe? Hammett never apologized, never explained, but never stopped writing. On his deathbed, he was still clutching *Tulip*, his unfinished autobiographical manuscript. Ironically, as new fictional ideas dried up, Hollywood turned his old novels into films and radio series, so that his fame increased during his inexplicable literary silence.

Hammett's personal life was paradoxical. The tall, thin man, laid-back and handsome like his later heroes, created many famous mysteries but also left several behind: enigmas often woven around an amalgam of veracity and deceit.

Like his tough investigators, Hammett walked the mean streets in search of honesty. He never played anyone's game but his own. He never faked, he never stooped. According to his daughter Jo, he never told a lie in his life (though she said he did confess to her that he had once lied to Bennett Cerf), and friends of Lillian Hellman report that Hellman told them he never lied. But he never told anyone much about anything. His inner world was private, a challenge for biographers. He was also on occasion extremely violent, revealing a frighteningly angry underside to a sensitive, quiet, often reclusive artist.

Curiously, this man who valued honesty admired attractive women who lied outrageously. Chief among them was Lillian

Hellman, who was accused of fraudulence and sued for lies and spent thirty years as Hammett's companion, fabricating and reinventing his life and hers. I have not only analyzed his domestic and sexual life with Hellman and unpicked fact from myth but have also produced new material on Hammett's strange but enduring relationship with his separated wife, Jose Dolan, and his two daughters, Mary and Jo. Previously, there has been scant insight and no worthy investigation into these relationships. Though largely an absentee husband and father, with a lifelong companion, he nevertheless remained devoted to his family, and they to him.

I discuss Hammett's controversial political activism against the most shaming erosions of civil liberty in American history. Together with Hellman, Hammett was a commanding presence in American political life. The two of them stood up for their beliefs during the late 1940s and the Red Scare of the 1950s, when they fought the McCarthy witch hunts. When summoned before Joseph McCarthy's committee, the Senate Permanent Subcommittee on Investigations, throughout the proceedings Hammett not only refused to name names, he refused to give even his own name.

Naming and not naming are a big part of this narrative. Hammett, who answered to several names himself (Dash, Sam, Dashiell, Hammett), was as cagey about his identity as he was savagely protective of his privacy. He signed himself in an early story as Peter Collinson, which in the underworld slang of the time meant "Nobody's Son." Hammett's first detective is the nameless hero known merely as the Continental Op. He gave later detectives names like Sam, his own first name, and other characters were named for people he admired, such as a former fellow patient nicknamed Whitey. Curiously, he signed several letters with the names of his characters, like Spade, Nicky, and Whitey, as if reluctant to use his own.

I decided to use the names he himself used or was called by others: "Sam" for Hammett as a boy and young man until he begins to publish under the name Dashiell Hammett; "Dash" if in affectionate relationship to Lily or his friends; and "Dashiell Hammett" or "Hammett" when talking about his work.

Lillian Hellman presented the same problem. I chose to use "Lily" for Hellman as a child and adolescent and as an adult if called that by her friends; "Lil" (her husband Arthur Kober's name for her) during her marriage to Kober; and "Lillian Hellman" or "Hellman" for her professional writing.

Hammett's policy of never naming names was an integral part of his ethical approach to his life and work. Hammett's moral vision became the stuff of literature, but set against that were his alcoholism, his tuberculosis, and his determination to avoid self-exploration.

Who wouldn't want to write or read a book about that man?

PART ONE
EARLY YEARS, 1894–1922

CHAPTER 1

In Baltimore on September 12, 1918, the bells of the City Hall rang out one hundred times. Military bands marched through the streets, and youths bursting with hope sang the "Star-Spangled Banner" out of tune. Maryland's men were invited to join up and throw in their lot with their countrymen. Every man between the ages of eighteen and forty-five had to register for the draft. Patriotic parades turned the draftees into heroes. Register today, they were told, hold a gun by Christmas. Prison awaited evaders. [1]

America had entered World War I the year before. President Woodrow Wilson had made a slow transition from neutrality to belligerence in the conflict that had wracked Europe for three years. It was, however, belligerence with a high moral purpose. He had told Congress, when asking a special joint session to declare war on Germany in a speech in early April 1917: "The world must be made safe for democracy." The declaration of war passed on April 6, and two months later, the first registration for the draft was held. The events in Baltimore on September 12, 1918, marked the third registration. Men in Baltimore were edgy, tense, excited.

One young Baltimore man had already made his patriotic gesture by joining the army three months earlier, in June 1918. He was twenty-four-year-old Sam Hammett, a private detective known as a Pinkerton man.

Sam was not new to Baltimore. He had lived there since he was a child of seven and understood the city, whose distinctive feature was said to be its "feeling for the hearth," its homeowners' pride in their residences. Yet the young Hammett did not consider himself a proud son of the city, unlike thirty-eight-year-old Baltimore writer H. L. Mencken, who would one day publish him. [2]

When America entered the war, Sam, an operative with Pinkerton's National Detective Agency, still lived with his parents, Annie Bond and Richard Thomas Hammett, and Annie's mother, Mrs. Dashiell, in her rented three-story row house at 212 North Stricker Street near Franklin Square in the western end of Baltimore. Most people on Sam's street were white. They rented or took in boarders. His grandmother had a boarder named Mrs. Crosswell. Taking in Mrs. Crosswell had improved the family's poor finances. Black families with poorer finances lived in alleys nearby. Most houses on Stricker Street belonged to hardworking tailors, clerks, or watchmen married to seamstresses, dressmakers, or, at the top end, salesladies. Sam's grandmother was a saleslady. It was a morning job, and later, in November 1924, Hammett told readers of the mystery magazine *Black Mask*, edited by that other, older Baltimore writer, H. L. Mencken, that his grandmother went to the movies every afternoon.

These ordinary people, among whom Hammett grew up, had tawdry ornaments in the crowded parlor. They had a privy in the yard, but little privacy. Six blocks south, on Hollins

Street where H. L. Mencken lived, most houses were owned by middle-class residents who had paintings in their front rooms. They had privacy.

From his bedroom window growing up, Sam could watch the orphan asylum on the opposite side of the cobbled street. He was not an orphan, although later he fell in love with one and married her. He had an older sister, Reba (Aronia Rebecca), born February 8, 1893, and a younger brother, Dick (Richard Thomas, Junior), born September 7, 1896.[3] Sam disliked Dick and tolerated Reba. He saw himself apart from them, apart from everyone, an only child with a single love, a sick and saintly mother who coughed incessantly. Annie Bond Dashiell had married Richard Hammett in 1892. She was a private nurse when she was well enough, but most times she was not. Sam adored her. He tried to help her when she was ill. He watched over his mom and watched out for his dad's bad temper.

The older Sam Hammett had been trained to watch. Watching people was his job as a detective. It was a silent, secretive occupation that matched his personality. He was inquisitive, adventurous, quick, and clever. He had been a Pinkerton for three years and thought the job suited him, where nothing else had. He could not count the number of times he had been fired. His father did, though—aloud, in front of the family. His father did not think Sam was either quick or clever. Father and son were not friends.

Sam was a loner; he was cynical and somewhat antisocial. To his own surprise and his mother's grief, the young man joined up. It was June 24, 1918. Private Samuel Hammett had taken leave of his parents, taken leave from Pinkerton's. His father thought the boy had taken leave of his senses.

Richard Hammett was both wrong and right.

Sam took the army exams, scored the second highest IQ of all the men tested, trained for three weeks, and became Private

Hammett of the 34th Company, 9th Training Battalion, 154th Depot Brigade. Sam was proud of his service. He was assigned to a motor ambulance company at Camp Mead, Maryland, only fifteen miles from his Stricker Street home and was surprisingly enthusiastic. He was expected to transport wounded soldiers who had returned from service in Europe and who brought with them Spanish influenza, which killed more soldiers during the war years than did bullets.

Recalling this later as the writer Dashiell Hammett, he says in his most famous novel, *The Maltese Falcon*: "He knew then that men died at haphazard and like that, and lived only while blind chance spared them." [4]

Within months of enlisting, Sam overturned his ambulance when it was full of wounded men. He was so traumatized by the accident that he resolved never to drive again, a resolve he kept for most of his life. Subsequently stricken by Spanish flu, he lay in an army hospital for three weeks, unable to sit up, wracked with coughing, and shaking with a high fever. His influenza developed into bronchial pneumonia, which, in a hospital rampant with the disease, led to tuberculosis, although in his case the tuberculosis was almost certainly contracted from his beloved mother. It was a crippling illness that he bore until his death.

His service record is studded with a history of constant chronic respiratory disease. Ironically, every promotion he received in the army was swiftly followed by another bout of illness.

On Valentine's Day, 1919, Sam was promoted to private first class. Nine days later, he was back in the hospital. Another diagnosis suggested acute bronchitis, catarrhal bilateral inflammation of the bronchial tubes. Both lungs were affected. The medical staff treated him as best they could. He left the hospital on February 27 and tried to resume his duties with a vigor he did not possess.

On April 23, 1919, he was promoted to sergeant. He felt dragged down by sickness, and May 29 saw him back in the infirmary. After that, the army finally admitted his disease was untreatable. The verdict: the tuberculosis was disabling. Sam would be forced to leave the service marked as a disabled veteran, although only a young man. In legal terms, he was a mere 25 percent disabled, worthy of a one-off fifty-dollar statutory award. In reality, he was a wreck. He would need considerably more than that, for never again would he be fit for any work that was physically rigorous. At twenty-five, he was an invalid. His immediate discharge was recommended and processed. Doctors offered him no hope that his condition would improve. He weighed barely 140 pounds. He had loved the army, loved being with ordinary men, for, though he had already attracted the attention of girls, it was men he was at home with.

His sudden disease was not the first time Sam had been struck down by events over which he had no control. Frightening episodes in his childhood had already prepared him, offered him a way of thinking to deal with those events. His daughter Jo Hammett suggests that, "As a boy, he had wanted to find the Ultimate Truth—how the world operated. . . . There was no system except blind chance."[5]

Hazard scarred Sam's earliest years as he watched his father, Richard Thomas, fail repeatedly, unable to hold a job, and even resort to taking Sam out of school to pull his weight. Did Richard Hammett think that a boy of fourteen could help repair family finances? He kept moving from one town to another, and his family followed. What else could they do? A farm in Saint Mary's County, Maryland; Philadelphia lodgings; a stint in Baltimore, worse than before. The three Hammett children never knew where they would live next, how long it would last, what job Pa would do. Pa drank and kept drinking. He abused his wife, found new women, became a tyrant.

Sam's home life was shaped by his mother's illness, his father's infidelity, poverty, turbulence, and violence. A boy with low expectations, facing a torpedoed life. He had few friends and felt he needed none. Sam developed a creed of stoical silence. He would need it to combat an unruly world. All he could do was to play at indifference. All he could count on was chaos and chance.

What was it like on that farm in St. Mary's County, Maryland, between the Potomac and Patuxent Rivers, where Sam was born and the first life-changing events took place?

CHAPTER 2

Chaos, quarrels, crowds, and noise. These were Sam's first impressions of Hopewell and Aim, his grandfather Samuel Biscoe Hammett's tobacco farm in St. Mary's County, Maryland, where his parents had lived since their marriage and where he was born on May 27, 1894.

At birth, baby Sam weighed eleven pounds. At age thirty, Hammett, who had been stick-thin for years, looked back in wonder at the chunky child. He gave Jo, his younger daughter, a photo of her papa aged about nine months, so sturdy, so large that his delicate white nightgown with the prissy Peter Pan collar looked absurd. The rosy, robust infant's sharp eyes stared wide-eyed at the camera without a hint of the frailty to follow. He was chubby but not always cheerful. He did not like loud sounds or noisy people. As he grew older, he became reclusive and sensitive, and the household's disorder deeply affected him.

His father, Richard Thomas Hammett, drank to excess and womanized blatantly. His Kentucky mother, Annie Bond Dashiell, a minister's daughter, suffered severely but would not stay quiet. She told her children, friends, and neighbors that all men had strong lusts and weak morals. When Annie could not moderate Richard's sexual behavior, she shocked neighbors by saying if you can't hold a man with love then you must hold him with sex. She even told Sam not to waste his time on a woman who couldn't cook, as she was not likely to be any good in the other rooms of the house, either! Sometimes, Annie's seductive behavior won, and Richard came home. Most times he did not.

Sam, who felt passionately protective of her, was *dislocated* (Jo's term) by Richard's drunken outbursts, casual sex, and brutal behavior, but of course he could not pit his small boy's strength against a father who was six foot three and two hundred pounds. Sam vowed that he would never abuse a woman the way his father abused his mother.

Sam's grandfather provoked local gossip by taking a young bride when his first wife died early. Though well over fifty, grandfather Samuel swept up twenty-three-year-old Lucy E. Dyer, who rapidly produced two sons, George and Samuel, and a daughter, Lucy, who shared the overcrowded house with Sam, Reba, and Dick and their parents. Sam, who shrank from their neighbors' disapproval, watched his grandfather's children rough-and-tumble with his siblings, all a similar age. This was yet one more disruptive element in his childhood.

Sam turned inward, hardly talking, except to Annie, whom he later saw as a strong survivor. Annie came from a family of French Huguenots who fled during the religious wars, emigrating first to Scotland, then, in 1653, to Virginia. She radiated an aloof superiority toward the uncouth Hammetts. Annie's relatives, descended from the De Chiels (later Dashiells), still lived in Baltimore where she was born,[1] and were proud of their ancestors' gold-shield coat of arms. The fact that Annie's ancestors had resided in the United States since the eighteenth century encouraged Sam's strong sense of self as an American.

The loutish Hammetts called her son "boy," but Annie, sure that Sam had inherited the romantic character of his French ancestors, had decided when he was born that his middle name would be "Dashiell." The unromantic boy remained "Sam" at school and later "Dash" to his buddies. In 1924, when he used Dashiell as his literary name, he told *Black Mask* readers that the only remarkable thing about his family was that there were on his mother's side sixteen French soldiers who never saw a battle.

The Hammetts by contrast were traders. The first Hammetts, small farmers, busy shopkeepers, tobacco growers, had reached St. Mary's County from England in the seventeenth century and had stayed. They were vigorous fighters in the Revolution and bitter survivors of the Civil War, which had ended only thirty years before Sam's birth. He grew up among kin whose farmlands and towns were occupied by Northern troops while their sympathies silently swung to the South. Though Maryland is a border state, Jo Hammett said her father felt "more like a Southerner than a Northerner, knowing he came from ancestors with solid roots in American history." This knowledge substantiated Hammett's unshakable belief that he was rock-bottom American, a boy raised as a Catholic who later elected not to side with God.

In interviews, Jo Hammett reported the sour effects of her father's childhood. "Papa gave such bitter accounts to me and my sister, Mary, about his pa's destructive behavior. He found what his father did hard to bear." In front of his wide-eyed daughter, Hammett had curtly ticked off Richard's excesses. "A womanizer, an alcoholic, a fancy dresser, Papa hated him for these things. He told us the smart outfits were to catch the attention of the 'lady friends' he consorted with when his wife was ill in bed. She was often ill, and Richard's behavior made her worse."

Sam remembered Richard angry, drunk on the farm, trying to involve Sam in farming. Whenever possible, the young boy escaped. This drunken behavior may account for Sam's desperate search for solitude, space, and silence, which he found fleeing to the woods and immersing himself in nature and wildlife. Young Sam would race to the stream, hide out in the woods teeming with game, until the noise of his quarreling parents was but a faint echo.

Jo described St. Mary's County as Tom Sawyer land, isolated on two sides by rivers and the third by Chesapeake Bay. She felt that a deep love of farming, fishing, and hunting infiltrated her father's blood early. "This intense passion for the outdoors stayed with my father throughout his life."

Years later, hurtled into the hysteria of Hollywood, sickened by sounds of celebrity, Dashiell still craved escape, still found it outdoors. Like many Southerners, Hammett felt at home in isolated places where there were animals, birds, and bugs. One year, he invited Mary and Jo to fish in the lake at Hardscrabble Farm, the 130 acres of wooded land in Westchester County, which at that point he shared with the trout, the turtles, and his co-owner, playwright Lillian Hellman. The girls later recalled the rare peace that came over him when he stayed nights alone at the boathouse.

The rough and restless Richard seemed unwilling to stay in one town or one house. Sam's earliest memories were of frequent moves, his father unable to stick at jobs or provide for his children. Sam was six when his family left the farm. Richard had failed in a bid for a political post after organizing such an ugly campaign that people in St. Mary's all but ran him out of town. Richard retreated to Philadelphia, Pennsylvania, in 1900. When Richard earned slightly more, he moved his family to 2942 Poplar Street, then a year later to 419 North 60th Street, Philadelphia.

When he failed to find his fortune there, he tried Baltimore in 1901, settling initially in the house rented by Annie's mother. Richard obtained the first of a series of poorly paid jobs as a salesman, followed by work as a foreman in a lock factory and as a bus conductor. Sam resented the fact that his mother had to work as a nurse to supplement the feckless Richard's wages.

As he grew into a tall redhead, Sam, left insecure by so many moves, so many unpaid bills, buried his head in books, often at the West Lexington library. He read voraciously: anything from mystery stories to science manuals, even Kant's *Critique of Pure Reason*, a catholic taste that would continue throughout his life and would focus on abstract philosophy, science, and technical manuals. Constant moves meant an interrupted education. By spring 1908, Sam was enrolled in Public School No. 72. Then that fall, on September 14, aged fourteen, he entered Baltimore Polytechnic Institute, where he might have flowered intellectually, as did H. L. Mencken, had he stayed long enough. Sam took physics, American literature, history, and English composition, the start of his passion for letter writing.

Sam also studied mechanical drawing, at which he became skilled, and math and technical subjects, which would later absorb him. His transcript showed him to be an average student, but before he could reap any genuine education, on February 9, 1909, Sam was withdrawn, after only one semester. His father needed help with a failing business, but when that business collapsed, the boy became a messenger. From then on, he read constantly and ultimately became a self-taught serious scholar with eclectic academic interests. His analytical intellect was bred from scant schooling. One consequence of his later poor health, which restricted physical activities, was his reliance on the life of the mind.

Sam's deep dislike of his father resulted in a weary cynicism about family life, hostility toward the breed of fathers, and by extension, toward those in power. He told young Jo that as a boy he fantasized he was adopted. He hoped one night his real father would come for him. This problem of paternity is pivotal to an understanding of Hammett's writings. Fatherhood forms the kernel of some stories and provides backbone for others. Conflicts between fathers and sons develop symbolically into conflicts between generations or between those with malevolent authority and those without: the drifters and doubters, the simple, the sensitive.

In some early stories that reflect Hammett's later hospital experiences, a young, sick soldier known as "I" or "Slim" rages against other figures of authority: authoritarian orderlies and medics.

In *Red Harvest* (1929), Hammett's debut novel, based on his experiences as a Pinkerton operative in Butte, Montana, his detective is known only as the Continental Op; he is nameless in the way in which a powerless, newborn baby is nameless. He is metaphorically fathered by the implacable Old Man, who runs the Continental Agency with iron discipline.

This is a novel of lost values, forgotten faiths, and corrupt institutions, where justice and order cannot be maintained. The city of Personville, where it is set, is so lawless it is known as Poisonville.

The worst instance of the evil, authoritarian father is Elihu Willsson, a man so obsessed with power that he effectively contrives to get his only son, Donald, killed before the Op, who has been summoned by Donald, can meet him.

The Glass Key (1931), Hammett's fourth novel, has some similarities to *Red Harvest* in its roster of crooked characters and Prohibition setting. Another small, unnamed city harbors a violent, lawless community controlled by evil mobsters and power-mad politicians. Gangster Paul Madvig, who wishes to marry Senator Ralph Bancroft Henry's daughter, runs the city by supporting two-timing politicians, including the senator. One night the senator's son, Taylor, is killed. As in *Red Harvest*, it is the father, Senator Henry, who is revealed as the murderer of his own son.

These are ruthless books with the same unbearable theme. There is a frenzy of violence and vengeance in which fathers commit terrible acts with the author's cynical acquiescence.

Hammett's fiction, which contains men who become sexual rivals with their sons or men who become predators of their children, shows fatherhood as a frightening concept: fathers maim, fathers kill, the law is unjust, authority is flawed.

Sam looked at his own father and saw a violent, uneducated man, unfit for gainful work, unfit for a career. Having no role model for reliable, steady employment severely penalized Sam. The bright boy without goals slunk into jobs slowly and shot out of them fast. He found no work that stimulated him, no women who interested him, so he turned to dice and cards, easy bets on horses, then alcohol and whores. The boy who loathed his father's drinking and womanizing was now addicted to both. Then to his horror, in 1914, he found he had contracted gonorrhea.

From 1909 to 1915 he could not get a job he liked and he could not keep a job he disliked. He tried and failed at Baltimore and Ohio Railroad, where he became a discontented presence before he left. He looked in at Poe and Davies Brokerage House then quickly looked out. He worked for stockbrokers, machine manufacturers, and canners. He became a freight clerk, a timekeeper, a stevedore, a yardman, a laborer, and a nail-machine operator in a box factory. Each job bored him. He abhorred routine, mindless tasks, and time clocks. He was unpunctual, uninterested, and refused to conform to rules. In a typical understatement, he later described himself as an unsatisfactory and unsatisfied employee. His employers felt the same.

A long, lean young man with high intellect but few skills, Sam seemed cold and detached. If disparagement or disapproval got to him, he rarely showed it. He felt superior to the jobs he mishandled, and he did show that. His insubordination or hopelessness meant most employers fired him. Only one manager, his boss at the Baltimore and Ohio Railroad, viewed him differently.

During his short stint as messenger boy, he arrived late every day for a week. Angrily, his boss told him to quit. Sam saw it as yet another expected setback from a capricious universe. He shrugged then began to walk out. His boss stopped him: "If you give me your word it won't happen again, you can keep the job." Sam hesitated, then shook his head. He knew he would again be late, so he refused to lie. Stunned, his puzzled but admiring boss let him stay. Hammett, unimpressed, soon quit.

In later years, Hammett embroidered that story because it illustrated not merely his pride and detachment but also his characteristic authority, which made people, even those superior to him, wish to be thought well of by him. But in the six spendthrift years of 1909 to 1915, with the single exception of his railroad boss, not one person saw Sam as worth deferring to. Only his mother, who recognized his walled-up talents, believed he could succeed when the right chance occurred.

Sam spotted an advertisement in a Baltimore newspaper for an intelligent person who fancied adventures. He was more than ready for an adventure that might reorder his life and, though he could not know it, turn the disorders of his past into the crime tales of his future.

The advertisement had been placed by Pinkerton's National Detective Agency, the nation's largest and most prestigious investigative organization, whose slogan was, "We never sleep." Like all Pinkerton operatives, Hammett was on call twenty-four hours a day for a mere twenty-one dollars a week. The agency founded by Alan Pinkerton in 1850 had formerly solved grand, scandalous, and sordid cases, even foiled assassination plots against presidents. Hammett absorbed not only principles of investigative procedures but also a romantic concept of the work of an investigator. Operatives did not merely crack down on crime, they also forestalled it. By Hammett's era, Pinkerton's had twenty offices, including the Continental Building in Baltimore where the Pinks kept watch on private property and supplemented local law enforcement agencies, the police, and even the US Security Service.

Sam had finally found work that was challenging and exciting. Some cases were routine, of course, others absurd. On one occasion, he shadowed a man who got lost and asked him for directions. Another time, he was assigned to catch a man who had stolen a Ferris wheel. Once, he spent three months in the hospital trying to collect secret information from the patient who shared his room. Such cases swiftly developed his understanding of inexplicable human behavior and increased his sense of irony.

In an early story that features his Continental Op, "The Gutting of Couffignal" (1925), the Op's satisfaction with detective work is expressed robustly: "Now I'm a detective because I happen to like the work. It pays a fair salary, but I could find other jobs that would pay more . . . I like being a detective . . . And liking work makes you want to do it as well as you can . . . You can't weigh that against any sum of money."[2]

Hammett modeled his Continental Op on James Wright, the short, fat assistant manager of the Baltimore office who taught Sam surveillance skills. "You simply saunter along somewhere within sight of your subject, and, barring bad breaks, the only thing that can make you lose him is over-anxiety . . . Even a clever criminal may be shadowed for weeks without suspecting it."

Sam learned not to worry about a suspect's face. "Tricks of carriage, ways of wearing clothes, general outline, individual mannerisms—all as seen from the rear—are much more impor-tant to the shadow than faces."[3]

Surprisingly, for a conspicuous man of six foot plus, he became an expert shadow. The obligations to become objec-tive, anonymous, invisible, to submerge his emotions beneath a cool investigative façade suited Sam, who was secretive and inscrutable. He adopted a public mask that was soon indistin-guishable from his private persona. A reclusive and distant young man, Sam had now fallen into a profession that encour-aged and validated those attributes.

He tailed, he trailed, he tracked, he stalked. Within a few weeks, he was an expert Shadow Man. A long, thin boy trained to avoid looking a man in the eye. The Pinkerton logo, an unblinking eye, became Hammett's logo, too. Eyes obsessed him. Eyes haunted him.

Three undated tales in the archives at the Harry Ransom Humanities Research Center at the University of Texas at Austin show that, though his stories might ignore chests or breasts, bums or thumbs, the eyes are there. Vittorio Corre-gione, the skinny little runt in "Action and the Quiz Kid," has "snapping black eyes." In "The Darkened Face," Fox, the operative from the Continental Detective Agency, stares at a mutilated woman with his "pale eyes—so deep-set and nar-row they squinted," while Rudolph Keupp from the Consul-ate General stares at Fox with "wide glassy eyes." In "Faith," fifty migratory workers in a canning factory have "raised brows over blank eyes" but never publicly express dissatisfaction with their employment. However, Feach, a rebel with "round maroon eyes," chuckles loudly, implying in the "sparkle of his red-brown eyes" he holds a secret. Later Feach, cowed, dwindles into a little man with "eyes that held fright when they were not blinking and squinting under fat rain-drops." As a shrunken man, his "eyes were more red than brown and dull except where they burnt with sudden fevers," until in a final fit of rage he sets fire to the buildings where the other men sleep, after which "the old sparkling ambiguity came back to his eyes."

Sam spent months engaging with the wealthy, the bankrupt, the workers, the bosses, the politically acute, the hopelessly naïve. He saw drama everywhere. He made notes, partly for his Pinkerton records, partly for his future. He loved detective work, but sometimes wondered about writing. He knew his adventures were formative and educational; what he did not yet know was that they would be crucial for his artistic development.

Yet, those seminal experiences provided more than a stock of authentic detective material. They also offered him a way of seeing the world, a philosophical code whose central elements were anonymity, objectivity, and morality.

At the expense of the company, Sam succeeded in his dream of going west. Pinkerton's provided money for train tickets, money for boarding houses. Sam loved journeys. He packed neatly, he was patient, punctual, alert, self-reliant, made do with little sleep, and became invisible on the streets. His trade fed into a philosophy that nothing is permanent, nothing is what it seems. If "honest" operatives could disobey conventional rules, could lie and steal in pursuit of their personal morality, which was to protect decent people from exploitation by evildoers, then in a conventional sense morality was questionable. Hammett's later politicization began at Pinkerton's.

Several extraordinary adventures are attributed to Hammett, though evidence leads a biographer to suspect that either he invented many of the most infamous tales or the stories are real but his participation dubious. The most imaginative tale is about Frank Little, retold here because it has significant implications for Hammett's philosophy and his politics.

In Butte, Montana, in August 1917, the radical labor union the Industrial Workers of the World (known as the Wobblies) was stirring up trouble among Butte miners, and their leader, Frank Little, was viciously murdered. Men with guns broke into Nora Byrne's boarding house at night, demanding to be shown the agitator's bedroom. They carried out a sleeping man with a broken leg. In the morning, Little was discovered hung from a trestle. Some said vigilantes had cut off his balls. A warning note to other radicals was pinned to the corpse's underwear. Hammett, said to be in the area at the time, always maintained that men came to him and other Pinks hired to prevent strikes in the mines, offering him $5,000 to kill Frank Little. Years later, Hammett told his companion Lillian Hellman he declined. Whether or not the vigilantes were ops, what was clear to Sam was that the actions of the strikebreakers were remarkably similar to those of the strikers. The agency's role in union strikebreaking eventually disillusioned him.

Sam caught gonorrhea again in 1917 but remained at Pinkerton's until he resigned in 1918 to join the army. While in military service, he fell ill to influenza, which left him vulnerable to the terrible series of lung diseases that would shadow his life. Still ill when he left the army, he went first to his parents' house to recover, then in May 1920 traveled to Spokane, Washington and the surrounding mining country, where Pinkerton's promised him more work. From October 15, 1921, he was reenergized as a Pink, then to his chagrin severe illness struck again. He quit detective work finally and irrevocably in February 1922.

When, at twenty-one, he had joined the Pinks with high hopes, did he imagine poor health would force him out in less than seven years? As he always earthed his imagination on stony ground and had such a poor work history, he probably did. But he never let on.

As he faced his young manhood stricken by tuberculosis, his two key strategies for coping with the disease were downplaying it and rarely referring to it. He deprecated his tuberculosis and fended off well-wishers with wit. Sometimes, he felt the need to wipe out every sign of illness.

When he wrote an account of his early army life for the mystery magazine *Black Mask* in November 1924, he omitted its most significant feature: contracting tuberculosis. "I spent an uneventful while in the army during the war, becoming a sergeant; and acquired a wife and daughter." When he mentioned Pinkerton's again he rewrote the script: "An enigmatic want-ad took me into the employ of Pinkerton's National Detective Agency, and I stuck at that until early 1922, when I chucked it to see what I could do with fiction writing."[4]

The truth was that fiction had become the only work he could do lying down.

Sam's response to all haphazard happenings was pragmatic. He fatalistically accepted indiscriminate disorder as if he expected nothing better. When he considered his childhood and adolescent traumas—frequent house moves, chronically ill mother, drunken father, his own binge drinking, removal from school, his string of jobs, constant quitting, and frightening disease—he concluded humans lived by chance, and died the same way. Every knock-back confirmed his view that life had no meaning. He packed this philosophy into his suitcase for his travels into manhood. It became his prevailing attitude and permeated his fiction. There was one curious difference in tone between his philosophical attitude to life and to literature. In life, his perspective was one of cool resignation, an unreachable detachment. But in his fiction, there is also heat, venom, and an occasional splinter of resentment.

Just once in his life and for a very short time, Hammett moderated his cynical outlook. He fell in love, genuinely, generously, with passion and with a kindness he would never show again. It is not surprising his love was for a young nurse, who cared for him as his mother, Annie, had, who was as proud of him as Annie was. She was Josie Dolan.

CHAPTER 3

When the Cushman Sanatorium opened in 1920,[1] there were seven army nurses, but Sam only noticed one, twenty-three-year-old Josephine Annis Dolan. Not only was she exceptionally pretty, with a riot of chestnut curls, but she welcomed patients with a kind smile as if they were co-conspirators.

People were always taken aback by her beauty. Years later, a former Pinkerton detective met Josie in middle age: "Jose was always lovely to look at. She had a beauty that came from a mixture of goodness and sexuality. That would have counted a great deal with Hammett."[2]

When Hammett was admitted, he was a sad scarecrow who weighed only 132 pounds, with 100 percent disability from tuberculosis. He flirted, and Josie thought perhaps he was not that ill. He helped her with her ward duties. She thought perhaps he was not that proud.

"Of all the patients, Samuel seemed to stand out. I thought he was very intelligent and striking—and his sleeping area was always very neat. Also, he was gentle." He seemed different from the country boys. Though he could hardly walk, he moved with pride. He dressed carefully even when he could wear only pajamas. Even the pajamas were neat. He made his bed in a military style, with a boyish smile. Determined to make up for his lack of schooling, he read every book that was available and took every vocational class granted to him. [3]

Josephine was born in Basin, Montana, in February 1897, the eldest child of Hubert Dolan, a West Virginia miner, and Irish Maggie, ten years younger than he. Maggie was dead at twenty-seven. Hubert drank heavily, then, when forced to return to work, left his three toddlers, Josie, three and a half, Walter, two, and baby Eddie with neighbors. Josie at first tried to take care of her brothers. Butte relatives took in Eddie, but when Hubert died three years after Maggie, Josie and Walter were sent to Montana's Catholic orphanage in Helena. Montana orphanages thought orphans were morally defective and should scrub sculleries. Josie was lonely, defiant, and frequently punished. One day, they locked her into the coal cellar then forgot about her. That was the day her remorseful aunt Alice Kelly, who already had a houseful of children, decided to visit. The previous night, Maggie had appeared to Alice in a dream, pleading with her to fetch Josie, who was instantly removed to the Kelly house in Anaconda. It was not a big improvement, for Uncle William Kelly, high on his job with the Anaconda Copper Company, regularly abused her. Josie could have told but kept quiet. This was family. Moreover, this family offered tastier food, better clothes, and more hope than the orphanage.

She got through grade eight at school then quit. Like Sam, Josie needed to escape. She didn't like blood, she didn't like death, but she knew nurses were respected. At fifteen, she trained for three years at St James' Hospital in Butte, then worked at St. Ann's Hospital before she enlisted in the army as a Red Cross nurse. After the war, she was accepted as a public health nurse first in New Mexico then in Tacoma. By the time she met Hammett, she was a second lieutenant.

"I outranked Sam, so he had to salute me," she said, still needing respect. [4] She did get Sam's approval if not ultimately his fidelity.

Sam understood Josie's story. Admired her pluck and felt compassion and loyalty, the same emotions he felt for Annie. Josie would ground him as Annie had done.

In Tacoma, Cushman had taken over ramshackle school buildings, laboratories, a lumber store, and a blacksmith's shop that was used by the former Cushman School for Puyallup Indians, hardly suitable as sites for treating respiratory diseases. Together, the seven nurses and four medical officers cared for a hundred needy veterans there.

In his last, unfinished novel, *Tulip*, Hammett recalled the friendly hospital as so sloppily run that patients could easily obtain passes for visits to Tacoma. As Sam's health improved, he began to court Josie seriously. They ate at good restaurants then walked and talked in the park. Sam obtained a pass to Seattle, where he rented an apartment for privacy. Within two months, they were lovers. Josie, overwhelmed by love, never believed that Sam's tubercular diagnosis had been confirmed. However, medical reports from the time said Sam was sick beyond repair. In 1921, he was transferred to Camp Kearney near San Diego for its warmer, drier climate. But the young, ardent patient had found sanctuary with a desirable, caring woman. From his new billet, he wrote to his beloved:

27 Sept [i.e., February] [5]

Dear Little Fellow—

We had just enough excitement on the trip down to keep away monotony, and landed here yesterday afternoon in pretty good shape . . .

. . . the going hasn't been any too smooth so far. Before we had our bags unpacked they flashed a set of rules on us . . . but we have broken all but a couple and none of us have been shot yet . . .

But that's enough of the Kearn[e]y talk—now for a little Cushman.

Which lunger are you taking out now and dragging into town when he should be sleeping? . . .

When you answer this *tonight* give me all the latest Cushman gossip—just the same as if we were sitting in the Peerless Grill.

Love
Hammett

Everyone called her Jose, except Sam. For five years, he called her his Little Fellow, his Dear, his Dearest, his Dearest Woman, Little Handful, Little Chap, Lady, Nurse, and Boss. Only when his life changed in November 1926 did he, too revert to Jose.

The Little Fellow did not write back. Days passed with no letter. Hammett wrote again:

Friday [probably 4 March 1921]

Dear Lady—

I didn't intend doing this—writing you a second letter before I got an answer to my first—but that's the hell of being in love with a vamp, you do all sorts of things. Before long, most likely, I'll have fallen into the habits of your other victims and will be writing you frequent and foolish letters. . . . And then I'll be getting so I can't eat or sleep, and will lose my immortal soul lying to you about the 15 and 18 hour naps I'm taking and the pounds of meat I am eating—for I'd never admit that I allowed you to interfere with my comfort and health. You'd enjoy that too much!

Sam wrote more often, and more openly than was usual for him. Josephine shyly held back, yet already she trusted him. His missives were flirtatious, funny, affectionate. He told her that his chums said "Little Miss Dolan" was a wonderful person, though the "regular and usual opinion" was that in comparison with the Little Handful "the Virgin Mary was a wild woman."

Sam recalled their good times. The worst part of the day was when the time was 7:40 p.m. and he knew that he should be in front of the hospital, in the rain, waiting for "Josephine Anna." By 6:00 p.m. on Jose's afternoon off, he knew he should be standing on the corner in front of People's Store, cursing her because she was fifteen minutes late. The rain reminded him of the times they had spent at the bridge "staging our customary friendly, but now and then a bit rough, dispute over the relative merits of 'yes' and 'no.'"

This was not the Hammett of later years, violent with starlets and even with Lillian Hellman, who feared his violence. Here the writer sounded gentle. He missed the Little Fellow's pert smile. He still awaited a photograph: "If I'm ever to get it I'll most likely have to come up and take it away from you. Maybe that's what I should have done about something else I wanted."

What he wanted now was her company. Was she still thinking of leaving Cushman? Could he persuade her to come to California? Had she answered his other letter? "God help you if you didn't."

Finally, the Little Fellow wrote back. It was March 9. He was "tickled pink," as he hadn't been sure she would write. He felt as if he had the world by its tail. He assured her that he was being remarkably faithful and admitted he loved her like a damn fool.

Hammett would always be better at expressing emotions in letters than in speech, but in this first love affair he admitted his feelings without self-mockery. "I may have done a lot of things that weren't according to scripture, but I love Josephine Anna Dolan—and have since about the sixth of January—more than anything in Christ's world. . . . You can't be missing me any more than I'm missing you, Sweet. It's pretty tough on these lonesome nights." He finished unequivocally: "I deserve all the love you can spare me! And I want a lot more than I deserve."

This emotion is unmistakable, unambiguous, a tender streak rarely shown in his later relationship with Hellman, except in some of his wartime letters to her.

On March 13, he wrote "Dear Nurse," telling Jose that he had nearly begun his letter with "Dear Mama," as her last note was filled with such motherly advice. Jose's instructions about taking the cure could have come from Annie. The letter was a harbinger. Jose would be as unremittingly devoted to him and as able to survive as Annie had been.

Sam wrote that this was the first time he had genuinely loved a woman that way. "That sounds funny but it may be the truth." A week later, he uncharacteristically expressed insecurity. "I never could figure out whether you liked me a little (I mean 'love'—I wouldn't give a God-damn to have you 'like' me) or were just giving me your evenings because you hadn't anything else much to do with 'em." He went into town frequently but came back "as much a virgin as when I went." Temporarily, he stopped seeing whores. [6]

Later, when they lived together, Sam wrote a story about a soldier making love to a nurse. He called Jose "Evelyn" and called himself "Slim" (his nickname from the staff and patients). In two sketches, Hammett captured some of their relationship but toughened it up. He wrote the first sketch at 20 Monroe Street, San Francisco, on October 4, 1926, where illness had temporarily separated him from his wife and children.

We would leave the buildings in early darkness, walk a little way across the desert and go down into a small canyon where four trees grouped around a level spot. The night-dampness settling on earth that had cooked since morning would loose the fragrance of ground and plant around us. We would lie there until late in the night, our nostrils full of world-smell, the trees making irregular map-boundary division among the stars. Our love seemed dependent on not being phrased. It seemed if one of us had said, "I love you," the next instant it would have been a lie. So we loved and cursed one another merrily, ribaldly, she usually stopping her ears in the end because I knew more words. [7]

Hammett's detached understatement is transparent in the notion that once an emotion is named, nailed down, it will then be false. Jose, young and guileless though she was, seemed able to accept Sam's gradual mask of verbal indifference and understood that it hid some of the emotions he had expressed openly in their earliest years.

In this first sketch, there is a distinct contradiction in tone between Sam's letters to the Little Fellow that were written at the time and this fictional fragment written later. His witty, gentle tone in the correspondence changes to an acid quality in the story.

By the time Sam wrote that sketch, their passionate courtship had altered into an affectionate domesticity, but that may only be part of the reason for the literary change. Here also was an emerging writer trying techniques.

Hammett, dissatisfied with this fictional version, later revised it, sharpened the landscapes so that the trees "made maps among the stars." In "Women Are a Lot of Fun Too" (undated), he removed the nurse's prettiness and concentrated on an erotic wrangle. Though Sam's letters to Josie were intensely romantic, to make Evelyn pretty would openly reveal this. He was not about to write romance, even if he felt able to live it.

> I was going to miss Evelyn. She wasn't pretty, but she was a lot of fun, a small-bodied wiry girl with a freckled round face that went easily to smiling. We used to leave the hospital around lights-out time, walk a little way across the desert, and go down to a small canyon where four trees grouped round a level spot. . . . We would lie there until late. . . . smelling the world and loving and cursing one another. Neither of us ever said anything about seriously loving the other. Our love-making was a thing of rough and tumble athletics and jokes and gay repartee and cursing. She usually stopped her ears in the end because I knew more words. [8]

In San Diego, Sam missed his male friends who broke Cushman rules without detection. Some played poker; some smuggled in drink. Sam's fellow patient Snohomish Whitey even committed strong-arm robberies near the hospital, then escaped back to his sickbed. The admiring Sam fictionalized Whitey first in an untitled story, then in "Women Are a Lot of Fun Too."

"Whitey shouldn't have hit the doctor, but he did. He poked him in the fat mouth and the doctor fell down on the board walk and squealed." Hammett's respect for the tough but powerless guy showed when Whitey cursed the doctor because he wouldn't get up to be hit again.

The nursing staff saw Whitey as "a filthy ignorant beast who doesn't know any better," while they saw the narrator as an educated man who knew a great deal better. For years, Hammett retained his liking for rough, boozy men, partly based on envy of the thin, frail invalid for the physically powerful male.

In the twenties, Hammett saw all doctors as authority figures who could be malevolent or, as in his own case, hopelessly inept. Whitey represented the rage of the ineffective against those in authority.

When Sam first met Whitey, men died around them in the merciless heat, but Whitey appeared fearless despite (like Sam) coughing up blood. Much later, Hammett inserted Whitey into his last manuscript, *Tulip*, where Whitey Kaiser became "a powerfully built squat blond Alaskan with most of the diseases known to man; he could hit like a pile driver, but his knucklebones would crumble like soda crackers."[9]

Twenty years after first meeting Whitey, when Hammett was back in the army during World War II and compared his sick, prematurely aged frame with the bodies of his young, fit fellow soldiers, he signed several letters "Whitey."

Separated by miles but joined to Jose by his letters, Sam, at twenty-six, already wrote well. Though Jose, twenty-three, was pregnant, neither of them seemed to be aware of her condition. Several notes, however, suggested that Jose felt ill. On April 30, 1921, Sam pictured her extremely sick, even dying. He went through the emotions of a man in love.

When Jose discovered her pregnancy, she quit her job, went home to Anaconda, coped as proudly as she could with her family's hostility, and wrote to Hammett. They arranged their marriage by mail. Of the two important letters that Hammett's daughter Jo knew Jose had saved but that subsequently were lost, one was from Sam to Jose on learning she was pregnant, the other was to plan their San Francisco reunion. The tone of the notes that preceded and followed the two missing letters was identical, both full of passionate love. Jo's family confidently assumed that Sam's desire to marry Jose and bring up their child was equal to hers. He had already written in March: "I really like to have you tell me what to do and what not to do. It's like being married to you."[10]

Discharged from Camp Kearney, he traveled to Seattle, where he lived briefly at 1117 Third Avenue. Then he moved to San Francisco to search for an apartment for them.[11] In June 1921, he rented a room at 120 Ellis Street. When Jose arrived in early July, he discreetly placed her in the nearby Golden West Hotel. On Thursday, July 7, handing her a bouquet of flowers, he took her by cab to St. Mary's Cathedral, where, despite Jose's Catholic observances, they were married in the rectory rather than at the altar. He had already warned her: "I haven't any God except Josephine."[12] Only when the ceremony was over did Hammett confess he was baptized a Catholic, so they could have had the religious wedding Jose wanted. Despite that first ripple of disagreement, in some strange way he took their marriage as seriously as she did. Though he did not long remain faithful, they never legally divorced. Until the end of their lives, she called herself and thought of herself as Mrs. Hammett, and Hammett told friends and later an irritated Lillian Hellman that he thought of her that way, too.

Their first apartment, at 620 Eddy Street, overlooking a park, was four blocks from the public library, where Hammett read Anatole France, Flaubert, ancient Icelandic sagas, and other works from Aristotle to Henry James, to whom he later attributed his ideas about style. He understood the grim, the greedy, the laconic, but now he seized on sophistication. He had good judgment, a flair for sorting literature from trash but so far no aptitude for making money.

Their three rooms cost $45 a month. His disability pension had been downgraded from 100 percent, worth $80 a month, to 50 percent, worth only $40 a month. Unable to pay rent, buy food, or manage a full-time job, Hammett returned part-time to Pinkerton's, in San Francisco's Flood Building, making about six dollars a day. He found the work enthralling, but what he later "remembered" from the time were four crucial cases that he may *not* have investigated, though he would take full credit.

Hammett's "memories" are looked on with fond indulgence by readers and critics alike. He was a fine detective, runs the myth, and therefore he almost certainly solved the cases. However, the only certifiable fact is that he was employed by Pinkerton's at the time.

The first sensational case was the Fatty Arbuckle rape and murder. Arbuckle, a popular film comedian, was accused in news reports of raping starlet Virginia Rappe in his suite at the St. Francis Hotel. Newspapers claimed that, when the grossly overweight Arbuckle climbed on top of Rappe's slim body, he ruptured her bladder and killed her. Arbuckle's defense team hired Pinkerton's for two trials. The first (September 22 to December 4, 1921) ended in a hung jury; the second (January 11 to February 3, 1922) acquitted Fatty on the grounds that Rappe's bladder problems were caused by venereal disease and a botched abortion. The sole evidence for Hammett's participation in the first trial was his own allusion to "the funniest case I ever worked on. . . . In trying to convict him everybody framed everybody else" that was picked up by the *New York Herald Tribune*, November 12, 1933.

By the second trial, Hammett had quit Pinkerton's, yet in his fragment "Seven Pages," he claimed he saw Arbuckle in the St. Francis Hotel lobby the day before the trial opened. "I was working for his [Arbuckle's] attorneys at the time, gathering information for his defense."

Though Sam was probably not on the case, he could not let go of the sexual absurdity. Fat crooks obsessed him. His triumph was Caspar Gutman, the Fat Man in *The Maltese Falcon*.

Hammett's second apocryphal detection was the 1921 Nicky Arnstein bond theft case. Arnstein was a gambler charged with organizing a $1.5 million securities theft and the theft of an additional $5 million from a Wall Street brokerage. Sam claimed he shadowed Arnstein, but both the thefts and the trials took place on the East Coast at a time when there is no evidence that Sam ever left the West Coast.

Hammett was similarly absent from his third infamous case, that of jewel thief Gloomy Gus Schaefer, accused of robbing the Shapiro Jewel Company in St. Paul, Minnesota, of $130,000 then fleeing to a roadhouse. Some Pinkertons found the roadhouse but no loot. No evidence supported Hammett's first implausible story about the case, which was that when alone on the roadhouse roof, he overheard Schaefer's gang discussing plans, fell through the roof, twisted his ankle, and allowed the gang to escape with the money. Hammett's second unlikely tale about this, set in a Vallejo street in 1922, had him shadowing Schaefer, who led him to some of the loot.

The fourth case concerned the robbery of gold coins from the freighter *Sonoma*. Hammett insisted this was his last case and his reason for leaving detection. According to him, he had been posing as an undercover agent on the *Sonoma*, and he quit the Pinkertons because he discovered the $200,000 gold coins just before the ship set sail, depriving himself of a trip to Hawaii to search for them while solving the crime.

However, the *Sonoma* case was solved on the very day that Hammett did finally quit the Pinkertons, making it unlikely that he had done the solving. That was one day after Arnstein's trial for conspiracy, three days before the first Arbuckle trial ended, and well before Schaefer committed his robbery. By the time Schaefer was arrested, the second Arbuckle trial was under way, and when the Arnstein case went to trial, Hammett was severely ill in bed.

The truth is, Hammett quit detection because he was desperately ill, with constant chest pains and dizzy spells. He weighed only 126 pounds. He was again an invalid who would die if he attempted to sail anywhere. He could no longer stagger four blocks to the library and needed a line of chairs between his bedroom and bathroom so he could rest on his way. The Bureau of War Risk Insurance Review returned his disability rating to 100 percent.

But this sick image did not suit Hammett. Better a false macho anecdote than the truth.

The Hammetts' daughter, Mary Jane, was born at St. Francis Hospital on October 15, 1921. [13] Jose budgeted, and Hammett was well enough to cook. The baby delighted him. He and Jose happily shared their child's care, until the doctor advised Sam to limit physical contact with Mary to avoid infecting her. Sam started sleeping on a Murphy bed in the hall, worrying about finances. Writing fiction seemed the only solution. In desperation, he wrote to his father, explaining his ambition, asking for money. His father refused, and Hammett never forgot it. When his beloved mother, Annie, died on August 3, 1922, he felt orphaned, like Jose. He was Nobody's Son, so he wrote four hours a day, signing eight stories Peter Collinson, the offspring of Peter Collins, the underworld name for Nobody.

In February 1922, he entered Munson's Business College as part of his vocational rehabilitation to train as a reporter, finishing May 23, 1923. He continued negotiating unsuccessfully with government agencies, resenting their authority and their indifference to the conflict between his bright aims and sick body. This resentment snaked through his first stories and cemented his hardening attitude of suffering blows and expecting nothing in the way of aid. Hammett's daughters remembered the terrifying rows their sick, scribbling father had with the Veterans Bureau. In October 1922, after several frustrating letters to Allan Carter, his enemy at the bureau, Hammett received "additional compensation" for Jose of $2.50 a month. The total disability payment was now $16.21.

A few months after the additional compensation in October 1922, the bureau said that once Sam finished vocational college, all compensation would stop. Sam, fuming, pointed out to Enemy Carter that he was so ill he could hardly walk, and his writings could not support his family. Carter referred Hammett's file to the District Board of Appeals, who kept Sam waiting without money for months. Carter consistently thwarted him. In October 1923, he even made Hammett resend his marriage credentials, in case he had recently become divorced! In April 1924, the District Board of Appeals awarded him retroactively $51.68 as a one-off additional payment, but then the vengeful Carter told him his last check would be May. Sam's angry protests won him $9 in June before sickness overcame him. He could no longer fight or write. For the remainder of his life, he continued an angry correspondence with the obstructive Veterans Bureau.

With enormous difficulty, he finished the journalism course, then, as his health broke down again, he took on a part-time advertising job with Samuels Jewelers, the oldest jewelry business in San Francisco. [14] Al (Albert) Samuels became the only loving father figure in his life. He learned his new trade fast, while he continued scribbling stories. Pulp magazines became an obvious market for him to earn extra income, since he could claim that his Pinkerton experiences gave his fiction authenticity. The pay was only one or two pennies a word, but if he exerted himself he could make thirty or forty dollars a month. (Pulps were cheaply printed gray-paper, book-length publications. In the 1920s, more than seventy pulps existed in various genres: crime, mystery, romance, adventure, and Westerns. Slicks were mass-circulation magazines printed on slick, or glossy, paper—for example, *The Smart Set*, *Redbook*, *Liberty*, *Saturday Evening Post*, and *Cosmopolitan*.)

In October 1922, the first story he would publish, "The Parthian Shot," was accepted by editors H. L. Mencken and George Jean Nathan for their prestigious magazine, *The Smart Set: A Magazine of Cleverness*, which paid almost the lowest rates in magazine publishing.

The tiny plot features Paulette Key, who dislikes her domineering husband mainly for his stupidity and obstinacy. The baby also makes obstinate demands for food and toys. Before Paulette leaves her family, she delivers her Parthian shot by having him christened Don. The reader can work out that the boy would grow up as Don Key.

Mencken and Nathan bought this one-hundred-word anecdote, for which they paid him only a penny a word, because they liked the narrative double twist.

Hammett was too ill to go to a restaurant to celebrate, but he and Jose had dinner sent in.

PART TWO
EARLY WRITINGS, 1922–1927

CHAPTER 4

Hammett burned with a new fever. Not sickness but success. *The Smart Set* showed him the way. It was sophisticated, ironic, iconoclastic. It had published Scott Fitzgerald, Eugene O'Neill, Sinclair Lewis, and Aldous Huxley, whose work he knew well. Mencken and Nathan believed in the talent of unknown scribblers, too, and the unknown Hammett thought his own burlesques, epigrams, poems, and stories might appeal to their taste.

Dedicated and determined, he slogged on an Underwood typewriter on the Eddy Street kitchen table. Real writers had desks. He moved to a larger apartment and built a desk. He made pencil notes, handwrote drafts, then typed clean copies on the typewriter. By one year later, October 1923, *The Smart Set* had accepted four more ironic short fictions.

Sam also tried nonfiction. In March 1923, *The Smart Set* published "From the Memoirs of a Private Detective," which consisted of twenty-nine satirical observations from Hammett's Pinkerton exploits that marked out his subsequent fictional territory. The cutting prose, similar to Hemingway's early experiments, had a bold, authoritative clip.

> I know a man who will forge the impression of any set of fingers in the world for $50.
>
> A man whom I was shadowing went out into the country for a walk one Sunday afternoon and lost his bearings completely. I had to direct him back to the city.
>
> The chief of police of a Southern city once gave me a description of a man, complete even to a mole on his neck, but neglected to mention that he had only one arm.

In mid-1923, Hammett dramatically changed style and market. He began to write almost exclusively for the pulps: crime, adventure, and mystery. Surprisingly, he retained the same editors, because two years earlier Mencken and Nathan had started the pulp story magazine *Black Mask* to subsidize their clever slick.

Already a *Mask* reader, Hammett, who later disparaged his "Blackmasking" to others, was nevertheless attracted by its earthy vigor. Feeling he could do better than their regular writers, he carefully studied the career of Carroll John Daly, whose hard-boiled detective, Race Williams, had appeared in *Black Mask* four months earlier, in December 1922. Daly's stories had a surface realism but no depth. His hero was unpolished, unintelligent, and unreal.

When Hammett began writing for *Black Mask*, his heroes were hard-boiled in a different sense. They were realistic but not insensitive. They had self-awareness rare in fictional detectives. They learned to accept criminality without showing their feelings. Their underlying fear was that constant immersion in an immoral society would render them emotionless.

Daly was a hack whose violence was gratuitous, plots were implausible, and dialogue lacked accuracy. Hammett's detective experience had given him not only authenticity but original ideas. When Daly later fell from fame, he blamed Hammett.

Hammett was already familiar with the literature and conventions of the so-called Golden Age of Detection, which started in April 1841 when the analytic Auguste Dupin solved Edgar Allan Poe's "Murders in the Rue Morgue." Fifty years later, Sherlock Holmes sprang from Conan Doyle's elegant pen to popularize classical detection. In 1913, E. C. Bentley established long detective novels with *Trent's Last Case*. He was followed by G. K. Chesterton's Father Brown. In the UK, Agatha Christie, A. A. Milne, Ngaio Marsh, and Dorothy Sayers added complex characterization to crime, while in the United States, S. S. Van Dine presented erudite investigator Philo Vance, who discussed philosophical issues with drawing-room facility.

Hammett saw Golden Age detection as a literary game with fixed formal rules. Authors never lied. Plots provided readers with a puzzle, clues, and a solution. Disguised clues were presented. However improbable the solution, physical laws were respected, and geographical settings and judicial procedures were rendered faithfully. Criminal motives gradually became clear. Police were seen as bumblers. Crime methodology must seem plausible, even if impractical or coincidental. Detectives were eccentric, intelligent, and middle or upper class. They were always in control. Faced with inadequate or false information, they would track clues to establish accurately "who did it" and to decide "the truth."

But in his stories, Hammett would break with the Golden Age tradition in several significant ways. He knew detection did *not* work like that. Sleuths did *not* sit in salons solving murders from clues on paper. In his experience, many investigators were working class; crimes were sordid; detection was rough, footslogging, arbitrary, and surprising. Hammett knew nothing was predictable. A successful detective had to be tough enough to peel away each layer of deceit and cynical enough to remain detached when he discovered beneath it another layer of pretense.

Before Hammett, the goal had been solving the crime. After Hammett, the detective himself would become a central subject. Hammett's experimental premise was that the biggest mystery was the self. Candid realism became his signature. He would invent the modern urban detective story, with street-smart dialogue, cadences, and rhythms and set crimes in dirty city streets, not in bright country houses. His knowledge of this territory meant that each detail was accurate.

"Zigzags of Treachery" (March 1924) turned on the way the detective, or operative, known as the Op, cleared a doctor's innocent wife of a murder charge. It was so realistic that it included the four rules of shadowing: stay behind your man as much as possible, never look him in the eye, act naturally, and don't ever try to hide from him. In walked a man shadowing a blackmailer who broke every one of the rules. Naturally, he got his neck broken.

An expert on chases, Hammett planted pursuits in dingy locations. In "The Gatewood Caper" (1923), his first story signed "Dashiell Hammett," he depicted a sinister alleyway where a male kidnapper on the run hid out to get rid of his female disguise.

Today, we see how Hammett's torrid tales crackle with credible characters and understated irony. Sophisticated plots have breathless actions, though sporadically he overdoes the whirlwind plotting. His narration is detached, objective, wry. His endings have sardonic twists.

Hammett's prose is muscular. Sometimes it throbs, some-times there are flat, underplayed statements. In "The Scorched Face" (1925), horror is evoked indirectly. A female corpse has been eaten by birds. Hammett's skill is to make much by saying little: "At the base of a tree, on her side, her knees drawn up close to her body, a girl was dead. She wasn't nice to see. Birds had been at her."

Even much later, in "Fly Paper" (1929), he uses a simi-lar technique in his held-in sentences to convey male men-ace: "Babe liked Sue. Vassos liked Sue. Sue liked Babe. Vassos didn't like that."

In these stories written in the twenties, Hammett's ficti-tious underworld of Prohibition-era gangsters and molls was extremely filmic, so it is little wonder that Hollywood would ultimately make a dozen movies from his novels. We see authentic-seeming organized crime as he counts the bodies in "Bodies Piled Up" (December 1923). The Op is "hotel-coppering" at San Francisco's Montgomery Hotel. The maid alerts the staff that "there's something wrong up in 906." Back inside 906, the maid stares goggle-eyed at the closed door of the clothes press. From underneath it, "a snake-shaped rib-bon of blood" moves toward them. The Op opens the door. "Slowly, rigidly, a man pitched out into my arms . . . there was a six-inch slit down the back of his coat, and the coat was wet and sticky." A second corpse suddenly pitches out "with a dark, distorted face"; then out tumbles a third dead man. A soft hat lies in the center of an unruffled bed, while in a puddle of blood on the closet floor lie two more hats. "Each of the hats fitted one of the dead men," sums up the laconic author. What an eye for detail. What an image for a movie.

Black Mask published Hammett's first hard-boiled Con-tinental Op story, "Arson Plus," on October 1, 1923. The nameless operative with the Continental Detective Agency (who would front twenty-six stories, two novelettes, and two novels) looked utterly unlike his creator: he was short, fat, balding, and middle aged.

Hammett told his *Mask* editor on October 10, 1923, that he hadn't deliberately kept his hero nameless. But as the Op had got through two stories without needing a name, he would let him continue. Certainly, the namelessness was related to Hammett's own desire for privacy.

The Op is a strange hero-detective. He has no home, no interests except his job, no goal except to get the job done, no motive except loyalty to his boss. His work code has two rules laid down by the agency: he must accept no rewards for solving cases, and honest work must be an end in itself.

The Op lives a bleak existence in an indifferent universe, epitomizing Hammett's belief that life is inscrutable, arbitrary, and does not match up to the orderly, ethical way people behave. Though the Op's job requires him to proceed in a methodical manner, he knows there is no order.

The Op is not always moral. Though he may do some good, his method is to use whatever tools come to hand, including violence or treachery. He can be as callous as the criminals. This paradoxical conflict between means and ends grows out of a similar conflict between the morality of the Op's employers and those he is employed to apprehend.

He appears to be the hired official of a respectable society, paid to clean up after criminals who operate in a crooked. world, but—and this is where Hammett differs from other crime writers of the time—the society is itself deceitful, malignant, and vicious.

"Arson Plus" is the first of many tales that would have a similar structure, where the Op inspects the crime scene, interviews suspects, cooperates with local police, and uncovers not one truth but layers of truths.

Here the Op is called to a burnt-out house that had been doused with gasoline, where a man named Thornburgh is supposed to have died. Central to the plot is the fact that $200,000 worth of insurance on the deceased has recently been purchased. A niece will benefit. The witnesses are Thornburgh's live-in servants, the Coomses, and Henderson, a traveling salesman. The Op discovers there is no niece, only a woman named Evelyn Towbridge impersonating her; there is no Thornburgh, only Henderson risen from the dead, impersonating him. There are no live-in servants, only the Coomses fabricating the movements of their supposed dead master. There *was* a fire, but it was started to defraud the insurance company. When the Op uncovers the "truth," it is the fabricated death of an imaginary man. The witnesses' story exists within the Op's story within Hammett's story.

Though the Op's methods parallel those of Hammett's successor Raymond Chandler's detectives, their underlying philosophies differed. Chandler would offer clues that led to "real" answers. Hammett's Op knew reality peeled away like an onion to reveal more plausibilities.

Chandler summed up Hammett's achievements in a December 1944 article in *Atlantic Monthly*:

> Hammett took murder out of the Venetian vase and dropped it into the alley. . . . Hammett wrote at first (and almost to the end) for people with a sharp, aggressive attitude to life. They were not afraid of the seamy side of things; they lived there. . . . Hammett gave murder back to the kind of people who commit it for reasons, not just to provide a corpse. . . . He was spare, frugal, hardboiled, but he did over and over again what only the best writers can ever do at all. He wrote scenes that seemed never to have been written before.

Hammett did more than that: he used his unique method, the double-layer effect.

In "The Tenth Clew" (January 1924), the Op is called to the home of wealthy industrialist Leopold Gantvoort, whose life has been threatened, and finds Gantvoort absent. Gantvoort's son hears that his father's head has been bashed in with a typewriter. A neat writerly touch. Nine clues await the Op. He discovers that one has been faked, and that discovery becomes the tenth clue. Beneath every clue lurks another puzzle. Again, Hammett suggests events are seldom what they seem and people rarely what they appear.

Gantvoort's fiancée, the exquisite Creeda Dexter, falls under Hammett's scrutiny. Characteristically, he fastens on Creeda's eyes—large, deep, amber, restless—always a key to personality. Those eyes expand, contract, and when Creeda becomes fearful "the restless black pupils spread out abruptly." The Op, willing but unable to trust Creeda, becomes suspicious. Hammett's theme of the beautiful woman who exploits a man's trust recurs frequently.

In "The House in Turk Street" (April 1924), redheaded gangster Elvira tries to tempt the detective. In "The Girl with the Silver Eyes" (June 1924), criminal Jeanne Delano attempts to seduce the Op, who resists and sends her to the gallows.

Though Hammett wrote about people's emotional experiences, they were rarely based on his own. One significant exception was the perceptive story "Holiday" (July 1923), written at the end of his first year as a professional author.

Paul Hetherwick, a tubercular patient at Camp Kearney hospital, was a lonely introvert who took a twelve-hour "holiday" in Tijuana. At the racetrack, he lost most of his pension check. At several seedy bars, he lost self-respect with second-hand girls selling thirdhand sex. The loner returned to the hospital having found neither love nor money. The sentiment

Hammett may have shared, though the story's style is coldly unsentimental. It is a fine story, but the autobiographical elements may have scared him from writing further confessional narratives.

Hammett preferred to ask abstract questions about the human condition: could one be a good person in an evil world? If shared values had collapsed, what did it mean to be good? Could we live our lives without trust?

In staking out new territory, Hammett had no mentor, no writer friends, merely a single burning ambition. But he kept it secret. The former loafer son of Richard Hammett senior who had been called stubborn and lazy did not seem ambitious to outsiders. Indeed, in a rare autobiographical outburst in *Black Mask* in November 1924, Hammett described himself as "very lazy," adding cautiously, "I have no ambition at all in the usual sense of the word."

Hammett's word was not always to be trusted, though. After a tentative start, the ambition he had concealed achieved an astounding success. By 1930, he would be recognized as an innovator in the hard-boiled school and would be likened to Hemingway.

While, in retrospect, Hammett was en route to success, privately Sam hedged his bets. If he had changed rapidly and irrevocably, Jose had not.

Jose wanted Sam to succeed. But she did not understand what writing meant to him. She prayed he would get a steady job. Meanwhile, she nursed him. His health had been on an increasing downward spiral since 1923. That October, he was diagnosed with active pulmonary tuberculosis. His weight was down to 131 pounds, and his disability was reassessed as 50 percent. Sick again in 1924, he was reported by public health nurses to be undernourished. Late in 1924, the doctors advised Hammett to separate from his family. His pulmonary tuberculosis had flared up badly, he was highly contagious, and there was severe danger of infection to his young family.

Mary and Jose first moved across the bay to Fairfax, California, while Hammett wrote "Ruffian's Wife" (*Sunset Magazine*, October 1925) about a devoted wife separated from her husband by San Francisco Bay. Then Jose and Sam decided she should take Mary back to Anaconda, Montana, until Sam had recovered. Mother and daughter stayed in Montana about six months while Hammett remained in the Eddy Street apartment trying to write but usually spending twenty hours a day in bed. In the late spring of 1925, Hammett's doctor advised him his condition had stabilized, so Jose and Mary moved back to San Francisco.

On May 24, 1926, their second child, Josephine Rebecca, was born at St. Francis Hospital. They were confidently expecting a boy, to be called Richard Thomas.

When I was about eighteen or twenty, Papa told me that before my birth he hoped I would be a boy. He didn't say it in a mean way, just kind of wistfully: "Oh, I really thought you were going to be a boy. Sorry about that!" What did I feel? I guess mad and resentful!

Years later, Hammett reassured Jo that a few minutes after she was born his heart swelled with love.

By 1926, he was still not able to earn enough to keep his family going despite the fact that between October 1922 and March 1926 he had published forty-two stories in thirty-nine months.

Frustrated at his inability to earn sufficient money in the pulp market, he had decided to quit writing fiction and look for a full-time job. In March, he put an ad seeking work in the *San Francisco Chronicle*, listing all his previous jobs from warehouseman to private detective and adding the words "and I can write."[1] Albert Samuels took him on full-time to write advertising copy for Samuels Jewelers. The pay was $350 a month, which was more than he had earned from pulp fiction. According to Samuels, he did a fine job, writing ads that were romantic yet astute, but the pressure of full-time work sent him back to drink. With his initial paycheck, he rented a second apartment at 408 Turk Street to use as a studio, where he would work, often late at night, on ad designs and layout.

His health could not keep pace with his energetic new interests, and he came down with hepatitis. Still at Samuels but becoming increasingly sicker, on July 20, 1926, he was found near to death, lying in a pool of blood from his lungs, and was forced to resign. The doctors at the Veterans Bureau advised him, yet again, to send away his children for fear of infection. While living in a furnished room at 20 Monroe Street, Hammett wrote regularly to Mary, who, with her sister and mother, was living in an apartment at 1309 Hyde Street. He enjoyed drawing rabbits, turtles, and elephants and pictures of himself at his desk. After eight weeks away from his job, Hammett reluctantly accepted he was not strong enough to work as a full-time advertising manager. On September 23, 1926, Samuels sent an affidavit in support of his claim to the Veterans Bureau, averring these sad facts. They finally agreed that Hammett was totally disabled. Grudgingly, they granted him $90 a month.

His relationship with Jose drifted, seeped at the edges, though his delight in his two daughters grew. This, however, was not helped when his illness returned and their family reunion was curtailed. The doctors again urged Sam to live separately, so although he moved with them on October 4, 1926, to 1309 Hyde Street, he was unable to stay more than a few weeks. Jose and the children continued to reside at 1309 Hyde Street until 1927, and while they remained there Sam lived alone within walking distance, at 891 Post Street.

During this and subsequent absences, Sam wrote regularly and fondly. The following letter, from October 4, 1926, is typical.

> Dearest,
>
> I did like the pictures very much: you look quite intellectual, or maybe it's artistic, with the bob . . .
>
> Here's the customary portrait for the nitwit [Mary]. Ask her what kind of dumbbell she is, and tell her to kiss Josephine Rebecca for me. I imagine the youngster is a darling by now. . . . And don't be worrying about my financial affairs. God knows we always staggered through somehow in the past, and I still can. I haven't missed any meals.
>
> Yesterday I wrote four poems, and I think maybe one of them is some good.
>
> > Love
> > D. [2]

As Sam slowly recovered, Joseph Shaw, *Black Mask*'s new editor, who took over in November 1926, lured him back to writing. Shaw would increase circulation to 92,000 copies per issue by 1929, but *Black Mask* was still not in the same league as the *Saturday Evening Post*. While the *Post* paid Scott Fitzgerald $4,000 for a story, Shaw paid Hammett $200. His first story in eleven months, "The Big Knock-Over," appeared in *Black Mask* in February 1927.

Hammett allowed himself to be seduced back to short fiction. By January 15, 1927, he also began to review mystery books for the prestigious *Saturday Review of Literature*. Joseph Shaw soon encouraged him to write book-length fiction.

Hammett needed no persuasion. He had made a promise to Jose:

"[T]his time I'll do enough of the murder-and-so-on to make a book. It's time we were trying prosperity. . . . Pray God I can keep my thoughts on it!"[3]

In some stories, he used plots similar to those in earlier tales (such as "The Tenth Clew" and "Corkscrew"), but he moved from plot-based fictions to character-driven narratives. For books, he would need a consistent theme. He began his search in the social forces that challenged contemporary detectives: political corruption and brazen criminality.

During spring 1927, Jose took the children to the country-side at Anselmo. She hoped they would all live together in the fall. But in their absence, Sam began an affair with the recently widowed musician/writer Nell Martin. He continued to love and respect Jose, but Nell offered him intellectual energy. It was she who had encouraged him to write reviews of detective novels for the *Saturday Review of Literature*.

To Jose, the biggest mystery about Sam was his divided self. She admired him when he was ascetic, disciplined, hard-working. She reluctantly accepted his second self: drinker and womanizer. They lived separately, loved each other and their children, but he no longer bothered to be faithful.

Jose felt as much resignation as distress. She knew what men were like. What she needed was his company and sense of family. He still tried, while, according to Jo, her mother con-tinued to love him steadfastly. She remained true to Sam even when eventually he lived another life in another place.

"Probably too true for her own good," said Jo reflectively. "She was still young and lovely and could easily have divorced and remarried, but it never crossed her mind."

Sam approved of Jose, valued her kindness, compassion, reliability, and dedication. He would never entirely discard his first love, his nurse, the sensitive lover who became his only wife. Jose would never quite accept that Sam had left her. He, in turn, never quite left her. He returned—infrequently, but he did return. Even during the middle years of his stormy relationship with Hellman, Jose earthed him with her natural- ness, loyalty, and care.

"He could escape the tensions and madness of Manhat- tan and Hollywood by returning to us," said Jo. "She always welcomed him home. If he came home ill or tired, she stayed around to look after him until he was well enough to go away again."

As late as 1950, Hammett bought Jose a house in western Los Angeles, and during a six-month period he spent a great deal of time living with her and the children in that house. She would remain poor; he would remain sick; she would hold on to their children; he would hold on to his writing. Neither of them would entirely let go.

Part Three
Professional Writer,
1927–1934

CHAPTER 5

Warren Harding, elected president in 1920, allowed cronyism, vice, and scandal to stain his administration. Key officials, including cabinet members, were accused of corruption while in office. His secretary of the Interior, Albert B. Fall, was later convicted of accepting bribes from wealthy businessmen in what became known as the Teapot Dome Scandal. His attorney general, Harry M. Daugherty, was accused of accepting bribes from bootleggers and tried twice, with both trials ending in hung juries. His director of Veterans Affairs, charged with the care of wounded veterans from World War I, went on "joy-rides" visiting hospital construction sites across the country, took bribes from local contractors, and sold off stockpiled hospital supplies for personal profit. When Harding died in 1923, his successor, Calvin Coolidge, restored some public confidence by his determination to achieve prosperity, but he whitewashed the previous government by not demanding the resignation of Harding's sleaze-tainted appointees. This was the era of Prohibition (1920–1933), when the sale, production, and transportation of alcohol were banned through an amendment to the Constitution, but even ordinary people broke the law. Bootlegging gangs made cities into war zones. Organized crime grew strong and terrorized the public, who, at the same time, were fed the notion by newspapers and films that there was something romantic about gangsters like Al Capone.

Against this context of corruption at all levels of American society, Hammett set the stories that he wrote in the 1920s and would also set his four great novels, on which he was now about to embark. [1]

Hammett continued to provide for Jose and his girls and to see them every weekend, but from 1927 onward he acted more often like a single man. He drank gin and whisky, often heavily. He had a brief fling with his former secretary at Samuels and began to see more of Nell Martin. She, like his editor, Joseph Shaw, was someone with whom he could talk about his plans for his first long fiction, which started life as a four-part serialization in *Black Mask* in November 1927 entitled "The Cleansing of Poisonville," but which soon became the novel *Red Harvest*.

"Poisonville" appeared monthly between November 1927 and February 1928 to enthusiastic promotion from Shaw. He told readers that the concluding story of the serial was one of the most startling developments ever placed inside detective fiction. In his biographical note about the author, he also upgraded Hammett's role at Pinkerton's to being "head of a large detective agency," thus creating for Hammett the persona of the only writer of contemporary crime fiction who had the inside story on the criminal world.

"Poisonville" is a savage tale of shameless sleaze in high places, and like *The Great Gatsby*, it exposes corruption at the center of American life. Its plot juxtaposes real terror and fake romance, and when the hard-boiled Op is summoned to investigate a murder, he stays to clean up the city and save his own soul.

The western mining city Personville, whose name symbolizes humanity, is called by the locals Poisonville, symbolizing a source of death. Four thugs—the bootlegger Pete the Finn, the gambler Whisper Thaler, the thief and fence Lew Yard, and the crooked police chief Noonan—run Poisonville, which Hammett based on Butte, Montana. Judging from his depiction, in Butte at the time it was hard to distinguish the rule of law from the rule of the mob.

The violent labor disputes in Butte between Frank Little's union, Industrial Workers of the World (IWW), and the mining companies, which Hammett had observed between 1917 and 1920, serve as a starting point for *Red Harvest*. Elihu Willsson, business baron, owner of banks, industry, and in particular the Personville Mining Company, has ruled the town for forty years. To defend his business interests against militant unions like the IWW, he brings in the four thugs to set up a protection racket. However, when the unions are broken, the thugs stay to terrorize the citizens and Elihu's family. Donald Willsson, Elihu's son, a newspaper magnate, summons the Op, but before he arrives, Elihu sees his son gunned down. Terrified, Elihu asks for the Op's help.

The detective's strategy is to provoke antagonism between the rival gangs so that ultimately, through about thirty killings, they destroy each other. In this way, the Op starts to replicate the violence he sees, turning it against itself. The poisoned city is a lawless place. The walls of the city are built on lies; truth is impossible to determine. Good and evil are not clearly defined, and though the gang leaders go, the corrupt Willsson remains. The Op's duty is to restore order in a place with no stable government, no organized religion, no social or moral standards. He is appalled to find that fighting arbitrary chaotic events means he becomes as duplicitous and violent as the crooks.

He confesses to Dinah Brand, hustler and gold digger, that he has gone "blood simple." Dinah is the most brazen of Hammett's heroines who use sex as a weapon of control. Each Hammett detective falls for such a woman, then has to choose between acting out his sexual desires and acting on his moral code.

The infatuated Op gets drunk with Dinah before she gives him laudanum to relax him. Instantly, he falls into a hallucinatory coma. When he awakens, Dinah is dead and his hand holds the ice pick plunged into her breast. The horrified Op moves from role of investigator to that of murder suspect.

Under the guise of crime fiction, Hammett has created an American existential novel. Like a bleak Kafka hero, the Op has to define himself. Hammett's sparse language, set off against the poisonous blossoms spattered throughout *Red Harvest*, is similar to Kafka's clinically controlled style in a story like "Description of a Struggle," which contrasts with the decadent, overwrought images of Kafka's peers in the Prague literary world. Both Hammett and Kafka use curt phrases to depict confusion and excess. In 1904, Kafka and his antiheroes do not know where they fit in their worlds. In 1928, Hammett's Op is as unsure of his place in society as Hammett is of his. *Red Harvest* investigates this moral and existential uncertainty.

By 1928, the effects of such uncertainty in Hammett's personal experience had solidified into a belief that existence was irrational and the world was unintelligible, yet even when arbitrary contingencies guided people's conduct, they saw their behavior as orderly and meaningful. Hammett translated this belief system into consistent literary themes from *Red Harvest* onward, and this, too, would help propel him to the forefront of American writing. *Red Harvest* would be published in book form on February 1, 1929, not long before the Wall Street Crash in late October of that year shook the foundations of the American Dream. The timing was singularly appropriate for a novel that exposed the gaps between how American political justice and social order were expected to work and how they did work.

In his subsequent books, Hammett would continue to investigate how people created their own sense of reality and produced alternative versions of it. In *Red Harvest*, those versions were linked to characters' fixations: The Op was obsessed with his job; Elihu blindly believed in control; Dinah was infatuated with money. Characters lived out those compulsions as if they were "truths." When their versions of reality collapsed, their lives disintegrated. [2]

On February 11, 1928, Hammett sent the typescript, unsolicited, in its four parts to Blanche and Alfred Knopf's New York publishing house.

> Gentlemen,
> Herewith an action-detective novel for your consideration. If you don't care to publish it, will you kindly return it by express, collect.
> By way of introducing myself: I was a Pinkerton's National Detective Agency operative . . . more recently, have published fiction, book reviews, verse, sketches . . . in twenty or twenty-five magazines, including the old Smart Set . . . [3]

Blanche Knopf was America's first female publisher of a major company in Western literary society at a time when women, Jews, and blacks faced major taboos in the publishing world. Her radical flair, energy, and discerning literary taste soon ensured her position as the woman behind some of the greatest writers of the twentieth century across the globe. By her death in 1966, twenty-seven Knopf writers had won Pulitzer prizes for literature and sixteen the Nobel Prize for literature.

Hammett was unbelievably fortunate to have found such an exciting, innovative house for his work. Blanche decided to take him on when no other literary publisher would touch crime. She took a risk on Hammett and his hard-boiled detectives, and it paid off.

Her reply came quickly:

March 12th 1928

Dear Mr. Hammett:

We have read POISONVILLE with a great deal of interest.

I would like to suggest some revisions, and I hope you won't object to them . . . the violence seems piled on too heavily; so many killings on a page I believe make the reader doubt the story, and instead of the continued suspense and feeling of horror, the interest slackens. One of our readers writes:

"I think the best way to cut this would be to take Lew Yard out of the story entirely. He never figures personally, but . . . he is responsible for a good deal of violence that could be left out . . .

"Another episode that could be entirely cut is the dynamiting of the Police Station. . . . The brief shooting episode on page 176 could be cut profitably . . ."

. . . you may have some ideas of your own regarding all this, and I certainly hope you will not in any way resent our suggestions. There is no question whatever that we are keen about the mss, and with the necessary changes, I think it would have a good chance. [4]

Hammett was stunned. Those words: "There is no question whatever that we are keen about the mss" were in front of him, on paper. Someone, some special person who knew about words, turned words into books, would turn *his* words into a book! It was a joy like no other.

Violence, eh? Too much violence? What did he think of that? Hammett *had* included a great deal of violence, like his fellow crime writers, but unlike them, he made a different use of its *effect*. [5] Although the exaggeration of the mortality rate made Blanche's reader numb, Hammett was surprisingly sensitive about bloodletting, and most murders occurred offstage. Even their later reports gave few brutal details. The prose, like Hemingway's, was drained of emotion. Where brutality arose, it was *not* from Hammett's language but from readers' responses to terrible events.

Blanche saw this, but she still wanted fewer deaths. Persuasively, she finished her letter on an irresistible question.

> Won't you tell me something about your ideas for detective stories, and whether you have any more under way?
>
> Hoping that we will be able to get together on POISON-VILLE (a hopeless title by the way) I am,
>
> > Yours faithfully,
> > Mrs. Alfred A. Knopf

Hammett's new special person wanted to see more. Of course, she was wrong about his title. Hopeless indeed! He tried "Poisonville" out on several retail booksellers. They agreed with Blanche.

"I'm beginning to suspect which one of us is wrong," he wrote back wittily on March 20, 1928, enclosing eight alternatives. She chose *Red Harvest*. He told her he would make the necessary changes; he did not, however, cut Lew Yard but revised the dynamiting of Yard's house to an offstage shooting.

Blanche was surprised when he told her that he not only had a new book, *The Dain Curse*, which would be finished next month, with serial rights already sold to *Black Mask*, but he had a new goal. He planned to depart from that type of novel. He would try "adapting the stream-of-consciousness method, conveniently modified, to a detective story, carrying the reader along with the detective."

He would show readers everything the detective found as he found it. The reader would receive the Op's conclusions as he reached them, and the solution would break on both reader and detective together. He told Blanche:

"I'm one of the few—if there are any more—people moderately literate who take the detective story seriously."

He wanted to write crime fiction without sticking to any tradition. He burst with ambition: "Some day somebody's going to make 'literature' of it . . . and I'm selfish enough to have my hopes."[6]

Blanche already believed in him. Together, they worked toward making this wild statement come true.

Red Harvest, dedicated to Shaw, appeared the same year as Hemingway's *A Farewell to Arms* and was so successful that some contemporary reviewers suggested Hammett's dialogue outstripped Hemingway's. Herbert Asbury in *Bookman* (March 29, 1929) said it was "the liveliest detective story that has been published in a decade." He added: "It is doubtful if even Ernest Hemingway has ever written more effective dialogue." Walter R. Brooks wrote in *Outlook and Independent*: "We recommend this one without reservation. We gave it A plus before we'd finished the first chapter" (February 13, 1929). Hammett and Blanche were delighted at the reviews. Later, André Gide wrote in his 1943 journal: "in *Red Harvest* those dialogues . . . are such as to give pointers to Hemingway or even to Faulkner."[7]

Over the years, the reviews kept coming in as each generation rediscovered the book. On February 7, 1944, in *New*

Republic magazine, Gide's admiration still had not dimmed: "Hammett's dialogues, in which every character is trying to deceive all the others and in which the truth slowly becomes visible through a fog of deception, can be compared only with the best of Hemingway."

Hammett's success as a novelist who wrote clever dialogue came not long after Warner Brothers released the first sound motion picture, *The Jazz Singer* (October 1927) with Al Jolson, who not only sang but spoke several lines of dialogue. By 1930, almost no silent films would be made. Movie producers wanted writers who could turn out crackling dialogue.

Early in 1928, Hammett had already begun to explore film possibilities. He sent Fox Studios in Hollywood several stories, including "Poisonville." By April 1928, he told Blanche Knopf that he would be using filmable plots for his future books. That same April, Fox Studios wrote back to Hammett thanking him for the material he had sent, but too restless to wait, Hammett went to Hollywood in June. He didn't succeed in getting a deal, but after Knopf had published *Red Harvest* on February 1, 1929, Paramount secured the movie rights. Paramount subsequently negotiated with him for original film scripts. They released the movie *Roadhouse Nights*, based on *Red Harvest*, in February 1930.

Hammett sent Knopf *The Dain Curse* (later serialized in *Black Mask*) on June 25, 1928. Alfred Knopf wrote to accept it on July 10, 1928, but advised Hammett the book needed heavy revisions. Blanche and editor Harry Block suggested he cut some characters and decrease the violence.

Hammett, hard at work on *The Maltese Falcon*, was less willing to spend time revising *The Dain Curse*. But he was not yet in a position to dictate, so he made some lengthy repairs. The plot, though highly complex, was experimental and powerfully symbolic.

He had developed the plot from his short story "The Scorched Face" (May 1925), which focused on a young, wealthy set driven to drugs by a religious sex cult. It featured another dangerous beauty, Gabrielle Leggett, who thought she had inherited the Dain family curse, which, in turn, compelled her to believe she had caused eight deaths. The Op's mission in the story was to clean up Gabrielle's morphine addiction.

In *The Dain Curse*, set in San Francisco, the Continental Op is called in to investigate what seems to be a theft of diamonds from the well-connected family of Edgar Leggett, a scientist who had the jewels in his possession. As in the story, the plot revolves around an alleged curse on the Dain family said to cause the sudden deaths of people close to them. Both Edgar Leggett's second wife and his daughter, Gabrielle, are Dains. The novel is divided into three parts; each relates to a different mystery, and each contains a murder. The Op soon realizes that the jewels are merely the starting point for his investigation when it appears as if Edgar Leggett has committed suicide with a pistol in his own laboratory. A note that purports to be a suicide note from Leggett is found by the body. In it Leggett confesses that under his real name of Maurice de Mayenne he had murdered his first wife, Lily, many years ago, had been convicted of that crime, imprisoned, then escaped, and now under his assumed name remains a fugitive from justice. The Op quickly discovers that the apparent suicide was a murder and the note was actually written because Leggett intended to run away again and did not want his second wife, Alice, or his daughter, Gabrielle, implicated in anything.

Gabrielle Leggett believes she has inherited the family curse, and that, as a four-year-old child, she herself had murdered her mother, Lily. The Op later learns that Alice, Leggett's second wife, was Lily's sister. Alice loved Leggett too, and it was she who had arranged Lily's murder. She had taught her young niece to play a game with guns so the child would be seen as the murderer, but Leggett took the blame. After he escaped from Devil's Island, he was found hiding out in San Francisco by Alice and Gabrielle, who had been searching for him. Alice then forced Leggett into marriage with her.

At the start of the novel, Gabrielle is addicted to morphine and involved in a religious cult. When she runs away from the cult, the Op protects her and helps her recover from her addiction. She later marries her fiancé, Eric Collinson. The Op confides his views on the case to his writer acquaintance, Owen Fitzstephan, who plays an important role in the plot. Fitzstephan is also a Dain and Gabrielle's second cousin.

The novel's first line, "It was a diamond all right," establishes a conflict between appearances and reality at the outset that the author continues to probe. Diamonds are set into the novel's fabric. Diamonds were a subject Hammett knew about from his years with Samuels, the jeweler, to whom he dedicated the book. [8]

The first trick in the story is that the scientist, Leggett, has used artificial coloring to make imperfect diamonds that he has borrowed from a diamond company look perfect, thereby disguising them. He tells the Op that a burglar has stolen them from the cabinet he kept them in, but the diamonds are in fact not missing, merely disguised. The apparently stolen diamonds are thus only a facet of Leggett's "robbery." This theme of "knowing what is real" pervades all Hammett's fiction. The Op becomes the sole arbiter of reality. Yet, each time the Op destroys one fiction produced by a character, he realizes there is another fiction behind the one he just destroyed.

Unlike the Op's role in *Red Harvest*, where he was an active participant in the action throughout, here he is largely a bystander, analyst, interpreter. Yet, even as he interprets the disorderly events, he is honest enough to say that any order and clarity he brings to the chaotic situation may only be one possible version of reality. At one point, the Op tells Fitzstephan that "one guess at the truth is about as good as another."[9]

The Op has to force himself not to seduce Gabrielle before he is able to cure her addiction. He discovers that the murderer is Owen Fitzstephan, who is revealed as a psychopath who has fallen obsessively in love with his cousin. It turns out Fitzstephan had persuaded Gabrielle to join the dangerous cult. He tries to persuade her stepmother, Alice, to murder Leggett, and when Alice refuses he kills him himself. He then murders Alice; Gabrielle's doctor, when the doctor learns of his connection to the cult; and Gabrielle's husband.

The writer Fitzstephan may be the murderer, but his symbolic role is also as a fellow novelist. He and Hammett both engaged in the creation of a reality. Both were dedicated to the pursuit of what was truth to them. Fitzstephan, like Hammett, discovered that we could make sense only of what we knew, and yet that knowledge was always limited and changeable.

Each section of *The Dain Curse* presents readers with a puzzle and ends with an apparent solution. But just as in Paul Auster's *New York Trilogy* (where each of its three novellas also proposes a puzzle and concludes with a solution that changes the previous ending), in *The Dain Curse* each solution in turn alters the meaning and answer to the previous riddle.

In the legend of the Holy Grail, innocence and purity in the figure of a heroic knight are set against evil forces. *The Dain Curse* is a twisted Holy Grail allegory, and it was the first American novel to paint an accurate picture of Californian mysticism. At that time, there existed approximately four hundred cults in Southern California alone, according to one estimate. But the fact that there are no final answers in this Op inquiry made it a literary work that developed Hammett's central theme: the arbitrary basis of truth.

Knopf published *The Dain Curse* on July 19, 1929. The critics were highly complimentary. They called the plot gripping, the dialogue cutting, and the revelation of the novelist as the criminal surprising yet explicable. The first review, in *The New York Times*, was favorable. The *New York Herald Tribune* praised the book for its astonishing speed and weird characters. In *Outlook and Independent* (July 31, 1929), Walter R. Brooks wrote: "We can think of only one story of this kind better than the second book of Mr. Hammett's and that is his first book."

The sales of *The Dain Curse* were better than for *Red Harvest*, and it was the first Hammett novel to be published by Knopf in England as well, where it would appear in January 1930. British reviewers would call Hammett fresh and inspired.

Happily, he reviewed his life.

In Jose, he had a nurse for his fragile body. In Blanche, he had a mentor for his writing. What he lacked was a companion he respected intellectually, who would stimulate his mind and challenge his views.

His final brief stab at family life as a young San Francisco–based writer was in the fall of 1929 at 1155 Leavenworth Avenue. But he wavered. He knew New York was the center of publishing. Ambitious and enthusiastic, he was certain the only way to establish his identity as a writer and obtain material success was to move to Manhattan.

Nell Martin, Hammett's part-time lover, was already in New York and had invited him to stay with her. Did she believe that she was the draw? That his writing would last and so would their affair? Certainly, she dedicated her novel *Lovers Should Marry* to Hammett. He admired her radical ideas but privately thought she wrote fluffy fiction. He did not respect her work as she did his.

Hammett's reliance on Jose's trust meant that he told her about Nell's invitation. Jose was not bothered. She knew Nell would not last. She was right.

By October 18, 1929, Hammett had left for New York and got an apartment at 155 East 30th Street. Intellectually, he had left several years before, and Jose knew it. Yet, ambivalences remained. Though he left Jose in 1929, when *The Maltese Falcon* was published on Valentine's Day, 1930, his dedication was "To Jose."

She did not feel Sam was deserting her but was following his ambition. Jo recalls: "Mother took Mary and me by train to Los Angeles. I don't think she felt that she was being abandoned or that it was the end of the marriage. There was sort of a celebration before we left. My father bought her a big steamer trunk and sent out for a Chinese dinner. From the tone of his letters you can feel the mood—he'd made it big, and their money problems were over."

Jose looked forward to the move to Los Angeles. Her Montana relatives visited there in winter, and she had the chance to have a house and yard. Jo's mother had never been a city girl. As Jose prepared to depart, she proudly labeled her luggage "Mrs. D. Hammett," the name crucial to her.

As Sam packed his smaller case, his new name, Dashiell Hammett, was now crucial to him, too. When Sam had signed his early stories Nobody's Son, after his mother Annie's death, that label had reflected not only grief but feelings of isolation in a writers' world he was not yet part of. Now it *was* his world.

CHAPTER 6

Blanche Knopf knew that, in publishing Dashiell Hammett, she had discovered the real thing, a genuine new man of letters, an eccentric who was a streetwise litterateur, some said the equal of Hemingway. Eagerly, on the brink of summer 1929, Blanche awaited the manuscript of *The Maltese Falcon*.

But when on June 14, 1929, Hammett posted her the final draft from San Francisco, she was abroad. He wanted Blanche to admire his new racy title (certainly not "hopeless") and to appreciate his growing artistic mastery. He had to make do with the words "swell title" from editor Harry Block. Hammett told Block on June 16 he was "fairly confident that it was by far the best thing that I have done."

Confident, yes, but also financially stretched. Humorously, he told his savior publishers in his cover letter "I am . . . desperately in need of all the money I can scrape up. If there is any truth in these rumors . . . about advances against royalties, will you do the best you can for me?"

He felt excited enough to ask Block to "go a little easy on the editing."

Block agreed on only minor revisions. He said the new detective Sam Spade's desire for the dangerous Brigid was described too bluntly, and he objected fiercely to some homosexual parts. He told Hammett that, whereas they might have been acceptable in an "ordinary novel," they did not fit the detective genre. Hammett was having none of this.

"I'm glad you liked *The Maltese Falcon*. I'm sorry you think the to-bed and the homosexual parts of it should be changed. I should like to leave them as they are. . . . It seems to me that the only thing that can be said against their use in a detective novel is that nobody has tried it yet. I'd like to try it" (July 14).

Hammett's view prevailed.

Persuasively, Hammett wrote to Block: "While I wouldn't go the [sic] the stake in defense of my system of punctuation, I do rather like it and I think it goes with my sort of sentence-structure."[1]

However, Hammett *was* making significant changes to his style and structure. His two previous books had relied on an episodic structure following the *Black Mask* installment method. The first novel, *Red Harvest*, was in four installments in *Black Mask* before it was published as a novel. The second book, *The Dain Curse*, was in four installments in *Black Mask* but was published as a novel with a three-section structure. This third novel was nonepisodic, which allowed more intimacy, and greater unity. Instead of an elaborate plot with many subplots and a huge number of characters, Hammett has a small cast of suspects, fewer storylines, fewer misleading clues. He has only four murders, all offstage.

Hammett has also moved from first- to third-person viewpoint, which is sharper for dialogue and a better fit for his drama. The first-person viewpoint offered intimacy and openness: no use to Hammett now. A third-person narrator could instead be rigidly neutral and detached. Spade, like Hammett, was private and closed. No one understood Spade. Using the third person made him morally ambiguous. It also allowed Hammett to analyze Spade in the way that the Op had examined other characters.

The Op—dumpy, middle aged, and unappealing—had been supplanted by a stand-alone private eye. A loner, a survivor, a tall romantic hero (whom it is difficult to distinguish from Humphrey Bogart, his most famous film persona), Spade was as reclusive, solitary, unpredictable, and occasionally as cruel as Hammett, who gave him his own name: Sam.

The names of Hammett's characters were rarely random. Before he became a professional writer, Hammett called himself Sam. When he stopped writing novels and, desperate for some structure, reenlisted in the army in 1942, he again called himself Sam, proudly signing his letters "Private Samuel D. Hammett." During his short time as an established novelist, he used the name Dashiell, yet when it came to his most famous novel, he labeled his alter ego Sam, not Dashiell.

Sam, the sick scribbler, had invented the author Dashiell Hammett along with Dashiell's five exceptional novels. When Dashiell later failed to keep writing, Sam at least was immortalized in *The Maltese Falcon*.

Hammett described Spade as a "dream man in the sense that he is what most of the private detectives I worked with would like to have been and what quite a few of them in their cockier moments thought they approached."[2]

Spade did share several characteristics with the Op. He, too, was caught up in a shifting universe of random violence, where a detective survived only by adhering to an inflexible moral code of professional obligation and honor. Like the Op, Spade was a man who could be tempted but could not be bought. Persuasive enough to charm, he was also ruthless enough to survive.

The story in the novel is about a group of shady characters chasing a certain bird across two continents. The glorious falcon is said to be made of gold and encrusted with jewels from head to foot. The narrative hinges entirely on fraud and deceit, though, for the final twist reveals that the falcon is a fake. No jewels, no gold, merely an artificial bird of worthless lead.

Fat Man Gutman tells thin man Spade the legend. In the sixteenth century, the Hospitallers of St. John gave a falcon every year as a tribute to the King of Spain for the use of the island of Malta. The first year's falcon was not a living creature but a golden bird of inestimable value decorated with precious stones. Subsequently, the fabulous falcon changed hands, then disappeared.

Gutman, a crook who wants the bird badly, hires beautiful Brigid O'Shaughnessy to find it. She links up with homosexual gangster Joel Cairo. They decide to double-cross Gutman, but Brigid betrays Cairo then outwits another violent falcon-seeker, Floyd Thursby, and arranges his murder.

Hammett later said that he drew the plot partly from Henry James's *Wings of the Dove*, but he also drew on his own earlier stories. He raided "The Whosis Kid" for another manipulative seducer who tried to tempt the Op before her avatar tried to tempt Spade. From "Laughing Masks," Hammett borrowed another exquisite heroine, rescued by a detective from an evil genius's tyranny. In "The House in Turk Street" and "The Girl with the Silver Eyes," he found models for Gutman and Brigid.

In *Falcon*, Hammett pays greater attention than previously to the relationship between his two main characters: the tough guy in the trench coat and the mysterious, treacherous liar. As the famous fog settles over San Francisco's shadowy streets, the beguiling Brigid bursts into Spade's office. Miss Wonderly, her first alias, flaunts provocative red curls, wears two shades of blue to match her eyes, and spins Spade a yarn about her missing seventeen-year-old sister who has run away from New York with Floyd Thursby, a married gangster. Miss Wonderly believes that Thursby is holding her sister in San Francisco. She begs Spade and his partner Miles Archer to shadow Thursby, who has arranged to meet her that night. Archer gallantly agrees.

Both Archer and Thursby are murdered. Miss W. checks out of her hotel, but Spade tracks her down and she reveals she has told him a "story." Spade reassures her: "We didn't exactly believe your story. . . . We believed your two hundred dollars."[3]

Trust me, Brigid implores Spade. No way, thinks Spade. For Brigid lies about everything. Yet, she uses the word "trust" like a leitmotif, initially seven times in nine sentences. Hammett hammers home her untrustworthiness. He writes some form of the word "trust" thirty times during the novel.[4]

Hammett refines his already curt dialogue here, too. Between Spade and Brigid it crackles crisply. "Help me. I've no right to ask you to help me blindly, but I do ask you. Be generous, Mr. Spade. You can help me. Help me."

Spade, languid, lean, and laconic, uses language hard as flint. "You won't need much of anybody's help. You're good. You're very good. It's chiefly your eyes, I think, and that throb you get into your voice when you say things like 'Be generous, Mr. Spade.'"

Spade does sleep with her, does confess "it's easy enough to be nuts" about her, but ultimately hands her over to justice. Brigid does not understand when Spade tells her that when a man's partner is killed, that man is supposed to do something about it. She is shocked at Spade's ultimatum. "Well, if I send you over I'll be sorry as hell—I'll have some rotten nights—but that'll pass." He admits he probably loves her but is adamant: "I won't play the sap for you."[5]

This novel provided an accurate record of a period blanketed by crime and corruption. Between 1910 and 1930, the number of police in America doubled as the urban crime rate increased. Corruption was common in many city police forces, partly because the average police wage was only $1,500 a year. Crime victims now turned to private detective agencies.

Hammett's novels often depicted repellent prejudices he had absorbed. In the *Falcon,* we clearly see his lifelong fear and hatred of homosexuality. Hammett cynically mocks the effeminate characteristics of Wilmer, Gutman's homosexual gunman, and Spade calls him a "gunsel," a derogatory term for a catamite or boy kept for lewd sexual purposes. Hammett's venomous hostility toward homosexuals in fiction and in life, together with his increasing inability to enjoy heterosexual sex (except with whores), seemed to spring from fears about his own masculinity.

Critic Sinda Gregory describes the novel's central theme as the omnipotence of mystery and the failure of human effort to dispel it. Biographer Richard Layman says it is the destructive power of greed. *The Maltese Falcon* does incorporate these themes, but like *Red Harvest* and *The Dain Curse,* its primary theme is how appearances belie reality, how nothing is ever as it seems, how order and meaning are mere human fabrications, and blind chance is the only thing on which we can rely.

Hammett uses the falcon, whose reality is that it is an imitation with no value, to emphasize his point that we all construct our own realities and make of them what we need. In the novel's most important passage, memorably a nonfiction one, Spade tells Brigid an anecdote to illustrate this. It is about a man named Flitcraft.

Flitcraft was a stable, content, and prosperous real estate dealer in Tacoma. One day, he left for lunch and never returned. Mrs. Flitcraft searched in vain for five years, then arrived at Spade's agency to say she had seen a man in Spokane who looked like her husband. Spade discovered that the man, now known as Charles Pierce, was indeed Flitcraft, who had a new wife, baby son, successful automobile business, and usually played golf after 4:00 p.m. on weekdays, just as he had in Tacoma.

Hammett's preoccupation with philosophical puzzles shows in the name Charles Pierce, for Charles Peirce (one letter rearranged) was a nineteenth-century American philosopher who wrote about chance, probability, and how people lived according to their illusions.

When Spade talked to Flitcraft, he learned that after lunch five years previously, as Flitcraft had passed a building being erected, a beam suddenly fell ten stories and smashed into the sidewalk, narrowly missing him. Flitcraft, frightened, felt that somebody had taken the lid off his life and let him look at the works. Until that moment, Flitcraft had led a happy life in step with his surroundings. He believed his safe life had meaning. Now, a falling beam had shown him life was disorderly and unsafe. His new view was that, by sensibly ordering his life, he had got out of step with it. So he decided to make a radical random change: he would disappear. But after two years' wandering, he settled in Spokane with a new wife and a new routine, astonishingly similar to his old life and old routine.

Spade tells the uncomprehending Brigid that the part he loves best is that Flitcraft did not appear to know what he had done, that he had adjusted himself to beams falling, then, when no more fell, he adjusted himself to their not falling.

Despite everything Flitcraft had learned about the random disorder of existence, he persisted in behaving as if life was rational. For Hammett, this provided an explanation of what guided both Spade's conduct and his own.

That he dared to insert into a crime novel a long *nonfiction* passage of deep philosophical meaning showed that he was now prepared to experiment with literary content in a genre novel.

In 1941, Humphrey Bogart, Mary Astor, Peter Lorre, and Sydney Greenstreet helped make Hammett's book a massive bestseller. Did Hammett appreciate the irony that his most famous and meaningful passage, which gave *The Maltese Falcon* its point and stood as a symbol for all his work, was entirely left out of this iconic film directed by John Huston?

The Maltese Falcon became a five-part monthly serialization in *Black Mask* the month before Hammett finally left San Francisco in October 1929. The published version by Knopf came out on Valentine's Day 1930. Hammett dedicated it to Jose for her unwavering support and commitment during the long years of unbearable illness and financial insecurity. It was reprinted seven times in America in its first year. The film rights were sold to Warner Brothers.

Nevertheless, despite the golden notices, the sales for *The Maltese Falcon* were disappointing. Blanche, Alfred, and Hammett all thought that the novel's enormous potential for commercial as well as literary success was cut short by the Great Depression. During the preceding autumn, on October 24, 1929, a day that became known as Black Thursday, Wall Street crashed. Investors ordered their brokers to sell at any price as the bottom fell out of the market in stocks and shares. During that first terrible day, 12,894,650 shares were sold. Investors lost as much money on that day as the United States had spent fighting World War I. Herbert Hoover, America's president at the time, was unable to hold back or deal with the oncoming recession. Automobile sales, the heart of the twenties' consumer boom, collapsed, and manufacturing fell drastically. The economic disaster rapidly spread worldwide. Unemployment and poverty dominated the lives of most people in Europe and the United States. In America in 1929, the unemployment rate had averaged 3 percent. Now, in early 1930, between a quarter and a third of all American workers were unemployed. [6]

By 1932, 5,000 out of America's 25,000 banks had gone out of business. By a year later, four years after the crash, the stock market had lost almost 90 percent of its value. As early as 1932, 34 million people belonged to families with no regular, full-time wage earner. By 1933, family incomes had dropped by 40 percent, a quarter of all workers and 37 percent of nonfarm workers were unemployed and in a tragic situation. While Hammett wrote on and on during the Depression, in those same years 13 million other Americans became unemployed.

When Hammett looked around him, he could see thousands out of work, their lives ruined. Yet, as America's bubble burst, he himself seemed safe inside a small bubble of his own. Startlingly, good fortune set in for him at exactly the point it ran out for other people. His financial success was astonishing. Just as he was now healthy after years of being sick, so he was now becoming wealthy after years of being poor. Both conditions, good in themselves, had terrible effects on him. Already, in the summer of 1930, he was heady with too much money. He claimed later that he had made $800 a week during that first year of the Depression. The contrast between Hammett's sudden comparative wealth and the fate of his 4 million unemployed countrymen, or even the few employed people—whose average annual salary of about $1,600 was less than Hammett's fees for two weeks—must have seemed dreadful. But there is no record of what he felt about it, and his actions were those of a careless, callous, materialistic Gatsby.

He more than anyone knew what living on the breadline meant. But high on his new status, his focus suddenly and ruthlessly was on expensive restaurants, stylish clothes, and ever more alcohol.

His behavior also changed. Gone was the sick, sensitive young man. His attitudes began to resemble the worst aspects of Fitzgerald's, Faulkner's, and Hemingway's machismo.

A lifetime of illness and poverty had exercised some restraints on Hammett's masculine excesses. Now that his disease was in remission and his fiction earning him wealth beyond dreams, those fetters were lifted. When sober, he was still the shy, secretive writer who had been valued by Annie Bond and Jose Dolan. But when drunk, he no longer respected anyone's feelings. He became abusive, violent, heartless, and cruel. He had lost his capacity to treat women lovers as equals or friends. Drunk most nights and half the days, he saw women as commodities whom he preferred to buy. Hammett was also bad-tempered with fellow crime writers. On April 5, 1930, he began a six-month job as a book reviewer of mysteries for the *New York Evening Post*; by October, he had reviewed eighty-five books, but he had become impatient and terse with poor writing as more alcohol and months went by.

His talent, however, was recognized everywhere. By mid-1930, he was viewed as America's best detective novelist and one of America's most talented fiction writers. His reviews were brilliant. And on March 10, Blanche's firm issued an advertisement proclaiming him "Better than Hemingway." This pleased Hammett greatly, as he was an enthusiastic admirer of both Faulkner and Hemingway.

Otto Penzler called *The Maltese Falcon* "possibly the best American detective novel ever written." Blanche used Penzler's words as the jacket quote.

Franklin P. Adams in *New York World* said that *The Maltese Falcon* was "the only detective tayle [sic] that I have been able to read through since the days of Sherlock Holmes."[7] L. F. Nebel (*St. Louis Post-Dispatch*, March 21, 1930) wrote: "It seems a pity that this should be called a detective story . . . it is so much about a detective that he becomes a character, and the sheer force of Hammett's hard, brittle writing lifts the book out of the general run of crime spasms and places it aloof and alone as a brave chronicle of a hard-boiled man, unscrupulous, conscienceless, unique."

Alexander Woollcott praised *Falcon* as "the best detective story America has yet produced,"[8] and *New York Herald Tribune* (February 23) suggested that "It would not surprise us one whit if Mr. Hammett should turn out to be the Great American Mystery writer," yet both still saw Hammett as a crime writer, albeit at the peak of his powers. Many critics, both at the time and certainly today, believed Hammett had elevated crime writing to literary fiction.

New Republic critic Donald Douglas suggested Hammett's novels displayed "the absolute distinction of real art." In *Outlook and Independent* (February 26), Walter Brooks confirmed: "This is not only probably the best detective story we have ever read, it is an exceedingly well-written novel. There are few of Mr. Hammett's contemporaries who can write prose as clean-cut, vivid and realistic."

William Curtis (*Town and Country*, February 15) believed that Hammett was "an amalgamation of Mr. Hemingway . . . Morley Callaghan and Ring Lardner." Hammett had something "quite as definite to say, quite as decided an impetus to give the course of newness in the development of the American tongue, as any man now writing."

Hemingway remained the main comparison. Listen to Ted Shane: "The writing is better than Hemingway; since it conceals not softness but hardness" (*The Judge*, March 1).

Hammett was most thrilled with two pieces of praise. When Herbert Asbury in a letter to Hammett praised the book, Hammett wrote to him on February 6: "I can't tell you how pleased I was with your verdict. . . . It's the first thing I've done that was—regardless of what faults it had—the best work I was capable of at the time I was doing it."[9]

When Gilbert Seldes in the *New York Evening Graphic* said: "[T]his is the real thing and everything else has been phony," Hammett was so pleased that he copied out the best parts and posted them to Jose.

Years later, in 1983, critic William Marling pointed out that the estimation of *The Maltese Falcon* as Hammett's best work had not changed. By 2012, the verdict was still the same.

In 1930, Hammett knew that with *The Maltese Falcon* he had broken through genre barriers. What he had created was a work of art.

What he wanted to do now, he said to himself, was to write a literary novel. That was his goal for *The Glass Key*.

CHAPTER 7

During the first half of 1930, Hammett worked on *The Glass Key* with surprising dedication and seriousness. As Knopf had brought out *The Maltese Falcon* in the spring and Blanche did not want to publish two Hammett novels in one year, publication of *Key* was delayed until 1931. [1]

The delay disturbed Hammett. He worked, he stalled, he fretted, he finished, then was desperate to see results. The patience sickness had forced on him had not carried over to his healthy self.

The new novel meant a great deal to him. This was probably because it came closest to a literary novel and showed a deeper understanding of his characters' psychological makeup. It had greater elegance and seriousness than his previous work, a polished, lucid style, and a more ambitious subject. It also reflected some emotion deep inside him to do with male honor.

Hammett was always happiest in male-only society. Think about Pinkerton's, hospitals, army, even jail. Those were places where a man's loyalty to another man could be tested. Where what could be lost was irretrievable. In *The Glass Key*,

Hammett wrote a book with male bonding at its core. The novel's themes of male friendship, male competition, male loyalty, and male betrayal dug as deep as the ultimate treachery of a man murdering his own son. For the first time, Hammett dealt with commitment to another person. Spade could not make the ultimate emotional connection to Brigid, whose villainy saved him from trying. But Ned Beaumont, *The Glass Key*'s antihero, does try for commitment and to another man, Paul Madvig.

This book has an assured, easy tone, a feeling of camaraderie that the previous novels lack. It rests on what Hammett knows about his kind. Men don't talk things through; they lean on one another, they stand with one another, they stand side by side. They laugh at the same poor jokes. Jose understood this about Sam.

Though *The Glass Key* contains murder, the investigator, Ned Beaumont, is not a detective but a gambler on a losing streak, as well as an advisor and confidant to Madvig, his corrupt political boss. The setting is a city based on Hammett's own Baltimore, where Madvig intends to support Senator Ralph Bancroft Henry's reelection, partly because he is in love with the senator's daughter, Janet. Janet, however, despises Madvig for his social inferiority and begins to take an interest in Beaumont.

On the night of Janet's birthday dinner, Beaumont finds the senator's son, Taylor Henry, dead in a street. Taylor had seduced Madvig's twenty-year-old daughter, Opal, and appears to have paid the price. Later, Beaumont begins a relationship with Janet, who is convinced Madvig killed her brother. Complexities ensue when Madvig falsely confesses privately to the killing. Ned, out to defend his friend, swiftly discovers that it was the senator himself who murdered his child.

Ned wants above all to remain committed to Madvig. But male friendship breaks down when Madvig comes to Ned's apartment to thank him for getting him off the murder rap and discovers Janet in the bedroom.

Though she apologizes to Madvig for the harm she has done him, Madvig and Beaumont are fixated on each other. With no expression on his face or in his voice, Beaumont says: "Janet is going away with me." Madvig turns white, mumbles something about luck, then stumbles out of the apartment, leaving the door open. Hammett continues: "Janet Henry looked at Ned Beaumont. He stared fixedly at the door."

Ned may have won Janet, but he has lost Paul and in so doing lost a part of himself.

The book ends with a most enigmatic scene involving Hammett's most ambivalent character. We don't know why Ned wouldn't accept Paul's apology during a fight they had earlier. We don't know whether Paul was frightened because he knew Ned wanted Janet for himself or because he suspected Ned wanted Paul for himself. The man is as mysterious as his motives.

Ned is Hammett's most fallible hero, the nearest to a self-portrait. Tubercular, principled, uneasy in a new world, a gambler, a man who sleeps with a woman of a higher social class.

Hammett, too, had now moved into a society quite different from his origins. However, he still sent money and letters to Jose and the girls, who were settled in Los Angeles, where Mary and Jo attended a Catholic school. The Kellys, Jose's relations, saw them frequently, and their Uncle Dick and Aunt Reba regularly wrote to them.

Hammett was exhausted. He had written four novels in three years. He had endured a thirty-hour writing session to finish *The Glass Key*. Later, he attributed his subsequent writing block to this marathon. Still good friends with Nell Martin, he decided to dedicate the novel to her before he finally left both her and New York.

When the lure of Hollywood was suddenly presented to him in summer 1930, he found it irresistible. Hollywood producer David O. Selznick offered Hammett a four-week contract at $300 a week, with an option of a further eight weeks at the same salary, plus $5,000 for an original story. He was to work on a Paramount gangster movie called *City Streets*, starring Gary Cooper.

In July, Hammett accepted Selznick's offer and headed for Los Angeles. It was a turning point in his career and life. He left behind his shiny success as a fiction writer. If he had known he would write only one more novel, would he have stayed? Hammett's philosophy does not even allow such speculation.

Hammett sent a telegram to Blanche's team on July 19 about copyrights for *The Glass Key*. "JUST HOW ARE WE TIED UP WITH WARNER BROTHERS ON THE GLASS KEY STOP THINK I CAN PUT OVER BETTER SALE WITH PARAMOUNT." He begged Knopf to send him proofs of *Key*.

Knopf reassured him *Key* was not tied up with Warner and they were sending proofs. By August 14, 1930, Hammett was worrying them again. Was *Key* going to be published? When? He hoped to place the *Key* movie rights before he returned east again; meanwhile, he assured them Hollywood "has been a lot of fun, except that I haven't found time to do much work on the new book."[2]

Under contract to write one original story for Paramount, he took a mere weekend to handwrite the seven-page version of "After School" and the eleven-page version of "After School" called "The Kiss-Off." His first assignment completed. Then he went on to develop it as *City Streets*, directed by Rouben

Mamoulian, which would be released in April 1931. Hammett felt moderately satisfied with the script and with Gary Cooper as "the Kid," its tough hero. Delighted, Paramount assigned Hammett to work on scripts for William Powell in *Ladies' Man* (1931) and Marlene Dietrich in *Blonde Venus* (1932). Despite Hammett's new work, his sole screen credit for Paramount before he left the studio at the end of 1930 remained *City Streets*.

Though he started work in Hollywood with a burst of creativity, more drink and more money led to feelings of elation, which translated into wild, erratic behavior and further promiscuity with prostitutes. He felt optimistic. When, however, he suffered a renewed bout of illness, many of his fears returned.

One of Hammett's new friends at Paramount was the screenwriter and playwright Arthur Kober, the amiable husband of Lillian Hellman. Lily was a young woman who desperately wanted to be a writer of significance. Like Hammett, she had been working in Hollywood, in her case at Metro Goldwyn Mayer, where she read manuscripts and wrote reports. She was less happy in her marriage than people generally thought, though she herself was not sure of the cause, since she loved and trusted her husband. But like the work she was engaged in, her relationship lacked some sparkle, some stimulation. She began to feel that the long drive to MGM, which had often depressed her, had become a symbol of something wrong in her marriage. She and Arthur decided to separate for a while, without ill feeling, and she returned to New York. While apart, they wrote streams of letters, offering each other lifelong loyalty and continued love. There was no definite break. Lillian and Arthur were as loyal to each other for years in the way that Dash and Jose were, so no one was surprised when she drifted back to Hollywood.

She made new friends with Hollywood writers and artists, including Ira and Lee Gershwin. Now Lily felt less dull, less aimless, more flamboyant, more like an intellectual party girl waiting for a challenge that might be around the corner. And she was in luck. Around the next corner lurked a meeting place for two people—herself and a stranger—that would become legendary. The location of this much mythologized corner was disputed at the time and has been disputed ever since.

Lee Gershwin remembered producer Darryl Zanuck taking her, Ira, and the Kobers to a movie premiere, after which they accompanied him to a crowded corner of the Roosevelt Hotel for Bing Crosby's opening concert. Helen Asbury remembered the legendary corner was situated in a party on Vine Street. Some biographers suggest Zanuck was hosting a party at the Roosevelt. Hellman herself decided years later, memory failing, that the corner must have been in Hollywood's Musso and Frank Grill on Hollywood Boulevard.

If no one knows the location, no one is quite sure of the date, either.

Richard Layman gives the date as "late in 1930 or early in 1931" in his first biography, then alters it to a robust and definite "22 November 1930," in his updated Literary Masters series.[3]

Diane Johnson confesses she is unsure but adds, so was Lillian, who told her years later she had no idea. Hellman the memoirist retrieved this disorderly situation by choosing November 25, 1930, as the date to be celebrated.[4]

If date and place are variable, the name of the stranger is not. In the most popular version, Lillian at the hotel party saw an extremely tall, rather rumpled man, who strode from his corner to the toilets. He had a shock of white hair, a twisted nose, intense brown eyes, and the rangy walk of someone aware of his talent and looks.

"Who's that man?" Lillian asked Lee Gershwin.

He was, by everybody's account, Dashiell Hammett.

CHAPTER 8

Hellman was twenty-five and Hammett thirty-six the day they met. Legend, disseminated initially by the Gershwins, suggested that when Lillian saw Dashiell she leaped up from her seat, raced to his side, and talked to him all the way to the men's room.

Legend assured readers that within minutes they left the party, rushed out to the parking lot, and sat in the back seat of Lillian's car, talking animatedly until daylight. Dashiell was startled by the way the stranger sharpened her wits as she spilled her words. He stared at this woman who liked Pushkin and fishing, grasped literature, believed in justice, and understood politics, art, and culture.

She was not one of the beautiful women who always lay in wait for him, but her vibrant energy masked her ugliness. Later, he told her she was "better than pretty," a cruel line that destroyed her confidence. His humiliating phrase would spread like a canker through her plays.

She had spent hard years, plain and lumpish, fighting the importance of beauty. The expectations of New Orleans society, where you *could not* be better than pretty, were that she would be a Southern belle like her exquisite mother, Julia, or her fellow artists, beautiful Zelda Fitzgerald, delicate Sara Haardt, and exotic Tallulah Bankhead. The two requirements were beauty and money. She had neither.

She had a determined jaw and an aggressive nose. She was a Jewish ugly duckling who scorned the shy, pretty girls and the boys who found her forbidding. Her anger, uncontrollable, was often directed against her father, Max, whom she loved with a passion more than was wise.

Max, the feckless president of a New Orleans shoe company that went bankrupt, never protected Lily financially or emotionally. Losing his house, he bundled his family into the home of his sisters, Lily's caring aunts Hannah and Jenny, who took in lodgers.

Would Lily get security with Hammett? In late 1930, overawed by Hammett's sophistication, she thought about his lifestyle. He knew tweeds were classy but never wore them with silk socks; he hired two black men, Jones and Jones's lover, as chauffeur, valet, and cook, and lived in swell hotels. But a rich hotel client was not a homemaker, something she needed.

Lily felt she had always been homeless. She was born on June 20, 1905, of no fixed address. In Lily's birth year, the New Orleans household records did not list Max Hellman, her thirty-one-year-old father, or Julia Newhouse Hellman, her twenty-six-year-old mother, both from German Jewish families, as either owning or renting a property in New Orleans.

Her mother, Julia, came from a wealthy intellectual family who moved to New York. Her father, a self-educated tradesman, was always poor. When the rash and restless Max lost his job, his firm, and his wife's dowry, he hustled his family to New York, hoping for help from Julia's rich relatives.

He underestimated their utter lack of faith in his business skills and so became a traveling salesman for a Gotham clothing firm, covering the Southern territory, placing his family in mean lodgings and sleazy apartments.

Max took long business trips for five months each year. At first, he left Julia and Lily in so many different towns that Lily later felt Memphis merged with Macon and Macon with Yazoo City. Then Julia and Lily returned to New Orleans for half of each year. Education became a frantic tennis game sometimes played with children whose strokes had force and brilliance, sometimes with those who could barely hold the racket. She rarely succeeded in school or college. She preferred solitary reading to schoolwork.

From 1918, Lillian and her aunts lived in the main Orthodox Jewish area of Dryades Street in New Orleans, which was steeped in Eastern European traditions. But as Max and his sisters became assimilated New Orleans citizens, comfortable with Southern rituals, they lapsed into cultural rather than Orthodox Jews. Julia was spiritual but, to her daughter's shock, prayed in churches as well as synagogues. Lillian told Dash she *felt* Jewish, and later he watched her follow Jewish ritual in burying her aunts and her parents.

She grew up even hazier about money than about religion. The riches of her grand New York relatives protected her. But in New Orleans, her family scrapped for pennies, wasted nothing, had nothing to save. For the New Yorkers, wealth had an almost fanatical status. For the New Orleans aunts, money was useful but less valuable than art and literature.

Too many schools, too many homes, too many religions, and too little money made Lillian rootless and impatient. Yet none of those challenges was as hard as the problem of her appearance. She felt out of control and spent her days organizing, making plans, being bossy, punctual, neat, contriving order and meaning. Suddenly, she found herself captivated by an enigmatic man who believed in neither.

Lily was amazed by Hammett's breadth of reading and, ironically, even more by his productivity. In the time she had turned out a few short stories, he had written three acclaimed and bestselling novels, and his fourth would be published soon. He was supposedly writing his fifth novel.

What Lily saw was a lean, laconic man, taller than her Jewish husband, Art, and her Jewish father, Max, and with a personality utterly unlike their outspoken emotional ones. Hammett, virtually silent, cool, observant, rarely showed emotion. He was secretive, private, inaccessible. That evening, the night they met, he was getting over a five-day drunken binge, the reason for his rumpled demeanor.

His form, figure, and style were those of the iconic Aryan, the goyisha forbidden fruit, the secret dream of the well-brought-up Jewish girl. A man who would never be accepted by Lily's Jewish family, who would always stand on the edge of their noisy world, surveying it with cynical detachment. He probably ate prohibited shrimp and unclean pork. Hammett himself was taboo. And since her unsettled New Orleans childhood, Lily had been seduced by the sinful.

What Hammett saw was a short redhead, with a husky voice, big breasts, a big nose, and an intense manner. That she was brash, Jewish, and spoke like a New Yorker in an attempt to lose her Southern intonation made her seem exotic.

Hellman's and Hammett's mutual unfamiliarity meant each felt more alive in the other's presence. A particle of that would last over thirty years.

Lillian, who always hoped for romance along with sex, decided she had fallen in love. Whatever Dashiell had fallen into, he did not term it "love." Suspicious of the label, he brutally dissuaded Lily from using it.

Dash's courtship of Lily was different from Sam's courtship of Jose. Different and less romantic. The raw emotions he had expressed in early words to Jose were not repeated with Lillian. Occasionally, he *wrote* the word "love" in letters, usually when Lily was in another town. Even then his affection was self-deprecating. On March 4, 1931, he wrote from Hollywood: "The emptiness I thought was hunger for chow mein turned out to be for you, so maybe a cup of beef tea."

Writing in late April 1931, he ended with the line: "I, as the saying goes, miss you terribly," with which she had to be content. [1]

Dashiell thought this headstrong creature might be good to take to bed. This was a frequent thought of his about women and carried no provision for long-term commitment. In bed, he demanded women who were docile, passive, and allowed him the kind of behavior, often edged with cruelty, usually purchased from whores. He was amused when the forceful Lily appeared as submissive as his other women. He did not know that Lily took sexual risks because she was not beautiful.

Hammett informed her that he would not give up other women: neither Jose, nor Nell, nor any other affairs.

Lily raged with unbounded jealousy. Her hysterical reaction to Dashiell's affairs stemmed from childhood nightmares induced by her father Max's greedy sexual appetites. Lily, who had yearned for Max's love, was eight when she trailed her father and their sexy lodger Fizzy down Jackson Avenue. She saw them kiss then drive off in a cab. Her black rage made her want to kill them. Instead, she threw herself down from her favorite fig tree and broke her nose. She always saw *herself*, not her mother, as the woman betrayed.

She ran to her black nurse, Sophronia, her "first and most certain love," who warned her against telling anyone about Max and Fizzy. "Don't go through life making trouble for

people."[2] Not to name names, not to inform, those become
Hellman's precepts, ones she would share with Hammett when
they entered politics.

Dorothy Parker, now Lily's friend, warned her that Hammett was cruel. Lily should stick to sweet-natured Arthur.
When Hammett was sober, he was mild-mannered, introspec-
tive, sensitive. When drunk, which was most of the time, he
was indeed cruel, heartless, violent. Worried friends heard
their rows, saw Lily's blackened eyes, bruised face. She refused
to talk about it. During one public argument, Dashiell punched
Lily so hard she fell to the floor. Later, she said furiously: "You
don't know the half of it. I can't bear even to be touched."[3]

Hammett did not confine his intimidation to Lily. With
stupid pride, he treated many women abusively. It was as if this
former invalid, suddenly living on borrowed time, was trying to
match up to some Last Frontier ideal of manhood, lashing out
in alcoholic rages, degrading women and himself.

With an exotic starlet, Elise De Viane, he went too far. Elise
had met and charmed little Mary and Jo on a shopping trip for
a gift for Jose. Already they knew they must keep quiet about
Papa's ladies. Mary whispered to Jo: "Don't tell Mama."[4] During winter 1931–1932, Dashiell invited Elise to supper in his
hotel room. Later, she called the police and had him charged
with assault, claiming that Hammett had raped and beaten
her. She sued him for $35,000 damages in California's Superior
Court. On June 30, 1932, he was found guilty in absentia, and
The New York Times reported Elise was awarded $2,500.

Sometimes Dash wished to share his starlets with Lily.
He liked to watch the pretty woman and the feisty woman
have lesbian sex. Sometimes he joined in. Just as Lily started
drinking heavily to keep pace with him, so she allowed these
sexual threesomes. But it was not only to please Hammett.
She realized that making love with another woman pleased

her, too. She did not mind her male lover watching. She grew afraid. Female sexual behavior with another woman was not merely outlawed in a Jewish household, it was seen as so gross it was invisibilized. One evening in a cab en route to a lesbian fling, the other woman started stroking Lily's leg. Lily instantly ordered the cab to stop. She hurtled out, told Dashiell it must stop. After Hammett's death, she admitted to a young bisexual companion that she feared liking it too much.

She had after all been strictly brought up in the South. Significantly, Hellman's experiences of and responses to lesbianism, still taboo in the late twenties and early thirties, prior to Radclyffe Hall's groundbreaking work, would become the controversial theme of Hellman's first play, *The Children's Hour*.

Hammett's participation in those threesomes was less about sex than power, another way he could control Lily. The threat of violence even more than its practice kept Lily "in line" but did not entirely subdue her spirit. She often walked away. Frequently, during their first years, she escaped to another town, hoping he would stop his violent ways. He did not.

Jose, whose early life had taught her the abusive ways of men, put up with Sam's drinking and his "ladies." Perhaps it was her gentle, unswerving loyalty that saved her from any hint of violence. Lily's early life had taught her the same lessons. Her father's constant infidelities and betrayals had savaged her spirit, yet she chose to take on a quintessential philanderer, then bucked at his behavior. She would not accept what Jose had accepted. She expected Hammett to change.

She grew angrier about Hammett's use of the double standard. He insisted she stop "juggling oranges" (other men). But he could not make this rule stick. Like an old-fashioned belle, she knew her flirtations would keep him close. He called her "a she-Hammett!"[5] But she was far from that.

Despite women's new sexual liberation, Lily was still uneasy about sex.

Lily and Dash appeared publicly as a couple. They hung out at the Trocadero, danced at the Café Montmartre, drank at the Brown Derby, and dined at Hollywood's Musso and Frank Grill. Gossip columnists linked their names. They made newspaper headlines. Angry Montana relatives sent Jose the humiliating newspaper clippings. Across the miles, Jose read those stories and was at first disbelieving, then ashamed.

Lily was often late home, distressing Art terribly. Sometimes, she did not go home at all, though she did not lie about her meetings with Hammett, merely trivialized them.

Lily thought it wise to stick by Art, to make bigger efforts to show how important he was. Their mutual dependence and respect meant that Arthur would never lose a place in Lillian's life. But that place was changing in ways Lily recognized and Arthur denied. Lily still needed Arthur's emotional security. But she also hankered for adventure.

So Arthur, already Dashiell's friend, became part of their trio. The three drank and dined with Sid and Laura Perelman and Pep (Nathanael) West, Laura's brother. Lily arrived for Perelman and Gershwin parties with Arthur on one arm and Dashiell on the other. One evening, their closeness to the Perelmans misfired. Dash played a trick on Sid by paying a hooker to strip nude in his bathroom. Sid went upstairs, was away a long time. Laura, enraged by catching them having sex in the bathroom, escaped to San Francisco for a brief fling with a more than willing Hammett. Lillian never forgave either of them.

Arthur could see Lily was besotted with Hammett but downplayed their relationship, deluding himself that Lil would return.

Then Jose tracked Arthur down in Hollywood, deeply concerned that her husband might commit himself to Lily.

Arthur reassured her that he was not divorcing Lil. There was no need to take Dash's affair seriously. Arthur had good reasons to believe this was true, remembering the loving letters Lily had written to him after her miscarriage, when she had taken a leave of absence from MGM and had stayed at the St. Moritz Hotel in New York City. Lil had written to say she was distressed because she had had a period. She had thought she would have been a natural "super-creator of babies," but she had failed. She had assured Art they could try again. Yet, even then she knew she would not return to him.

Hellman, hopeless at ending relationships, preferred blurred edges. Dash and Arthur both wanted her back. Kober said he needed Lil by his side if he were to write well. Dash, also missing her, wrote provocatively that he was being more or less faithful, then taunted her by saying if she did not come home he would have to go on "practically masturbating." Lily did not come home, and as a consequence of several mindless affairs, Dashiell contracted gonorrhea for the third time in his life. This was the start of renewed illness.

In the world outside their circle, President Hoover and Congress were unable to stave off the collapse of the US economy, but inside their Hollywood bubble Hammett was rich when he met Lillian. In 1930, he had earned $100,000, which covered the high expenses of the Ambassador's accommodation and his gifts to his children and Lily. He gave her a jeweled brooch, pearls set in black metal. Did it cost more than $500? she asked. Yes, he said, but not as much as $600. He put her down as the five-hundred-dollar type.

She recalled in later years that one of the kindest things Dash did was to support her until she earned enough to support herself. He constantly left money on his bureau for her to take whatever she needed. No mention of it was ever made.

"He fed me," she said. "You never forget somebody who does that for you."[6]

He was so profligate with money, loaning or giving it to anyone in need, that he rarely kept any for himself or laid away any for what might be hard times in the future. Meanwhile, Lily remained as sensible with his money as she was with her own.

Dashiell encouraged Lillian to meet his daughters. She disliked children and felt jealous of Mary, nearly ten, and Jo, four, who lapped up the glamour of Hollywood. They watched Lillian pretending to be fond of them and saw cracks in the pretense. Dash was buying the girls new clothes in a store when Lillian arrived, petulant and irritable. The counter clerk asked her if she'd like to sit and wait. Lillian snapped: "No, I'm not going to sit there." Mary thought Lillian's attitude was not unreasonable. Why should this rich, smart lady like them? Lillian wanted Papa's attention, but he was giving it to her and Jo.

Jo knew Lillian was married, but she behaved like Papa's rich, bossy wife. Not his real wife. Not Mama. Jo recalled that generally Lillian tried to be kind to her: "Though she would try to sway me in lots of ways. It was always, 'Well us girls are on an equal level, and I'm telling you this because you'll understand.' I was, of course, terribly flattered to be considered on her level!" Jo recalled that when she was about seven or eight, on one occasion Lillian was deliberately unkind.

> I was in the swimming pool. . . . Out of the blue sky, Lillian suddenly asked me in a mocking tone if I was devout, knowing I was a Catholic. What do you say to a question like that? Fortunately, my father said very offhandedly: "Oh well, she figures if she's wrong she's only lost a little time, and if she's right why you know she's saved." He did it just to turn Lillian aside from me. . . . Today, I think she was being bitchy . . .

One difference Jo noticed between her mama and Lillian was that Lillian ran a "tight ship": "There were rules for everything, and order, whereas Mother ran a pretty loose ship. We were kind of lippy. She was very lenient."

Jo pointed to a central contradiction in her father's character:

> In one way he could be free, talking about things like sex and what went on in Hollywood when ordinary fathers wouldn't have told those horror stories. On the other hand, he was very much the Victorian father. "You do what I tell you and don't answer back" would be his terms. He made my sister wipe lipstick off her face when she was fifteen. There was this big contradiction between easygoing and "Never forget that I'm Daddy."

Jo felt he was not fit for the domestic scene. "Even when I was in high school and had a date arranged, if he was due, I would cancel it and stay home. When Papa was there, you were there. He was our focus."

About Hollywood, Jo said: "Papa hated it and most of the people in it. He had a contempt for the gross ignorance and commercialism that was rife there. . . . I think he also had contempt for himself for taking the money then not doing what he should be doing. So to come to our house, where Mama helped him stop drinking, was to be some place where he could get away from all that."

Hammett found a peace with his wife and children that he never replicated anywhere else. "Mother was kind of passive with him and would act as his nurse. He might be in bed a lot of the time. She'd bring him food then encourage him to get up. She loved him and never until the very last days said in her head that they were really separated. It was like she was still his wife, even though he might be off with other women."

Dashiell continued the pattern toward his family he would maintain all his life. He would write to them, send them money irregularly, visit them laden with gifts, and spend time with them, often collapsing with exhaustion and being nursed back to recovery by Jose.

Lillian always grossly underestimated Dashiell's love and loyalty toward Jose, Mary, and Jo. They were his only family. Sam had told Jose that if she took care of the children, he would take care of her. Jo said her mother held on to those words as long as she could, and her father did, too. Even when his support checks were late, nobody doubted that they would come. The three of them always knew they were his family, even if they lived apart.

Although his family knew about his relationship with Lillian, what they didn't know about were his drunken excesses and constant partying. They certainly were not privy to his mounting anxieties about his novel writing.

Hammett, though successful in Hollywood, felt something ominous was happening to his fiction. Instead of drinking less to tackle the problem, he drank more, as if to deny the problem existed.

Yet another bout of gonorrhea in March 1931 accompanied his sexual excesses. More significantly, severe tuberculosis struck. Terrible head pains and trouble in breathing forced him to stop drinking for a brief recuperative period. Then, back on the bottle, he was again seriously ill.

Hammett had left Paramount at the end of 1930, and in January 1931, Warner Brothers executive Darryl Zanuck hired him to write an original Sam Spade story. It would star Powell, who, like Hammett, had come from Paramount. On January 23, 1931, Zanuck gave Hammett $5,000 (the first of three equal installments) on signing the contract for "On the Make." When Hammett delivered the treatment, he received the second $5,000, but when he completed his assignment on April 28, Zanuck rejected it and refused to pay the final installment.

Released from his contract, in spring 1931, he began then abandoned a fragment called, like his later novel, "The Thin Man." As Blanche wanted to delay the proposed delivery and publication date of *The Thin Man* so that it did not clash with that of *The Glass Key*, Hammett thought it pointless to turn the fragment into a book. Instead, he offered it to his new literary agent, Ben Wasson of the American Play Company, to hawk around as a teaser.

The Glass Key, first published in England on January 20, 1931, was published in the United States on April 24, 1931. Hammett's spirits rose at the ensuing critical acclaim.

The reception was even hotter than for *The Maltese Falcon*. In the first two weeks, *The Glass Key* sold 11,000 copies, and by December sales had reached 20,000. In the first two months, there were five printings at $2.50 a copy. Movie rights were sold to Paramount later in 1931 for $25,000.

The book was praised as one of the most excellent American detective novels ever published. Bruce Rae in *The New York Times* (May 3, 1931) said there could be no doubt about Hammett's gifts in this special field and no doubt about *Key's* success. The *New York Herald Tribune* (April 26) described it as twice as good as *Falcon*, while in *Outlook* (April 29) Walter Brooks proclaimed Hammett had now written the three best detective novels ever published.

It was the high point of Hammett's writing career, marked as such by Dorothy Parker, whom Hammett had not yet met but who suddenly discovered him for *The New Yorker* (April 25): "It seems to me that there is entirely too little screaming about the work of Dashiell Hammett. My own shrill yaps have been ascending since I first found *Red Harvest*, and from that day the man has been, God help him, my hero." She heaped exuberant praise on *The Maltese Falcon* and said that, though the hero of *The Glass Key* could not "stand near Sam Spade," she found the book "enthralling."

Hammett's own later appraisal was that *The Glass Key* was his best book.

Blanche urged him on by post to make progress in his next novel. He answered her by telegraph on April 17, 1931: "THOUSANDS OF APOLOGIES FOR NOT HAVING ANSWERED YOUR LETTER BEFORE. . . . JUST BACK FROM A FEW WEEKS IN SAN FRANCISCO EXPECT TO STAY HERE SEVERAL MONTHS BUT EXPECT TO HAVE NEXT BOOK THE THIN MAN FINISHED IN A COUPLE OF MONTHS." [7]

The Knopfs hoped to publish *The Thin Man* in January 1932, but they would have to wait much longer than they could have imagined.

Hammett's depressions and disease worsened. He was unable to write and unable to quit drinking. His frail, tubercular condition could not take that amount of alcohol. Determined to commit suicide, he left the accommodating Knickerbocker Hotel, where he did not want to upset the management, checked in to the Roosevelt, and declared his life was not worth living.

A stranger told Jose Hammett was threatening suicide. She raced to the Roosevelt, but he refused to open the door. Then someone told her it was a false alarm and she left. It was in fact a warning signal of how frail his mental condition was and how afraid he was of not being able to write again.

When Lillian arrived, she pounded on the door until Dash, who believed drink and TB would kill him soon anyway, opened it, saying weakly: "I'm a clown." Lily, dismissive, entirely failed to understand the depths of his despair.

On August 6, 1931, Hammett entreated Knopf for money in order to leave Hollywood. Broke and self-destructive, he settled into New York's Hotel Elysee to write *The Thin Man* with absolutely no success. Instead, he communed drunkenly with William Faulkner. After a full day's drinking, he and Faulkner went to a Knopf party for Willa Cather, at which Hammett passed out and Faulkner was abusive to the Knopfs.

By May 1932, Hammett and Hellman were living in grandeur at the Biltmore Hotel in New York, while poor Jose, in despair because she had received only $100 from her husband in seven months, wrote to Alfred Knopf. She said she was desperate, the children needed clothing, and she didn't have enough money to feed them the right food.

"I feel as thou [*sic*] he is not getting my letters—someone is holding them back—I know he loves his family—would hate to hear they are in this condition."[8]

The Knopfs said Hammett had checked out of his New York apartment, leaving no forwarding address. Hammett did love his family, but at this point he felt as incapable of helping them as he was of helping himself.

No wonder Lily clung to Kober and was distressed when, in 1932, she and Arthur together told Julia and Max they planned to divorce. Julia adored Arthur, disliked Hammett, and felt ashamed her married daughter was living in sin. Though Max felt certain wayward bonds with Hammett, he was concerned that his daughter was linked to a non-Jewish drunk.

Kober told *his* family he would never love any girl as he did Lil. "Lillian is all cut up about the divorce," he wrote his mother in the Bronx. "She is still very much in love with me."[9]

In court, chivalrously he insisted that Lil prefer charges of cruelty against him: a laughable but sad procedure.

Kober's unpublished autobiography was called *Having Terrible Time*,[10] and at that point, privately he, Lily, Jose, and Hammett were doing just that.

CHAPTER 9

Hammett and Hellman's outrageous public behavior was still making headlines, which continued to distress Jose. "Mother was terrified Papa might marry Lillian," said Jo. "Publicly, she told everyone that she and Papa were temporarily living apart because he needed solitude for his books."

Jose's pride did not allow her to speak negatively about Lillian. "The only time Mama spoke harshly was after Papa's death, when she said Lillian should have given us some of Papa's possessions."

Jose, who had acquaintances but no close friends, was lonely. She would endure years alone until, as Jo said reflectively, age put out the final spark of hope. "Mother's life was more tragic than Papa's. He chose his privacy, but Mama just let her isolation happen."

But, fearful, Jose was also strong. "The tough thing about Mama was she never chickened out."

In 1932, the Hammett family moved around in Southern California. First they stayed in a bungalow court in Hollywood, then in a house in Beverly Hills, with a Swedish live-in maid.

"It did not last," Jo said. "With Papa away, we became even naughtier, crayoning on walls, disobeying the maid, who left quickly. Mother . . . did not replace her. We moved to Burbank Glendale in West LA, where Papa bought Mama a fancy Packard."

But Dashiell forgot to keep up payments, so Jose watched a well-paid stranger drive it away.

By the mid-thirties Jose had settled in Santa Monica. She and Hammett communicated regularly, which temporarily allayed her fears of divorce.

"It's hard to remember how disgraceful divorce was, especially for a Catholic," Jo recalled. "Lillian was the Boogie Man of my childhood. Her name in my mother's mouth had a cold, scary sound. It was always 'Lillian,'—not 'Lillian Hellman' or 'Miss Hellman' . . . but 'Lillian' as if she knew her." [1]

Jose could not believe that she was the object of Lillian's jealousy, while Dashiell made it clearer than ever to Lillian that his family was out of bounds of her malice. His unique relationship with Jose was his business, not Lillian's.

Jo remembered that her father overspent on extravagant gold-link name bracelets for her and her sister and elaborate boxes of European chocolate for their mother. "Mary and I had Raggedy Ann and Andy dolls as large as we were. Another day he sent us a trunk . . . from F. A. O. Schwartz . . . every child's magical present."

Lillian stood by uneasily, but knew better than to comment. Then the reckless father's money began to run out. By September 1932, Hammett, still at the luxurious Biltmore on Madison, had few resources left. He was so broke he had to leave the Biltmore.

Needing a cheap base where he could write seriously, he moved with Lillian, but, incomprehensibly, to the equally expensive Hotel Pierre. When the first month's bill of $1,000

Dashiell Hammett as baby
(Private collection)

Dashiell Hammett as a
young man in civvies,
1918 (Private collection)

Dashiell Hammett in the army as a
young man, 1918 (Private collection)

Josie Dolan, Dashiell Hammett's wife, as a nurse
(Courtesy of the Dashiell Hammett Estate)

Dashiell Hammett's two daughters, Mary and Jo (Courtesy of the Dashiell Hammett Estate)

Lillian Hellman as a young woman, at the time she met Hammett (Associated Press)

Dashiell Hammett and Lillian Hellman chatting at a table at 21 Club, December 31, 1944 (*Time* and *Life* Pictures/Getty Images)

Blanche Knopf, Dashiell Hammett's publisher (Photography Collection, Harry Ransom Humanities Research Center, the University of Texas at Austin)

Dashiell Hammett before the House Committee on Un-American Activities, March 27, 1953 (Bettmann/Corbis)

Dashiell Hammett is handcuffed to fellow Civil Rights Congress representative W. Alphaeus Hunton as he approaches car at Federal court to be taken to Federal house of detention, July 9, 1951 (Hyman Rothman/*New York Daily News* Archive/Getty Images)

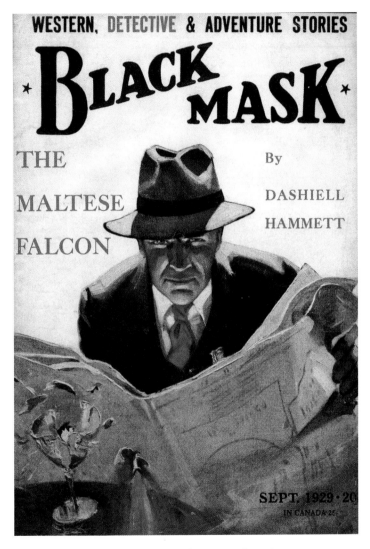

Cover of *Black Mask* September 1929, featuring part one
of *The Maltese Falcon* (Private collection)

Window display of Hammett's *The Thin Man* (Photography Collection, Harry Ransom Humanities Research Center, the University of Texas at Austin)

arrived, he sneaked out, wrapped in thick layers of clothes, his cheeks padded with cotton wool to change his gaunt appearance. Pep West, acting as hotel manager at the Sutton Club on 330 East 56th Street while completing his novel *Miss Lonelyhearts*, offered them refuge there, along with writers Edmund Wilson, Quentin Reynolds, Erskine Caldwell, and James T. Farrell.

Two separate decisions changed his life. First, he stopped drinking and settled in to writing *The Thin Man*. Second, he read *Bad Companions*, a compendium of criminal case histories by William Roughead. He discovered the Great Drumsheugh Case, in which two female teachers were accused of lesbianism by a pupil who hated them. Hammett had wanted to write a play, and this could have been his material, but instead he would hand it over to his lover.

Lily and Dash had finally found a way to be together— Hammett, writing *The Thin Man*, which would be his last published novel, and Hellman, mentored by him, soon writing what would be the first of twelve major Broadway plays.

On September 29, 1932, Hammett warmed up by reworking minor stories. He tackled some published Sam Spade tales, produced two new stories and the novella *Woman in the Dark*, a mystery without a detective that focused on Luise Fletcher, the usual, exotic woman with the usual brand of brains, betrayals, and bewitchery. After those rehearsals, Hammett worked on his novel without pause. He finished *The Thin Man* by May 1933.

He borrowed from his early sixty-five-page fragment, also called "The Thin Man," its title and two names: Guild, the fragment's detective, who is now the novel's policeman; and Wynant, the fragment's writer, who is now the novel's inventor. The plot centers on missing scientist Clyde Wynant, who, implicated in a series of crimes, is then discovered dead.

To Lillian's surprise, her alcoholic lover stopped drinking, resisted parties, and refused to go for walks in case he lost his creative thread.

"Life changed. . . . The locking-in time had come and nothing was allowed to disturb it until the book was finished. I had never seen anybody work that way: the care for every word, the pride in the neatness of the typed page itself." [2]

While Dash wrote, Lillian made mischief. Pep West was engaged to Alice Shepard, a beautiful model. One evening, when Pep drove Alice to Grand Central Station, Lily decided to join them. She made a play for Pep. Alice recognized the signs but felt paralyzed. When she arrived home, Alice telephoned Pep, but her fiancé, already in bed with Lillian, did not answer.

What were Lillian's motives? They were mixed: she felt rejected by Hammett's concentration on his novel; she was jealous of Alice's outstanding beauty; and she wanted revenge on Pep as the brother of Laura, who had seduced Dash.

Hammett dedicated The Thin Man to a delighted Lily and told her his witty protagonist Nora Charles was based on her. Lily was less pleased when he added sardonically she was also the model for his villainess.

In this witty novel, Nick and Nora are stylish spoofs of Lily and Dash, though Hammett omits their financial problems, his violent streak, and Lily's insecurities. Nick at forty-one and Nora at twenty-six mirror the ages of Hammett and Hellman, who were forty and twenty-seven on publication day. The clever banter between Nora and Nick reflects Hellman and Hammett's witty discourse. Nick's drinking habit and cynical philosophy that life is arbitrary and often bleak are recognizably Hammett's.

But there are significant differences. In previous novels, Hammett's concern was to analyze the way men behave toward men, with a consequent stereotyping of his female characters. Here, in his description of an affectionate marriage, a product of the new sexual freedom of the 1920s and 1930s, Nora is a three-dimensional woman almost equal to her man.

This time, *The Thin Man*'s characteristic theme that the nature of reality hidden behind plausible appearances is hollow, worthless, and morally ambiguous is presented with humor. Fake falcons abound under other guises, but the context is a sun-spattered society of party people rather than a tormented world of corruption, cruelty, and vicarious violence. *The Thin Man* still shows shocking brutality in a universe that is randomly predatory, but the style is ironic. All of the three deaths in the novel take place offstage, so that they can be handled with sleek throwaway lines. Hammett has moved away from the graphic descriptions of several brutal fights in *The Glass Key* or the dehumanizing corruption of *Red Harvest* and *The Dain Curse*. Violence in this sophisticated comedy of manners is less grim than in *The Maltese Falcon*.

The cast is rich, cultivated, and leisured, and several characters are not related to the case—a big break with hard-boiled fiction convention—and include satirical portraits of popular contemporary entertainers, such as Jack Oakie and Oscar Levant.

The book opens in 1932. San Franciscans Nick and Nora Charles are Christmas shopping in New York, accompanied by Asta, their whimsical schnauzer. *The Thin Man*, like *The Glass Key*, no longer uses a working detective but a hero who does no paid work at all. Nick, a former PI and now a hard-drinking playboy, quit his job six years previously, the year after he married Nora, a wealthy lumber heiress who is as fascinated by detection work as was Lillian. Nora has an orderly, logical attitude toward detection, unlike Nick or Dashiell. The couple's opposing criteria are revealed when Nick explains they "probably" have enough evidence to convict the murderer. Nora won't accept the word "probably." She feels Nick's solution is "not very neat." Nick assures her with "It's neat enough to send him to the chair," but Nora is dissatisfied. "I always thought detectives waited until they had every little detail fixed in." When Nick explains that probability in an arbitrary world is the best that can be achieved and that "murder doesn't round out anybody's life, except the murdered's and sometimes the murderer's," Nora is still dissatisfied.

Hammett starts the novel elegantly, with Nick lazily leaning across the bar in a 52nd Street speakeasy. Nick is softer than Spade, brighter than Beaumont. The attractive Dorothy Wynant introduces herself as the daughter of Clyde Wynant, Nick's former employer. Dorothy is in New York with her mother, the villainess Mimi, once Nick's lover, now divorced from Clyde and remarried to Christian Jorgenson. They are hunting for the missing Wynant. Nick suggests they phone Herbert Macaulay, an ex-army pal whose life he once saved and now Wynant's lawyer. Macaulay later informs Nick that Wynant has vanished purposefully to work on a new invention. Suddenly, Wynant's secretary and mistress, Julia Wolf, is found murdered. Communications start streaming in, apparently from Wynant, desperate to prove his innocence.

The large cast begins to lie, deceive, and distort. Dorothy's childhood crush on Nick develops into adult passion, and she tells him her mother beats her and her stepfather abuses her. The strange sadistic teenager Gilbert, Clyde's son, also becomes infatuated with Nick, while Nick himself has to fend off moves from manipulative Mimi.

Hammett's own streak of sexual sadism shows when Nick watches Mimi slash Dorothy across the mouth with the back of her hand, then says lightly to her: "You must come over to our place sometime and bring your little white whips."

But his determination to refuse romance with anyone except Nora gives him a different role in Hammett's oeuvre from previous detectives.

Reluctantly, Nick agrees to take on the case. Hammett returns to the first-person viewpoint but uses it in the old-fashioned English classic style of keeping the reader in the dark about information Nick possesses. Nick, more flippant than previous investigators, also conceals clues from the police, a method of which Hammett had previously disapproved in other crime writers. In earlier novels, Hammett's detectives hunt hungrily for evidence; in this novel, the evidence arrives lazily at Nick's desk.

As in *The Maltese Falcon*, there is a sudden curious interruption to the narrative. Hammett writes a two-thousand-word nonfiction account of cannibalism, taken from Duke's *Celebrated Criminal Cases of America*, which focuses on the case of Alfred G. Packer, a prospector who murdered and ate his companions. When Gilbert tells Nick he is fascinated by cannibalism, Nick points him to the Packer case. Nick has already noticed that the teenage boy with sadomasochist feelings is also a sly voyeur with incest fantasies about his mother.

The cannibal episode, though less successful than Flitcraft, probably stems from a similar thematic motive. It highlights people-eating qualities of several characters: Mimi, Dorothy, Gilbert, Jorgensen, and Macaulay. Certainly, cannibalism has an appeal to Hammett, whose own interest in sadistic sexual activities is evident in this novel. The motif of destruction for the pleasure of doing it is similar to that seen in previous novels, except here the context is social rather than criminal.

Considered risqué at the time, this was Hammett's most *commercially* successful novel. Yet critics debated its artistic merits. Some thought it the weakest of the five; others thought it nearest to serious literary fiction.

In the thirties, Nick and Nora's open marriage was viewed as scandalous. Several characters were visibly lecherous. The sadism was satirized, not contained. Several lines of dialogue drew protests. These included phrases by women about going to the can; Nick's flat-voiced comment that Mimi hated men more than any woman who wasn't a lesbian; and Nora's advice to Nick that he should keep his legs crossed when he saw Mimi. Most controversial was the discussion between Nick and Nora after Nick had physically restrained Mimi. Nora asked him: "Tell me the truth, when you were wrestling with Mimi, didn't you have an erection?" Nick replied "Oh, a little." Nora found this funny and said tartly: "If you aren't a disgusting old lecher."[3]

Redbook, the women's magazine, was anxious to publish *The Thin Man* but only in an expurgated condensed edition. In their December 1933 issue, they cut the offending lines. Knopf cleverly used the censored dialogue in a *New York Times* advertisement on January 30, 1934: "I don't believe the question on page 192 of Dashiell Hammett's *The Thin Man* has had the slightest influence upon the sale of the book. It takes more than that to make a best seller these days. Twenty thousand don't buy a book within three weeks to read a five word question."

Despite this, the Canadian government banned the novel. The first English edition censored the offending passage. Knopf brought out the unexpurgated US edition on January 8, 1934, and it sold 20,000 copies in the first three weeks and more than 30,000 in the first year. Hammett wrote his own jacket copy and included a self-portrait in an elegant tweed suit and wide-brimmed hat, casually carrying a cane. Though the title *The Thin Man* referred to Wynant, Hammett's photo on the cover led people to label the author and/or the hero Nick as the Thin Man.

Interestingly, in every publicity blurb Hammett described himself as married with two children. On January 22, he was thankful that he could at last write from the Lombardy Hotel to tell Jose their financial troubles were over. He said if God did not intervene, they would be out of debt and on the road to security.

He gave Jose three exciting pieces of information. First, his swell book had fine reviews. He sent her the clippings. The previous week, it had sold better than any other in New York, Philadelphia, and San Francisco. Secondly, he told her MGM was buying the movie rights for $21,000. He promised to send her a thousand as soon as the money arrived, then more each week, regularly. His third piece of news amazed her. He was to write the story for a cartoon strip for Hearst's syndicate. That would bring him in a regular income.[4] In its first eighteen months, *The Thin Man* sold 34,000 copies at $2 each.

The following week, on January 29, King Features, owned by William Randolph Hearst, launched *Secret Agent X-9*, a daily comic strip with words by Hammett and drawings by Alex Raymond. We are out of the woods, he told Jose. He promised her this time he would stay out.

As he wrote his letter, the Thin Man was rich again.

Many other writers, clerks, and tradespeople in the United States and elsewhere in the Western world were not faring so well. Many thousands were still suffering dire unemployment and unbearably low wages.

The previous year, 1933, when Adolf Hitler, the forty-three-year-old leader of the National Socialist German Workers (Nazi) Party had become chancellor of Germany, in Hammett's America, Franklin D. Roosevelt had become the thirty-second president of the United States. Roosevelt had immediately set into motion his New Deal to alleviate the Depression. He focused on three areas that have become known as the three Rs: relief for the unemployed and the poor, recovery of the economy to pre-Depression levels, and reform of the financial system, so that a repeat of the disastrous situation could not occur.

In his first hundred days, he sent bills to Congress and set out a number of optimistic programs that included cutting pay of government workers; cutting government spending by 15 percent; insuring people's deposits in banks against losses to restore their confidence in the banking system; an Agricultural Adjustment Act (1933), which paid farmers to limit the amount of crops they grew, or to dig back into the ground crops already grown; and an act that forced employers to deal with trade unions and allowed workers to take part in collective bargaining. He signed an act in March that permitted sale of 3.2 beer and wine—thus effectively ending Prohibition before the Twenty-first Amendment repealed it at the end of 1933, while generating tax revenue for the government and allowing the community to feel better about drinking.

But his programs to restore the economy worked slowly, and by 1939, there were still ten million unemployed.

In his fiction, Hammett rarely depicts the effects of the Depression directly. The world of Nick and Nora in *The Thin Man* is complete escapism, perhaps necessary for his readers. Hammett and a princely group of well-paid artists and writers stood apart from their fellow men and women and appeared to barely comprehend their hardships.

Between 1933 and 1950, Hammett's total earnings from the novel, its spin-offs, and its characters used in movies produced in the thirties and forties amounted to almost a million dollars. MGM made a successful film of *The Thin Man* starring Myrna Loy, released in June 1934, for which the screenplay was written in a mere three weeks by Albert Hackett and Frances Goodrich, who became Hammett's good friends.

Five successes behind him, Hammett turned his attention to Lily's career. He had been saving powerful material for a play that he wanted to write himself but which he saw as perfect for Hellman's first drama.

During winter 1933–34, Dashiell and Lillian left the Sutton Club Hotel for Homestead, Florida, to work on it. They got drunk for a few weeks in Miami, then moved to a primitive fishing camp in Key Largo, where they stayed through the spring and summer, fishing by day, reading at night, and working on the play. Hellman decided it was one of their finest years, because they discovered they got along best in the country and without people.

In Homestead, Hellman feverishly drafted *The Children's Hour*, the play based on the plot Hammett had found for her. Hammett read and reread every draft, criticizing, mentoring, editing, judging, making her write, rewrite, rewrite the rewrites, over and over. He was determined that she would achieve his own goal of meticulous perfection.

They put money down on a small lot and planned to build a house there. When they eventually returned to New York City, they missed Homestead so much that in spring 1934 they returned for a few weeks.

On March 24, 1934, Hammett's last short story, "This Little Pig," a satirical tale about the movie industry, was published by *Collier's*. Later in the year, on September 27, Universal would buy his screen story "On the Make," which they would release under the title *Mister Dynamite* in May 1935, but Hammett's output was now quite sparse. As Hammett's writing life wound down, Hellman's began to take fire.

PART FOUR
HELLMAN AND HOLLYWOOD, 1934–1936

CHAPTER 10

Lily wrote. Dash edited. Homestead, Florida, was ablaze with activity. And rows. Long days. Hard nights. Dash ripped up page after page. "He tore them to pieces," Lily said later. The fight was over *The Children's Hour*. "There was a great deal at stake, great deal of feeling at stake."

Dash staked their whole relationship on the fact that he wanted Lily "to be some good." He was "pleased and proud" when she was. His constant criticisms came from his belief that Lily was "good enough to fix things." On an early draft, Lily wrote, "he spared me nothing."

Hammett forced her to rewrite dialogue, use fewer words, shape the structure. Never give up.

Hellman whined that she wanted to give up. "Don't be a writer," he baited her. "Nobody asked you to be a writer. This is what it costs." She whined some more. "If you never write again," he said coldly, "what difference will it make?" Try again. She tried again. They were both worn out.

She attempted to intimidate him into sparing her. "If this isn't any good, I'll never write again. I may even kill myself."[1]

He did not spare her. She did not die. The disciplined work went on. She called him "teacher." She was not unhappy. She would have other critics but none as sharp. She would have other audiences but none as necessary.

One of Dashiell's most appealing characteristics was his generosity toward other writers. What he downplayed was his sense of shame about his own inability to write. The writer's block seemed to have settled into his spirit and could not be shaken off. Over the months, it got steadily worse until he wrote to Lily a poor attempt at a joke, with the typing diagonally down the page like a poem, admitting, "What little imagination I've got is used up."[2] He felt as if he had suffered a stroke. He thought the writing side of his brain had become paralyzed.

Lily was grateful for his constant attention, but her savage yet kind mentor was simultaneously playing the fond father and affectionate, absentee husband. Dash wrote two loving letters to Jose and a gentle one to Josephine and Mary, telling them he had gained weight, had managed ten days on the wagon, was suntanned, felt better than for years, was becoming expert at deep-sea fishing. He planned to return to Homestead next year but promised to come and see them first. He sent them kisses. He did not mention Lily or Lily's play.

But the play preoccupied him. The Great Drumsheugh Case concerned a Scottish girls' boarding school forced to close in 1810 because a mixed-race schoolgirl lied about her two headmistresses, who were subsequently accused of lesbianism. The girl's grandmother believed the accusation and influenced parents to withdraw their children. When the teachers sued for libel, the case dragged on for ten years. When they were finally exonerated by the House of Lords, their lives had been destroyed.[3]

Hellman relocated the story to New England, changed and added to the plot. Manipulative, white schoolgirl Mary tells her seemingly liberal grandmother, Amelia Tilford, the school's major funder, the lie about teachers Karen and Martha doing unnatural things, then blackmails her fellow pupil, Rosalie, to substantiate her lie. Mrs. Tilford phones other parents, who remove their children. Karen's and Martha's careers are destroyed; Karen's engagement to Mrs. Tilford's nephew, Dr. Joseph Cardin, is ruined, as he half-believes the lie; and Martha, who suddenly recognizes she might be a lesbian, kills herself.

Eric Bentley, reviewing the 1952 version, believed Hellman spoiled the play by telling two conflicting stories simultaneously. "The first is a story of heterosexual teachers accused of lesbianism: the enemy is a society which punishes the innocent. The second is a story of lesbian teachers accused of lesbianism: the enemy is a society which punishes lesbians."[4] Hellman refuted this by saying the play was about a lie, not about lesbianism.

My new evidence shows the close relationship between Hellman's play and the novel *The Well of Loneliness* (1928) by Radclyffe Hall, whom Lily met in Paris when Hall was finishing writing it in early 1928.[5] Dash and Lily watched the fierce flames of condemnation overtake Hall's book, and Lily's fears for her own play probably tempered this early insistence that her drama was not about same-sex.

When the play was produced, several concerned in the production were also fearful. Lee Shubert, owner of the Maxine Elliott Theatre, watched the confession scene rehearsal where one woman recognized her love for the other. "This play," he said to Lily, "could land us all in jail."

While she polished the play, Lily was working as a fifteen-dollars-a-week reader for thirty-six-year-old Herman Shumlin, one of Broadway's finest directors, so Dash felt she stood a good chance of having the play staged. He was right. When the manuscript was finished, Lily put it unsigned on Shumlin's desk. "This is the best one I've read," she said. Even before he discovered her identity, Shumlin was so excited about the writer's power, he took it on. "I was all a-tremble, it was so good," he said. "When I finished the second act, I was afraid to go on, for fear it couldn't last. As soon I was through reading, I immediately agreed to produce it."[6]

Shumlin soon mattered to Lily almost as much as Kober and Hammett. He became her theatrical mentor and, after *The Children's Hour*, produced and directed *Days to Come*, *The Little Foxes*, *Watch on the Rhine*, and *The Searching Wind*. He would intermittently also be Lily's lover for a decade from 1934.

For years, critics have asked whether Hammett wrote *The Children's Hour*. Some anti-Hellman reviewers implied Hammett wrote all Hellman's plays. Lily discussed themes and symbols with Dash. She followed his every criticism to the letter. She openly acknowledged his help. But the archives show *no* evidence of Hammett's original rewriting, just many of his edits and ideas. Hammett's granddaughter Julie Rivett saw such detailed editing on *The Children's Hour* that she thought he could be regarded as a cowriter. However, many writers have substantial editing help but do not credit editors as cowriters. Hammett himself always said it was entirely Hellman's play.

Lily dedicated it: "For D. Hammett With Thanks." She said that without his initial aid, she would never have become one of the four most famous Broadway playwrights along with Edward Albee, Arthur Miller, and Tennessee Williams.

"I'm not at all sure that I would have written without Hammett because I had written. . . . I had stopped writing. I had decided I was not going to be any good and that I wasn't going to be bad. It was he who teased me back into writing, annoyed me back into writing, baited me back into writing. And then watched for as long as he lived."[7]

Telegrams arrived before the show opened on November 20, 1934. Laura and Sid Perelman wrote: "WE HOPE IT'S A BOY LOVE AND KISSES." Lee and Ira Gershwin wrote: "A GIRL WHO CAN MAKE LEE SHUBERT CRY DESERVES THE NOBEL PRIZE." West wrote: "IT IS REALLY A SWELL PLAY DARLING A REALLY SWELL PLAY." Moss Hart's telegram said: "TO TELL YOU HOW THRILLED I WAS WITH THE PLAY AND I WISH I WERE IN YOUR BOOTS TODAY." Her Newhouse relatives characteristically cabled: "MAY YOUR OPENING BE CROWNED WITH SUCCESS AND FINANCIAL GLORY," while her Hellman family wrote: "LILLITH THE LITHE, LILLITH THE LOVELY, LILLITH THE MAZELTOV."

Hammett, who had left for Hollywood on October 26, hired by MGM at $2,000 a week for ten weeks to write a film sequel to *The Thin Man*, did *not* send a cable. Nor a card. Nor flowers. He felt his faith in his pupil was justified by the queues outside the Maxine Elliott Theatre. She felt his loss at her side. Was he to become an absentee mentor, an absentee lover, in the same way he had become an absentee father and husband? Lily did not know. She still lacked faith in her talent. She needed Dash.

Two nights before the opening, she began to drink and did not stop for several weeks. She went to see Max and Julia, who had not read the play. Both were proud, but also frightened for her in a world they could not comprehend. They were right to be frightened. For despite Julia's view that Lily had been the sweetest-smelling baby in New Orleans, on opening night, Lily smelled only of drink. She saw the play from the back of the theater, holding on to the rail.

At the opening night party, Lily passed out on the floor by the elevator. Nobody missed her. But she missed one person in the crazy crowds. Missed him bitterly. Dash was not there in New York to share their triumph.

She had promised to phone Dash after the opening. She put through a call to Dash's rented house in the Pacific Palisades, which contained a soda fountain. After many rings, a woman answered, said she was Hammett's secretary, admonished Lily for calling at such a strange hour. Two days later, Lily realized she had called at 3:00 a.m. California time but that Hammett had no secretary. In her explosive version of events, she impulsively took a plane to Los Angeles, went immediately to the soda fountain, smashed it to bits, then flew back to New York on a late-night plane.

Hammett did in fact have a secretary, Mildred Lewis, of whom he was fond, whom Lily always "forgot" about. But any one of the beautiful women who surrounded Hammett could have answered that phone call. The nearly impossible plane times made the story unconvincing, but Lily's rage was not in doubt.

Six days after the opening, Dash wrote Lily an abject note. "I love you very much please. I haven't a single bit of news beyond what I told you over the phone except that I still love you very much please and would ask that you might find it possible to return my affections if it so happens you could do it without too much trouble."

He had already written from Hollywood: "I miss you awfully honey. . . . I hope the rehearsals are going smoothly and I hope you are being a good girl."[8] As he had ignored all her rehearsals and, worse still, had been absent for the first night, she saw no reason to be a good girl. She slept with both Kober, who had not fallen out of love with her, and Shumlin, who suddenly fell in love with her.

Lily had taken revenge and found some comfort. But in behaving as Hammett behaved, she had lost something irreplaceable in their relationship.

In 1973, in *Pentimento*, Hellman referred to an infamous trip that she claimed she made during this period to see her friend Julia, who she said was involved in anti-Nazi undercover work. There is no sound evidence to back up this statement, made by the much older Hellman, who had become an unreliable though compelling narrator. Possibly, her distress over Dash's absence and her subsequent low self-esteem caused her to invent this tale of herself as heroine in a fight against the Nazis.

The reviews for *The Children's Hour* cheered her immensely. She wrote about the first night: "I remember Robert Benchley pressing my arm and nodding his head as he passed me on the way out of the theatre. . . . I don't think I knew what he meant."[9] The next morning, newspapers revealed exactly what Benchley meant. Every critic congratulated her on a stunning, well-crafted drama. Brooks Atkinson in *The New York Times* (December 2) called it a "stinging tragedy." Walter Winchell (*New York Daily Mirror*, November 21) elevated Lily to stardom by saying she was "perched high on the pedestal." Robert Benchley (*New Yorker*, December 1) thought the play had "too many endings" but praised her for an outstanding event in American footlights history. Her bold hit ran and ran, for 691 performances. It would have the longest run to that point in the Maxine Elliott Theatre's history.

Suddenly, Lee Shubert's fear was proven prescient. *The Children's Hour* was banned in Boston, banned in Chicago, banned in London, where only private performances were permitted. Bans increased its fame and audiences.

Dash and Lily hoped their play would win prizes. But *The Children's Hour* was a *scandalous* triumph. Radclyffe Hall had won two literary prizes and had been expected to win another for *The Well* but failed to do so because of subject matter deemed inappropriately inflammatory. Hellman expected to win the Pulitzer Prize, but her subject matter also was deemed inappropriate.

The New York drama critics were so appalled when it did not win the Pulitzer that indignantly they formed the prestigious New York Drama Critics' Circle Award, and, though Lillian did not win it for *The Children's Hour*, she did win it twice later.

Dash faced new problems. On May 2, 1934, he had come to the attention of the FBI for the first time. The director of the Investigation Division for the US Department of Justice dispatched a note to Special Agent R. E. Vetterli in San Francisco. The division had been advised that an alarming series of illustrated stories about Special Agent K-9 [*sic*], supposedly a former Justice operative, was running in several West Coast newspapers. The director wanted information immediately about the storyteller's identity. Did he (surely not she?) have any departmental affiliations? Vetterli amended the fictional special agent's name to X-9 and revealed that Hammett was the author of the humorous features in the *San Francisco Call-Bulletin*. Vetterli reassured the director that Hammett was not a special agent. A second agent, H. R. Phibrick, added that this man was known to be very successful in his field and had made considerable money from his "detective yarns." Temporarily satisfied, the FBI put the case into "closed status." [10] But within five years, the FBI would reopen that file and start to scrutinize Hammett's activities with much more serious consequences.

In Hollywood that fall and winter, Hammett was feted, photographed, and publicized. He fraternized with Marlene Dietrich and Frank Tuttle, a Fox movie director who specialized in crime films. Dash told Lily he was surprised at the fuss *The Thin Man* had made in Hollywood, where "people bring the Joan Crawfords and Gables over to meet me instead of the usual vice versa! Hot-cha!" [11] He went to cocktail parties at Dorothy Parker's. He joined Charlie Chaplin, Walt Disney, and Alexander Woollcott for dinner. There were distinctly shabby japes. He stole a cat's-eye ring, his producer Hunt

Stromberg's good luck charm. At the Basque speakeasy, he suddenly scooped up handfuls of knives and threw them around the room. He slept with Sis, a doped-up woman who insisted he sleep with her mama first. He fell flat on his face at the Trocadero and was found prostrate in gutters.

Charming one minute, boorish the next, always unpredictable, he was usually drunk.

He hung out with Nunnally Johnson, currently writing screenplays for Twentieth Century Fox. Johnson said Hammett's behavior could only be explained by his assumption that he had no expectation of being alive beyond Thursday. The recurrence of his clinging sickness made this assumption not unreasonable. Did he wish Jose were there to take care of him? He never verbalized it, and his willful disregard of increasing alcoholism paralleled his stoicism in the face of fate's blows. He continued his binging with Edward G. Robinson and Arthur Kober, who had another successful screenwriting job at Fox.

Even Hammett's laconic friend Budd Schulberg had left his well-paid post as head of production at Paramount in 1932 to produce original movies. It was painful for Hammett to mix with such productive people. Unable to write anything, he fended off messages from Blanche, who was being hounded by Hammett's public about the next book. As Hammett had contractual obligations, Alfred suggested they bring out "The Big Knock-Over" and a related story, "$106,000 Blood Money," in hardcover.

Foolishly, Dashiell would not let Alfred do it. Six months later, he was forced to confess to Alfred: "Yellow fellow that I am, I turned tail before the difficulties the new book was presenting and scurried back here to comparative ease and safety."

"Here" was the tinsel world of MGM where he would stick it out through the summer of 1935, while reassuring Alfred that he would try to get in "some licks" on his book meanwhile. [12] The Knopfs were not reassured.

MGM's disapproval of his tardiness was more urgent than Knopf's. On January 8, 1935, Hammett finally submitted his story to Stromberg before briefly returning to New York. By June, he had signed a three-year agreement with MGM, which would be canceled before its term because of his alcoholism and unreliability. By September 17, he managed to give Stromberg a 115-page typescript of *After the Thin Man*, which MGM released on Christmas Day 1936.

During fall 1935, Hammett moved restlessly between New York's Plaza and Hollywood's Beverly Wilshire, utterly unable to write. Between 1934 and 1936, six movies were made from his original or adapted stories, as though his talented past had risen up to taunt him. Even an income of around $100,000 in 1934 failed to keep him from debt. Between 1933 and 1936, five lawsuits for nonpayment of debts were filed against him. He gained temporary creditworthiness when the film of *The Glass Key* was released in June 1935. He moved his writer's block from his luxury hotel to a six-bedroom penthouse at 325 Bel Air Road. Jones, his black chauffeur/butler, and Jones's lover, Winston, cared for him.

The studio would not leave him alone. Every day, they sent twenty-year-old Mildred Lewis to his home. Some days, Hammett never got up. So Mildred, notebook in hand, waited till 5:00 p.m. then slid into the studio's limousine to go home. Some days, Hammett came downstairs in pajamas and suggested she help him with the crossword puzzle. If it was Thursday, the servants' day off, she cooked, badly. This was Mildred's first job as an untried secretary. But Hammett told her she was attractive and clever. Occasionally, he called her into his bedroom, where he lay quietly in bed. Nothing would happen, he promised. He would merely hold her tight if she lay beside him. She had no idea if this was in her contract, but she preferred the crossword, or better still, dinner out with a fully clothed Hammett. Sometimes at the Clover Club (gambling with his chips), she met scary Dorothy Parker, but even worse, some mornings she saw a series of black and Oriental fancy women from Madame Lee Francis's house tiptoeing downstairs from Hammett's bedroom. Mildred got used to the letters that arrived regularly from his wife and daughters, who lived nearby, and at the photo on the piano of his girlfriend Lily. Mildred told her husband very little about her position, but when the famous writer filled their house with flowers, the husband wondered about her job. It's the way writers work, the secretary said loyally. But the truth was that this writer and this secretary did no work at all. [13]

Throughout the rest of 1935, Blanche sent long, persuasive letters encouraging Hammett to send them the book. She visited him in California and reported to Alfred he looked "simply superb" and was going "to write a novel soon."

Meanwhile, Knopf's hopes for a new novel faded when Hammett cabled: "WILL YOU DEPOSIT MY CCOUNT [sic] GUARNTY [sic] TRUST SIXTIETH AND MADISON ONE THOUSAND DOLLARS AND WIRE ME. . . . THANKS AND BEST REGARDS AND DON'T BE SURPRISED IF YOU GET A BOOK BEFORE SNOW FLIES=DASHIELL HAMMETT."

Alfred, cynical, sent only $500. Hammett, unable to write books or screenplays, was managing a fine line in cables. His riposte arrived at Knopf's mailbox less than a month later. "CAN YOU DEPOSIT THAT SECOND FIVE HUNDRED TODAY AND LET ME KNOW=DASHIELL HAMMETT." [14]

If Hammett found Blanche hard to face, his shame with Lily was greater. Unable to write, instead he had to watch as Hellman became one of Hollywood's biggest screenwriter successes.

When her play opened, Lily had $55 in her bank account. The theatrical production earned her $125,000. Unused to large sums of money, she spent it instantly. "I bought presents—expensive luggage—for my friends, most of whom couldn't use it because they couldn't afford to travel."[15] She also bought herself a mink coat.

She began research for her second play, *Days to Come*, but was perfectly happy to accept Sam Goldwyn's offer of $2,500 a week to return to Hollywood. "I'm going back to take a job at just thirty times what the movies paid me the last time I worked for them."[16] She was now one of the highest paid screenwriters in town.

Hammett's own income in 1934 was also huge, around $100,000. In 1935 it topped $100,000. He was still unbelievably rich but, unbearably, no longer a novelist.

CHAPTER 11

Hammett, employed by MGM as a $2,000-a-week screen-writer, was brilliant but unreliable. He drank, sharpened pencils, thought about Communism, and monitored Hellman's sudden fame.

Lily's *Children's Hour* triumph had offered her a splendid reentry into Hollywood. As a lowly paid reader at MGM, she had worked in Culver City's dusty gloom. Now, in 1935, as a high-salaried screenwriter, she had a desk in Sam Goldwyn's palatial Formosa Avenue studio. Dash and Lily never pretended to feel degraded by film work, as did some screenwriters. Instead, Dash taught Lily toughness and to use her quick temper, which Hollywood moguls would respect. It worked with Goldwyn, for whom Hellman wrote five screenplays, starting with *The Dark Angel*, which was censored and not allowed distribution until Hellman had removed all sexual implications between the two main characters. Goldwyn, mightily impressed with its 1936 Academy Awards, paid $40,000 for screen rights to *The Children's Hour*, whose title he was not allowed to use and whose purchase he was not allowed to advertise because of Hays Office objections.

In 1922, movie producers who believed Hollywood culture was immoral had appointed a censorious regulator, Will H. Hays, president of the Motion Picture Producers and Distributors of America, where his job was to insist on rigid Christian principles from screenwriters, casting directors, and producers, promulgated in a Motion Pictures Production Code. He was especially fierce with anyone Jewish or Communist. Hammett had helped ensure that Hellman, left-wing, Jewish, and feisty, managed all right within the Code. Now he advised her to be pragmatic about the fact that their "baby" was being retitled *These Three*, under which label all suggestions of lesbianism were removed, and its publicity material contained no direct or indirect reference to Hellman's drama. She could not even receive credit for writing the play.

As members of the Screen Writers Guild (SWG), Hammett and Hellman had begun negotiations in 1934 for rules to help writers, which infuriated the studios. The guild was a quasi-union that stood up to studio heads determined to keep writers anonymous, divided, and largely underpaid. Thirty percent of Hollywood writers earned less than $2,000 yearly, and only 10 percent more than $10,000 at a time when the average wage in the United States was $1,600. Hammett, though a high earner, believed in protecting fellow workers. He recalled his strikebreaking Pinkerton days and soon took leadership roles in both the SWG, where he would become a board member in 1937, and the League of American Writers. The League of American Writers (LAW) was founded by the Communist Party in 1935 to unite Hollywood's left-wing political forces against the rising Nazi threat. Hammett would become president of the LAW in 1941.

Hammett's nascent political activism also included attending Communist Party meetings in Hollywood, and later joining the party and participating in writers' groups sponsored by it. (I'll discuss this at length in the next chapter.)

Samuel Goldwyn, like many other studio heads suspicious of employees' unions, felt employees should be absolutely loyal. On May 11, 1927, several Hollywood studio heads had established the Academy of Motion Picture Arts and Sciences to maintain their power. Radical screenwriters, including Hellman, Dorothy Parker, and Hammett's friends Frances Goodrich and Albert Hackett, found unionization gave them shared commitment and some bargaining power.

Dash no longer took much pleasure in his sexual relations with Lily. He feared his new impotence in his writing would be mirrored in his sex life. So he used Lily as he used his chippies, but made clear that although she came free, she did not have their skills. Lily became very disturbed by this new situation. Dash told no one that sex with Lily had gone badly wrong. Lily told her diary. She speculated that it was because they no longer had a "grand passion." Immersed in her own exciting writing, it did not occur to her that the reason might be the absence of Hammett's own passion: writing.

Neither Dash nor Lily could decide what might improve their relationship. Lily thought their unwed status might be one cause. So she shocked Dash by finally asking him to marry her. He refused. He said Jose was a Catholic. She would never divorce him. He did not say he had one wife and did not need another. No matter how carefully he chose his words, Lily felt rejected. She consoled herself by lunching with Art, who saw she was "very unhappy." Two days later, she told Art she felt distanced from Dash and now wished to act as if unattached. She started by sleeping more often with Kober, then when Shumlin arrived, she slept with him again, too.

Modest Kober had suddenly become a big name as a successful stage and screenwriter who, between 1930 and 1946,
would pen more than thirty screenplays and plays, including
two Broadway hits. He knew everybody and introduced his
ex-wife to them. Initially, Lily shared Hammett's suite at the
Beverly Wilshire and contributed half the rent. Despite her
"strong tie" to Dash, her deep affection for Art meant they
lunched, dined, went to bed together before she returned to
Dash. Increasingly, with Dash's sexual withdrawal, she used
sex with other men, including Kober, to gain approval. Dash
intimidated her when they made love; Art did not, so she
learned to relax.

Noticing her slight withdrawal, Dash, when invited to
meet Gertrude Stein, said he would accept if he could bring
"someone." He took Lily, whose recent artistic prestige
appeared to have bypassed Stein, for she lavished praise on
Hammett and Charlie Chaplin but said nothing to Hellman
or the other female guests, who included Paulette Goddard
and Anita Loos. Snubbed lady visitors were always left to the
attentions of Stein's wife, Alice B. Toklas.

Though dining out with Dash as a couple pleased Lillian,
she was unable to stop him from sleeping with chippies.

Jose suffered privately from Dash's absences, but Lily
shrank publicly from his cruelty. Wretchedly, she recalled her
mother's tolerant despair over Max's women. Perhaps Julia
had felt she had no other choice. Hellman was determined to
exert *her* options. But every time she bedded Art, she remained
compulsively attached to the unavailable Dash. The attention
Dash gave his family did nothing to raise Lily's spirits. Now
that they all lived on the West Coast, he saw his children
frequently and asked Lily to engage with them. Discovering
that young Jo wanted to learn to ride, he took her to a store
to select an equestrian habit. Lily, who came reluctantly, was

mercilessly sharp with the assistants. Jo was mortified, but her father laughed. Yet *he* never behaved like that or allowed them to be rude. Jo understood her mother's silent disapproval of Lillian, but desiring her father's love, she, too, kept quiet.

Jo had heard their Kelly relatives complain about the way her seemingly wealthy father ill-treated Mama. Jo, however, had also heard her father complain about the dollars that ran away. She was aware that often the dollars ran into generous gifts for her and Mary, the new riding coat, the matching hat and boots, and huge boxes of candy, even stuffed ducks over-flowing with goodies. The previous year, from Florida, he had sent Mary an expensive wristwatch and Jo an Alice bracelet. He bought Mama a silver brush and mirror and had given her garnets she was too shy to wear. Jo knew he had given Lillian a mink coat, which Lillian was not shy about. Papa even rented a Beverly Hills house for them and told Jose: "Get someone in to do the work."

Jo thought about the Kellys' comments. Could a grownup be mean as well as generous? Poor as well as rich?

Hammett was poor, said one friend, because he would give you the shirt off his back. Hammett was poor, said another, because money meant nothing to him. He appreciated people paying him back, but he never once asked for it. Hammett was poor, said Lily, because he did not care about money, made no complaints, and had no regrets when it was gone.[1] Hammett was poor, said Jo, because when he had money, he gave it to you, and when he didn't, he gave it to you anyway.

Hammett's already low self-esteem over his inability to write sank further. His fear that impotence in one area would be matched by impotence in another was accelerated when gonorrhea and other genital ailments returned. Lily became scared she would catch a sexual disease. She felt more lonely when Kober quit his job with Fox in April, saying it was a burden off his shoulders, then left Hollywood after a lavish farewell party on May 23, 1935, at which Dash became excessively tight, partly because he, too, valued Kober's friendship.

Hellman, who believed she could solve problems by traveling, escaped in June when *These Three* was completed. Although Dash felt he could treat Lily any way he liked and she would still not look for other men, except for occasional comfort, he was wrong. In Albuquerque, she met a bright, young man of twenty-five, Ralph Ingersoll, former managing editor of the *New Yorker*, currently managing editor of *Fortune* magazine, who for a brief time introduced Hellman to his bed and a more sophisticated form of politics. Yearning for Hammett, Lily nevertheless made love with Ingersoll. Soon, however, they began to have arguments. He was a married man, too. Dash noticed Lily was still juggling oranges, but what he didn't realize was that she still wanted him very much. The fact that Dash and Lily were rarely open with each other about their feelings meant that briefly she did consider marrying Ingersoll and told Dash she was semi-serious "about another man." But when later she mentioned that she had decided not to marry the man, her version was that Hammett had said, "I would never have allowed that, never."[2]

During 1935, Lily confided in Dash about her increasing concerns over the health of Julia, her mother. Dash seemed unable to work out how best to support her, and when untreatable colon cancer resulted in Julia's death on November 30, it was Kober who was there to comfort her. Dash kept away. Max could not contain his grief. Every time he mentioned Julia, he burst into tears. Lily longed for Dash's support, but he remained in Hollywood. Perhaps he knew he would seem out of place at a Jewish funeral. Perhaps he was drunk. Lil and Max quarreled over the funeral arrangements, while Arthur, who loved Julia, soothed everyone and quietly took charge.

Lily realized too late how much she had misunderstood her mother. Only now, suffering Hammett's philanderings, did she comprehend what Julia went through. But her belated respect for Julia was tempered by the strange relief she felt that the rival for her father was dead.

Max needed her desperately, wanted her love, desired her. Ironically, she suddenly fell out of love with him. Her desire was only for Dash. Max and Lily continued to argue into 1936, yet for years Hellman could not admit the roots of her twisted relationship with her father, until she wrote about it first in *Another Part of the Forest* then in *Toys in the Attic*. In Dash's absence, she slept with Kober through December's difficult days.

In the fall of 1935, Hammett had moved back and forth between New York and Hollywood, staying at the Plaza in New York and the Beverly Wilshire in Beverly Hills. By January 1936, his drinking and partying lowered his resistance to illness, and he again collapsed with lung disease. He entered Lenox Hill Hospital on January 11. Briefly released, he reentered on January 16 to be treated for venereal disease, lung disease, alcoholism, and generally dreadful health. That was the first of a series of Lenox Hill hospitalizations, which continued in March and July 1936, May and June 1938, June 1940, and December 1948. On finally leaving Lenox Hill Hospital in early February, clutching the books Blanche had sent for his convalescence, he took a room at the Hotel Madison on East 58th Street, where he was so financially insecure that the Knopfs rescued him with a Valentine's Day gift of an early royalty payment of $478.99.

Characteristically, he made light of his hospitalization. A letter to Mary postmarked January 16, 1936, from the New York Plaza said: "It's mighty nice being back in New York, though I haven't been feeling well enough to get around very much. Tomorrow I'm going to the Lenox Hill Hospital, 76th St. and Park Avenue, for a week or two to see what's the matter with me. Don't any of you worry too much about it. My doctor seems to think it's only that I'm run down and need a good rest."

He asked Mary to kiss Jo and Jose for him, then curiously signed it, "Love, Dash." A few days later in a letter to Jo, he asked her to "tell Jose I'm feeling a lot better." Reassuring them in a fatherly manner that there was nothing to worry about as the doctors kept him in bed where the nurse even scrubbed his face for him, strangely he yet again signed the note "Dash."[3] Until this point, Hammett had always signed letters to his children "Love, Papa" or "Love, Pop." This new signature might reflect a sudden distance from his role of father. But hospitalization is as likely to symbolize acute alienation from a sense of self. Such a change is not untypical of those who are institutionalized even briefly. When Zelda Fitzgerald entered her second mental hospital, the signature on her letters to her young daughter, Scottie, changed from "love, Mama" to the stark "Zelda." Time in hospital is life out of control. Perhaps his own name was all Hammett could cling to.

Dash wondered whether Lily would invite him to share her first New York apartment at 14 East Seventy-Fifth Street. She did not, and he said nothing. Their relationship was going through another phase of silences and misunderstandings.

In spring 1936, she spent a month traveling between Cleveland and Cincinnati, gaining background information for her new play, *Days to Come.* She invited Dash to Tavern Island off the shore of Connecticut to read a draft, but he was still too ill to give his expertise. Later, when Ralph Ingersoll joined her at Tavern Island in September 1936, assuming they would have time alone, he found Hammett at the head of the table, and Shumlin and Kober in residence.

In October, Hammett left New York City for Princeton University, where he had been hired to teach creative writing seminars. He rented a fashionable mansion at 90 Cleveland Avenue, ensconced his manservant Jones and his dog named Baby. Lily, in an anxious state, arrived with her revisions. Her second play was an astute evaluation of the crisis between labor and management during the Depression, but it was less a political argument than a moral one. Lily explored her characters' psychological intricacies as if in a novel, which Dash felt might not work on stage. But drinking heavily, he made only perfunctory criticisms, said foolishly the words were "fine." Both knew they were not.

When Lily returned to New York, he brought in Pru Whitfield, with whom he had begun an affair in January 1936 at the time of entering Lenox Hill Hospital and while he was recovering. Despite the fact that Pru's ex-husband, writer Raoul Whitfield, had been a fellow Black Masker, was a protégé of Blanche's, and had always been a decent friend to Dash, he did not hesitate to woo Pru and form an intimate friendship with her.

While neighbors in Princeton complained bitterly about Hammett's loud, boorish behavior, Hellman in New York worked to correct the play's faults. Without Hammett's discipline, however, she did not pare the dialogue or focus the action.

Dash nevertheless believed in the play. Shumlin eagerly directed it. A talented cast, including Florence Eldridge, William Harrigan, and Ben Smith, opened on December 15, 1936 at the Vanderbilt Theatre.

Hellman had analyzed society's ineffectuals, the incompetent bosses who let decay and evil destroy others. Later plays of hers would succeed magnificently, but without Hammett's help, the well-intentioned *Days to Come*, a rehearsal play, defeated her.

The audience grew restless. At the end of act three, applause was muted. Hellman vomited in a side aisle as the curtain went down. Hammett and Kober found her lying distraught in an alley behind the theater, weeping and crying: "It's a flop." It was. The opening night party resembled a wake. She yelled at Hammett that he was a son of a bitch. He *had* said her play was good. Hammett was silent, gathered his cloak, headed for the door. Then he turned. "I did indeed. But I saw it at the Vanderbilt tonight and I've changed my mind."

The play ran for only six performances.

She had dedicated it to Julia and Max. When it opened, her mother was dead and she was alienated from her beloved father. Lily had always felt Max had failed her. Now she felt not only that she had failed Julia, but for the first time Dash, their politics, and playwriting had failed her.

However, Lily, unlike Dash at that point, had enormous resilience, which helped her confront her failures. She knew Dash believed life had no meaning. She felt differently. Life had to have meaning. She must stay in control. Passionate politics and effective drama had to be her future.

Hammett, still unable to write, for the first time envied Lily's optimistic determination. He watched her yet again invent order out of disarray. If he was to survive his current writing failure, then he must construct something different; he must pay more attention to Lily's work, which he had neglected when drunk and ill; and he must further develop his interest in politics.

PART FIVE
COMMUNISTS, FOXES, AND ARMY, 1936–1946

CHAPTER 12

The world was in a terrible state. Injustice faced Hammett everywhere he looked. In Europe as well as his own country, social forces were becoming markedly right wing. Nazism had grown strong in Germany, which worried him and fellow writers. In 1933, Germany under Chancellor Adolf Hitler had withdrawn from the League of Nations, the organization set up to keep peace after World War I. In 1934, Hitler was awarded dictatorial powers as Führer by the German Reichstag. He had been inspired by the success of Benito Mussolini of Italy, who soon after he became prime minister obtained temporary dictatorial powers from the Italian parliament, making him Il Duce, the supreme leader. In 1935, German Jews were deprived of citizens' rights by the Nuremberg Laws. Among its repressive policies, the Nazi regime banned political opponents, boycotted Jewish businesses, hounded Communists and Jews from public office, expelled Jewish students from German universities, and forced blacks to be sterilized. They also started to burn "subversive" books, something that keenly worried Hammett and his left-wing and writer friends.

In 1936, the year that Edward VIII abdicated the British throne because of his romance with the American divorcée Wallis Simpson, Fascist Italy and Nazi Germany formed an alliance, the Rome-Berlin Axis. German troops occupied the demilitarized Rhineland between Germany and France, an act that violated the terms of the Treaty of Versailles, the treaty that had ended World War I.

Hammett looked at Spain but saw little that gave rise to optimism. Civil war had broken out in 1936 after a military coup overthrew the elected left-wing Popular Front government. General Francisco Franco's Nationalist forces were locked in struggle against loyalists to the Spanish Republic. Hammett's circle feared the spread of Fascism that would follow a Nationalist victory.

On the home front, the Roosevelt administration had made some political and social improvements. Unemployment had fallen almost by half, to 13.8 percent of the civilian labor force. Millions of Americans received government checks for working for new agencies like the Civilian Conservation Corps and the Works Progress Administration. Without that income, many would have starved. There was now an activist state committed to providing individual citizens with a measure of security against unpredictable market turns. Some African Americans achieved high office: William H. Hastie Jr., for example, appointed by President Roosevelt, became the first African American Federal judge, and Alabama-born Arthur W. Mitchell the first African American elected to the House of Representatives as a Democrat.

However, the United States remained isolated from events in Europe and isolationist in its foreign policy. In September 1938, Britain's prime minister, Neville Chamberlain, met with Hitler in Munich to try to avert impending war. Ed Murrow, CBS news chief, coordinated broadcasts from European cities to keep Americans informed on developments across the Atlantic.

Hammett's life during this period became without focus. He was depressed about social and political events and devastated about his writing. Fiction had given him up. No longer did it lurk at the corners of his mind. Anxiety about its absence filled up the space instead. With Hellman, except when they worked closely together on her plays, he couldn't seem to get his relationship to flourish as it had done. They loved each other, but that no longer seemed enough. He needed something in which to have faith. Everywhere, he saw social wrongs, and he strongly believed that there had to be a better system to correct them. His interest in Communism sprang from that belief and his earnest desire for social justice.

In 1935, the Hollywood section of the US Communist Party had been founded at the house of screenwriter Martin Berkeley. Berkeley later told the House Un-American Activities Committee the attendees had included Hammett and Hellman. The Hollywood branch was started with the hope that the party could draw on the resources of wealthy, powerful members of the movie industry. Although Hammett later showed Jo his Communist Party membership card, for many celebrities loyal to the party's goals, membership was not officially recorded in order to protect their privacy. These members, termed "members at large," did not pay dues but were expected to donate generously. They were not forced to attend public rallies or sell Communist Party publications, either. It was their resources the party expected to tap. Early in 1936, Hammett became a member at large of the party, as did many of his friends, including Lillian Hellman, Edward G. Robinson, and S. J. Perelman.

Hammett participated in several Hollywood Communist Party activities, including the Western Writers Congress and the Anti-Nazi League. He also sent $500 to the Abraham Lincoln Brigade and in 1937 asked the Party's permission to go to Spain. The party decided that Hammett, still famous, was more use to them in America. It was Hellman who went to Spain in October 1937 to make the radical documentary *The Spanish Earth*, written by Ernest Hemingway and John Dos Passos. On December 6, 1937, Hammett spoke at the League of American Writers' symposium on the topic, "Should writers mix in politics?" He was, of course, in favor of writers becoming political. In 1938, he was elected chairman of the Motion Picture Artists Committee, which, though not Communist, raised money for anti-Fascist causes.

From 1938 to 1940, Hammett was associated with two important political journals. The first was *Equality*, which defended democratic rights and fought anti-Semitism and racism. It was published by the organization Equality Publishers, which was headed by Hammett. *Equality*'s inaugural issue, in May 1939, contained an open letter to America's Catholic hierarchy warning them about spreading prejudice against Jews. Being Jewish was becoming increasingly perilous. At an authors' luncheon on January 9, 1941, at the Hotel Astor, Hellman would later identify herself as a Jew and writer: "I am a writer and also a Jew. I want to be sure I can continue to say what I wish without being branded by the malice of people making a living by that malice."

In 1938, Hammett also participated in the early planning of Ralph Ingersoll's New York newspaper, *PM*, which would begin publication in 1940. FBI agents watching Hammett noted that Hellman and Kober sat on the *PM* board, while Hammett was hiring Communist or suspected Communist writers.

What the Communist Party meant to Lily and Dash at that point was not what was later understood by party membership. It did not necessarily include any desire or obligation to overthrow the US government or to practice acts of subversion as it had in the twenties. By the late thirties, the Communist international policy-making body had started an initiative called the Popular Front, which focused on civil rights issues, women's rights issues, equal rights for minorities, and causes for well-known individuals who had been wronged politically. This attracted liberals into the party, as did the enthusiasm for the cause of republican Spain. Franco, of course, was supported by Fascists in Germany and Italy. Hammett and other liberal celebrities were seduced to the cause of anti-Fascism.

Politics did not motivate him to write. During winter 1936–1937, while Dash remained blocked, Lily adapted Sidney Kingsley's 1935 Broadway hit *Dead End* for a third hit screenplay at Goldwyn. She received virtually unanimous critical accolades. The movie was nominated for four Academy Awards, including Best Picture. That same year, to Dash and Lily's delight, Kober's hit play *Having Wonderful Time* opened at Broadway's Lyceum Theatre. After the first night, Dash wrote to Lily: "I love you and miss you. . . . I had a couple of drinks with Ralph [Ingersoll]. . . . A sweet guy, I think, but dull."[1] On May 5, 1937, Kober heard his play, which was later awarded the Roi Cooper Megrue prize, was runner-up for the Pulitzer. The movie version of *Having Wonderful Time*, starring Ginger Rogers and Douglas Fairbanks Jr., was soon being shot.

After Princeton, in mid-March, Hollywood had beckoned, and Hammett went back again. Goldwyn wanted him to write an "original." William Randolph Hearst offered him $50,000 to write a story for Marion Davies. When MGM suggested a third *Thin Man* movie for producer Hunt Stromberg, Hammett decided to sell MGM perpetual rights in Nick, Nora, and their dog Asta for $40,000.

Lily joined Dash in Hollywood from April till August, where they took over the six-bedroom Royal Siamese Suite at the Beverly Wilshire. Lily tried to emulate with Dash the familiar, relaxed intimacy she had with Arthur. Dash and Lily often dined together at Kober's with Scott Fitzgerald and Dot Parker and her husband, Alan Campbell. All of them were deeply shocked when, on July 11, 1937, George Gershwin, only thirty-eight, died a "terrible death" after having a tumor removed from his brain. At Gershwin's memorial service on Thursday, July 15, Dash, Lily, and Arthur mourned together. When Arthur remarked that Dash and Lily were acting like "quarreling married people," Lily confessed Dash had had a "change of feelings."

Despite being on the wagon since March, despite Lily's presence, despite their reawakened sexual life, Dash continued to frequent chippies. Lily tried to persuade herself it didn't matter because she was with him publicly. Once again, they discussed marriage and even set a wedding day. But when the day approached, Hammett fled town with another woman. Before Lily had recovered from his betrayal, she had become pregnant with Dash's baby. He told her he was delighted. He wanted the child. He wanted to be a father. He wanted them to be a family. He even said he would ask Jose for a divorce.[2] But he did not say he would change his behavior.

One afternoon, exultant and happy, Lily rushed back to the hotel, holding a celebratory bouquet of flowers. In their bed, she saw Dash with a chippy. She understood the symbolism: They were lovers; she was pregnant; he wanted their child; but he would not become sexually faithful. Nothing, Lily decided, would make her go through the public humiliation of sharing their baby's father sexually with other women. She went to Europe; she entered a hospital, as she had done several times before, and aborted their baby. Though she had terminated several earlier fetuses, this abortion was not merely one more in a series. In 1925, she had aborted Kober's baby, for she could not marry a Jewish man while pregnant. In 1937, she *could* marry a non-Jewish man even though pregnant, but only if he were exclusively hers. Did Dash know exactly what he was doing to their relationship, or was he so careless of other people's feelings that he simply acted without thought?

Lily finished a first version of her new play, *The Little Foxes*, in August 1937 then escaped Dash and left for Europe to visit Paris, Spain, and then Moscow. In her absence, Hammett felt abandoned. The doctors labeled his lungs fragile; he stayed off drink, but his health worsened. Would a divorce help? On August 26, 1937, Dash and Jose got a Mexican divorce. It was not recognized under US law, and neither Jose nor Hammett ever took it seriously. They continued to think of themselves as a long-distance married couple.

But Hammett felt he had tried, and he wanted Lily to know. He telegrammed her from Los Angeles on September 7: "HAVE DIVORCE AND FLU STOP REMAINING HERE UNTIL TWENTIETH STOP MUCH LOVE= DASH." Two days later he wrote again: "Dear Lilishka, There's a lot of missing of you going on round here, personally speaking." He repeated: "I was divorced in Nogales, Sonora, Mexico, on the 26th of last month. . . . I hope and imagine you had a swell time in Russia." Again, she did not answer. Hammett, a strange, reserved man, was sometimes able in letters to release his feelings. So throughout October, November, and December he plied her with love letters.

The day after Christmas, he wrote from the Beverly Wilshire: "The youngsters came in for lunch to bring me their presents: otherwise I saw nobody." He was still reworking changes on his "charming fable of how Nick loved Nora and Nora loved Nick and everything was just one great big laugh. . ." But as he wrote, "wish you were here," he was not laughing. By January 15, 1938, he recorded his tenth month without drink. "Lilishka may be generous in most things, but she's a postage-stamp miser." [3]

After returning to the States from her trip to Spain, France, and Moscow, Lily stayed with Kober for Christmas, dined with him on New Year's Eve, and saw him almost daily in 1938. By May 15, Lily suggested they consider remarriage.

Lily visited Max in New Orleans in February 1938. Hammett sent her a wire: "It is raining here but only on the streets where they don't know you are coming."

Then Dash, worn through with fatigue, having lost more than twenty-five pounds, stopped writing his weekly letters to Jo. "Your father the Ex-King" has abdicated, he said. Though his untitled novel remained untouched, he was more scared by sexual impotence. Unable to leave his bed, he saw Jose but felt useless. The hotel bill rose and was unpaid. He wrote cheerful notes to Lily, who had no idea of his condition. On May 14, after fourteen months of being sober, suddenly he sent down to the hotel pharmacy for alcohol. He drank and drank. His cry of despair to Lily told her he was drinking.

Frances Goodrich arrived at the hotel and found him pale gray, half-dead. She and her husband, Albert Hackett, knew he must be hospitalized at once, but the hotel would not let him leave till the $8,000 bill was settled. The Hacketts decided to airmail him to Lillian. After a doctor agreed to sign a paper saying Hammett was fit to fly to New York, they sneaked out his belongings and supported him through the lobby as he struggled, sipping whisky. Hammett had never felt so sick, so low, so helpless. Hellman had never felt so frightened for him. She had an ambulance pick him up at the airport. On May 31, 1938, she checked him into Lenox Hill, where his doctor, Irwin Sobel, recorded three months' loss of weight (he had lost twenty-five pounds), premature emaciation, low basal metabolism, low blood sugar, small heart, suspected adrenal, thyroid, and pituitary hypofunction, pyorrhea, impotence, a raging fear of insanity, and a range of neuroses comprising a severe nervous breakdown. His teeth were also infected. Hammett remained in bed, his teeth and diseased body cared for. Slowly, he regained his spirits. Within weeks, he put on weight. On his discharge in mid-June 1938, Lily rescued him and took him to Tavern Island to recover. When better, he helped her with *Foxes*.

Hellman suddenly, desperately needed Hammett's help with the play, which rested on Hellman's family history and was her most difficult one to write. More than her other plays, *Foxes* owed most to Hammett's editorial brilliance, which tamed her angry talents. Unruly himself, he rigorously insisted on Hellman's absolute discipline. Her genuine appreciation evoked a witty response: "You're practically breaking my heart with letters about the play. I think we're going to have to make a rule that you're not to tackle any work when I'm not around to spur, quiet, goad, pacify and tease you."[4]

The play was set in the living room of Regina and Horace Giddens's house in a small Alabama town in 1900, and there were strict instructions in the script that all accents be Southern. Hammett's teasing began when he read an early version in bed one night. The next morning, Lily found a note under her door:

"Missy write blackamoor chit-chat. Missy better stop writing blackamoor chit-chat." Hammett said it would be a good play someday, but for now, she should tear it up and start again.[5] She restarted and rewrote the black servants' dialogue.

Hellman, relying on historical truth (her maternal grandmother was the model for Regina), wanted her heroine to ride around the town on a horse while husband Horace died at the end of act three. Hammett objected that the sound of horses' hooves would make audiences laugh. Hellman said it was true to life. Hammett said truth and artistic truth differ. She changed the end. Horace, dying, begs Regina to get his medicine. She stands still, silently watching him. She does nothing, and he dies, with no extraneous clatter, no cacophony. A restrained, calculated murder.

Drafts and notebooks in the Hellman archives are filled with Hammett's revisions. She rewrites nine drafts. He scrutinizes, vandalizes, authorizes every phrase. Each change improves her script.

Lily said later that Dash was generous with anybody who asked for help. He felt it was wrong to lie about writing. Lily believed his toughness came from a mixture of dedication, generosity, and a ruthless honesty. When finally she thought she had got the script right, she put it outside his door. She hoped *this* version would satisfy him. It satisfied everyone.

On January 9, 1939, rehearsals began. The cast was led by Tallulah Bankhead whose scarlet reputation for temper tantrums matched Lillian's. Called an elegant tramp by Tennessee Williams, Bankhead was a "total bitch" to everyone except the director, Herman Shumlin, with whom she was sleeping.[6] Dash observed Lillian and Tallulah fighting frequently.

After the February 2 Baltimore opening, attended by Dash, Lily, Max, Dot, Alan Campbell, and Sara and Gerald Murphy, Hellman threatened to leave the company when Bankhead was too wildly praised, and she had to be calmed by Hammett. But the show opened to rave reviews February 15, 1939, at New York's National Theatre, ran for 410 performances on Broadway until February 3, 1940, then toured for two years. Hammett's efforts ensured that it became an American classic. The rights were bought by Goldwyn for another hit movie, which was nominated for nine Oscars.

Hammett was proud of Lily, but her success on two coasts overwhelmed her. Two weeks after the play's opening, she fled to an isolated village in Cuba, away from critics praising her, reporters besieging her, and her own drunken, "wasteful, ridiculous depression." She had shrunk from Dash's reckless drinking; now she feared for her own stability. She knew something was wrong when having the biggest hit on Broadway made her a miserable drunk. Unlike Dash, she determined to do something about it—for both their futures. In 1940, she consulted psychiatrist Gregory Zilboorg, who told her he wouldn't analyze an alcoholic. She managed to quit drinking and was virtually abstinent for six years before becoming a moderate drinker. This new regime enabled her to help Dash, too.

In 1939, using money earned from *The Little Foxes*, she had purchased in her name, as a joint investment for her and Hammett, Hardscrabble Farm in Mount Pleasant, Westchester County, New York. This rural retreat, where she would write five plays, allowed Hellman and Hammett an almost idyllic life for two years, their happiest time together. The property included a farm, stables, bridle paths, woodlands, fields, meadows, an eight-acre lake, guesthouses, and an exquisite white clapboard house. She learned to farm. They raised and sold poodles until they made enough to buy chickens, cows, and three thousand asparagus plants. They reared crossbred ducks, stocked the lake with bass and pickerel, raised pigs and young lambs, grew giant tomatoes. They were peaceful and productive together. Dash and Lily sometimes had separate lovers, but they shared a base. He felt at home here and at ease with Lily. Only his writing block caused him anguish.

By 1939, Hammett and Knopf had parted company amid frightening rows. After Hammett was released from his contract with Knopf, Random House paid him $5,000 for his next novel. Alfred told Bennett Cerf, president of Random House, that the novelist was a "terrible man."[7] Though Hammett reported optimistically to Cerf that he was plugging away at his new novel, called *There Was a Young Man* or *My Brother Felix*, he confessed to Jo that he had lied. At first, he shared the agony of his blockage with Lily, who did not understand. This was her mentor, the disciplined writer, who had taught her how to write well. She watched him buy a new typewriter, settle regularly to work, either having a drink to encourage the words or curtailing drinking so the words were clear. No words came. Nothing helped. No strategies prevailed. Yet Hammett kept trying to write, kept up those sad schedules for the next twenty years. He never gave up trying to write. He never succeeded. But he talked less about it to Lillian, then never.

When his daughter Mary later required psychiatric help, Hammett talked to Mary's psychiatrist about his writing trauma. Some days, he felt he had too much money, and if he lost it, spent it, or gave it away, then he would be able to write. He drank it away. He threw it away. Though he wrote the screenplay for *Another Thin Man*, he found no words for his fiction. Some days, he felt he had nothing left to write about. He wrote nothing, was nothing, yet his fame and wealth increased. He missed San Francisco and the obscurity and poverty that drove him to write.

In March 1939, Madrid fell to the Fascists. On August 23, Hitler and Stalin signed a nonaggression pact. When, a week after the pact was signed, on September 1, Hitler invaded Poland, England and France declared war on Germany. Two weeks later, Russia invaded Poland, leaving American Communists, including Hammett, confused as to how to respond. Should they oppose the war? Should they support Russia's invasion but not Germany's? Or, should America support a war to stop Fascism? Most Communists took the first stance. Hammett believed America should ignore the war temporarily and continue domestic socialist reforms. He was on the League of American Writers' Keep America Out of War committee in January 1940. Also in 1940, he was elected national chairman of the Committee on Election Rights, which promoted Communists as political candidates, his most proactive political commitment. In 1941, he became president of the LAW. That summer, the league ended its antiwar position when the Germans invaded the USSR.

Only at Hardscrabble did he relax from his political activities. He fished, he walked, he recalled his childhood farm, he listened to Lily's ideas for her new anti-Nazi play, *Watch on the Rhine*. Her protagonist, Kurt Muller, an anti-Fascist German, had similarities to Hammett. "I suppose there's some of Hammett in almost every character I ever wrote," Hellman said. "In everything I've written, Hammett has been somewhere, some form of him."[8]

In 1940, two auspicious meetings occurred. The first was Lillian's encounter with the child of a Jewish New Orleans friend, ten-year-old Peter Feibleman. The boy intrigued Lillian, who watched him grow up, saw him at intervals as he changed from a small boy to a young man, and who after Hammett's death would replace Dash in her affections and become her heir.

The second meeting was between Dash and Lily and Arthur Kober's fiancée, Maggie Frohnknecht. Art brought her to Hardscrabble to meet them. They both liked her immediately. Lily became matron of honor at Maggie's marriage to Kober on January 11, 1941, when her own marriage to Art finally ended. Maggie soon became one of Dash's closest, most devoted friends. Inevitably, the Kobers would ask Lily to be godmother to Cathy, their only child, born March 16, 1942.

Nineteen forty-one was a year of human suffering on an unbearable scale. Tragic examples included the Warsaw Ghetto, where more than 4,000 Jews died every month, and the Vitebsk Ghetto, where in October 1941, 4,090 Jews and several mentally ill Jewish children were killed. Of course, the mass suffering did not stop there.

In July that year, Jo, fifteen, and Mary, twenty, took the train east to stay with Dash in his apartment in the Fifth Avenue Hotel. He took them to shows, nightclubs, and Hardscrabble Farm, where he taught them to fish, plant, and understand nature. Jo was happy. Mary, who had binged on drink, drugs, and sex back home, began to reveal her wild ways. Perhaps she thought her father would understand. Perhaps she didn't care. Hammett either cared too much or too little, for he hit her, blacked her eyes, and grew crazier than she was with anger and distress. Jose had concealed from him the tragic turn Mary's life had taken. He had no idea where to start to help. Irritable and powerless, he would not allow Lily, who despised Mary, to intervene. When the girls returned to California, Lily was relieved but Hammett was icily morose.

They spent some of the next weeks at Hardscrabble and then, on Sunday, December 7, 1941, Hellman, Hammett, the Kobers, and Shumlin were relaxing there when the news came through the radio that Japan had bombed Pearl Harbor. One hundred and eighty-eight aircraft were destroyed on the ground. The number of Americans killed was 2,403, including sixty-eight civilians. Roosevelt told Congress: "No matter how long it may take us to overcome this premeditated invasion, the American people in their righteous might will win through to absolute victory."

Lily's *Watch on the Rhine* had opened at the Martin Beck Theatre in New York on April 1, 1941, and exceptional notices meant that on January 25, 1942, *Rhine* was chosen for the Washington celebration of President Roosevelt's birthday. Warner wanted to film the play as an anti-Nazi movie, and since Hellman was still working for Goldwyn, she recommended Hammett as screenwriter.

On January 30, Warner signed him up for $30,000. Hammett approved of the way Hellman handled the issue of conscience in the play, so he determined to keep close to her original in the screenplay. However, the initial scenes were overladen with slow philosophical dialogue, and Herman Shumlin, the anxious director, found he needed to encourage and prompt Hammett into finishing the script. He finished writing the script in pencil on April 23, 1942. Lillian typed it and took her version to Hollywood on May 20. In her contract, Hellman had added the proviso that *she* would polish the script at $3,000 a week before filming started, so in a curious role reversal, she rewrote Hammett's lines to sharpen them. When the movie was released in August 1943, the credits read: "Screenplay by Dashiell Hammett, Additional Scenes and Dialogue by Lillian Hellman." Neither of them mentioned the irony. Hammett was nominated for an Oscar, and the movie was nominated for best picture but narrowly lost to *Casablanca*.

During 1942, he began to frequent Harlem whorehouses, where they understood impotency. He found black and Asian girls the most useful. If sex didn't work, the whorehouses offered pornographic shows that sometimes satisfied him. With Lily, there were always struggles of power or sentiment. Lily's practice of seeing herself as the equal of her male counterparts often undermined his masculinity. With whores, there was a straightforward understanding of desires that Lily's "nice girl" side shrank from.

Just as Lily had not forgiven him for driving her to abort their baby, so Hammett had not forgiven her for the abortion.

One night, when Lily was driving him to town, he pawed and leered at her, wretchedly plastered, demanding sex. She had never before refused him. But that night, appalled at the degrading waste of his life and the insecurity of hers, she said no. She would not make love when he was in that state.

He sobered up with shock. If she refused him now, she could refuse him again. He could not cope with that.

Hellman told Diane Johnson that Hammett made a decision never to sleep with her again. In that public version, Hellman said Hammett never apologized, never mentioned the decision. Subsequent biographers made a good case that just as Lily punished Dash for his behavior with that abortion, so now, by withholding sex, he was punishing her for going through with it.[9] That case has not been believed by everybody, however. Hellman privately told Peter Feibleman a different version. He writes:

> That theory is wrong. *Lily* stopped sleeping with Hammett. He did not decide to stop sleeping with her. If you are sexually in love with somebody who likes whores and the neighbors then one day you say "OK. Enough!" Lily told me that was what she felt. I know what other critics have said. . . . Their view made a better story but it was fictional. I knew Lillian. Hammett would always have kept up an affair with her. She emotionally couldn't afford it.[10]

Hellman's version in public. Hellman's version in private. No version from Hammett. Silence: always Hammett's version of events.

If Feibleman was correct and it was Lillian's decision to end their sexual relationship, then was it a face-saving loyalty that made her change her story and protect Hammett from a further slippage of his masculinity?

What mattered was that when Lillian decided on the termination and when she said "no" that night, she had no idea of the consequences.

Hammett had tried to enlist that year but the recruiters sent him away, scornful of his age and ill health. Then on

September 17, 1942, he read that the army had relaxed their rules. He went to the Whitehall Induction Center carrying X-rays that showed his TB had been arrested. As an alcoholic with a history of chronic illness and nervous breakdown, he could not credit they would take him. However, the psychiatric officer was a fan of Hammett. As a famous writer, you are not a nervous person, are you? he asked. Hammett calmly said he wasn't. The officer decided writers knew a great deal about human nature. They could be useful in the US Army. He signed the forms.

Hellman was aghast. Dash was running away from his problems, their problems. Dash would get sick. Dash would get killed. Dash glowed with excitement. "This is the happiest day of my life," he said. [11]

CHAPTER 13

The military that had accepted Hammett's enlistment knew his speeches at anti-Nazi rallies. In 1940, for instance, he had spoken at a meeting in protest against Nazi atrocities against Jews and Catholics in Germany. He had also spoken at a meeting of the Professionals Conference Against Nazi Persecution, of which he was president. The military knew, too, that he led campaigns to protest discrimination against Communists. Yet, they inducted him at the age of forty-eight, an old man by army standards, still on a disability pension from World War I, and assigned him to a signal training unit at Fort Monmouth, New Jersey, where he wrote training manuals. A year later, on August 8, 1943, the army sent him to Adak, Alaska, not a quiet bolthole for elderly invalids but an area of fierce fighting, where the Japanese Imperial Army had invaded US territory. Hammett became a corporal, then a sergeant, and helped secure the Aleutian Islands. He remained in Alaska for the duration of the war.

Dash thought about Lily often while he was away. It was always easier to think about her when he or she was absent. Lily felt lonely and useless. She talked at rallies, wrote speeches for people in Washington, planted a granite field that broke two ploughs, waited for Hammett's war missives but contrarily didn't always answer them. The early ones seemed dull.

> 27 September 1942, Fort Monmouth, New Jersey
> Dear Lily—
>   Army manners seem to have changed a lot for the better since my last experience . . . our food is put on the table in platters, from which we dish it into our mess-kits. The man who takes the last full portion from a platter carries it back to the counter to be refilled. . . .
>
> Love—
> Pvt. S.D.H. [1]

His constant flow of letters to her should have told her what he felt. In them, in letter after letter, especially the later ones, he expressed the depths of his feelings, which he had rarely shared with her, according to what Lily told Diane Johnson. But in his absence, her jealousy grew unbounded. Lily suspected Dash wrote as regularly to Jose as to her. He had given Jose's address to the army, not hers, as next of kin. That rankled. Perhaps he wrote regularly to other women as well.

She was right about Hammett's letters. He wrote often to Jose, to Jo, to Mary, to Lily's secretary, Nancy Bragdon, and a great deal to Maggie Kober, who was diagnosed with multiple sclerosis in October 1943, and to Pru Whitfield, whom he had installed in the Princeton house, who received seventy-five letters during his army years. "Family letters" were always dispatched to Jose.

Fort Monmouth, New Jersey
[Postmarked September 28, 1942]

Dear Jose,

Well, here I am, back where I started twenty-four years ago—a private in the United States army . . . am training for combat duty, with, I think, a fair chance of making it, though Army regulations say men over forty-five must be non-combatants.

So far my middle-aged bones are holding up pretty fair under the strain of romping around on the drill field with a lot of kiddies, and I feel fine . . .

Hammett told Mary on July 15, 1943, that her name and address were on his dog tags. "You are the one the government will notify if it has any news to give out about me, like . . . 'DESERTED,' or 'MISSING IN ACTION,' or 'WE CAN'T GET RID OF HIM.' If any such news comes along, wire Lillian, will you."

Hammett lent his Abercrombie credit card to Lily and asked her to become his shopper, banker, and not-quite-wife, whom he instructed to mail food parcels and to purchase "low brown shoes" size ten and a half C. At first, she was unaware then later shocked to discover that Dash was making long-term provisions for Jose and trying to secure his children's future.

"There'll be the usual amount of money for you and the children for some time to come," Hammett reassured Jose on September 28. "But I don't know how the more distant future will work out, so I'd suggest you try and save as much as you can. I took out $10,000 insurance—$5,000 in the name of each of the children—and the Army allotment . . . will come to Josephine each month. I couldn't claim Mary as a dependent, since she is more than eighteen . . . I think we'll make out all right financially."[2]

Hammett had been bonded to Lily, treating her as his not-quite-wife for twelve years, but when he said "we" he meant the Hammetts.

In October 1942, Dash wrote and told Lily that the men, who called him Pop, had seen through his anonymity. He had blossomed as the camp celebrity. One man got past the name Samuel "to the D." Autograph requests followed, including one from his company commander. One lieutenant thanked Hammett for his books, which gave him back much-needed self-respect. Hammett told him it was the nicest thing anybody could say to a writer. He finished his note to Lily: "I love a girl like you, Dash."

In December 1942, Dash told Lily the truth about his feelings when she left New York for Hollywood to work on *The North Star*, her movie script about a group of Russian villagers. "I am left behind to face the war practically single-handed . . . I suppose I'll first really miss you when I can't phone you in the morning. Maybe I'll phone anyhow just to keep my hand in."

He managed to calm her spirits by sending her one army letter she loved. It began, "Dear cutie and good writer," written after he had read her script.

> I kind of guess it's kind of all right. I like. Maybe you're going to have to cut the early parts a little . . . but . . . It's nice and warm and human and moving.
>
> And so are you.
>
> Love
> Rookie[3]

As Hammett foresaw, more trouble between Lillian and Goldwyn instigated the stormy end of their professional relationship. Their successful film of *The Watch on the Rhine* was

controversial. Lily needed Dash to face the outcries. Instead, in
May 1943, she went to Hardscrabble to recover. "Please write
me," she asked. Dash wrote to her constantly.

Why was Dash happy in the army? Why did an eccentric
man who largely lived by his own standards find hard discipline pleasant and entertaining? He loved the army's order, rituals, regulations, and admiring male comrades. One called him
a "male Garbo," others made him a hero, everyone called him
Sam. He was "liked because he was likable—pleasant, mild
and frank."[4]

Maybe a life ruled over by other people solved some of his
problems. Maybe he got a sense of pride that he could stand up
with men half his age. Was it simpler? That he liked his country? That he felt it was a just war?

Still, he sent Lily loving letters. "New York tonight . . . and,
with very pleasant finality, to the quarters of a girl named Hellman, who had better be heading in the same direction herself . . . Love, Whitey."

On May 9, 1943, came a witty note: "What do you look
like? . . . What are your hobbies? Would you like to correspond
with one of our soldier boys in a New Jersey camp? . . . His
hobby is Jewish playwrights."

Then came a telegram from Seattle, Washington, July
17, 1943: "I AM A PATIENT ELDERLY MAN WHO SAYS TO ARMIES
QUOTE ALL RIGHT I WILL LIE ON THIS BUNK UNTIL YOU TELL ME
WHAT TO DO UNQUOTE AND WHO LOVES YOU=DASH."[5]

The war brought her warmth not seen in peacetime.

One significant note asked Lily to buy him a ring. On May
27, 1943, she had missed his birthday.

"You say you love me, but you haven't yet given me the birthday present due last May." He wanted to have "some very nice
little thing to hold on to." He wanted a symbol of their bond.
"I want a ring." Not any old ring but a platinum-mounted one.

"I'll leave the details to you. All I ask is that the ring be sturdy, beautiful and valuable: I don't want any Japanese hacking off my finger to get at some trifling bauble." He asked her to engrave something inside the band. She wrote instantly, saying how glad she was. "I'm glad you're glad I asked for the ring and I'm glad you're glad to send it," he replied. [6]

Perhaps at last there would be peace between them.

By 1943, Dash's teeth were so infected that the army would not let him go overseas. Immediately, he suggested having every tooth pulled out. Lily's toothless lover reported in May that he was now completely out of teeth, having given up his jawbone. For three weeks, he would be gumming eggs and soft bread. That weekend, the man with the sunken face, like the face of death, met Lily in the "21" and ordered soft-boiled eggs. Lily screamed.

Later, she told Dash that she and Shumlin had emotionally come to the end. Dash, never jealous of, though sometimes exasperated by, Lily's affairs, said in a letter to her on February 29, 1944, that he couldn't help her because he had never understood Lily's relations with him. But he was intensely interested in how she was managing without his play-doctoring. Lily, anxious about writing her new play, *The Searching Wind*, without Hammett's help, leaned on him long-distance.

"I hope the play is coming along better than if I was on hand to get into quarrels with you about it, and that therefor[e] you are devoting to sheer writing those periods you used to take out for sulking because I was hampering your art." [7]

When Dash received his copy of the play, his letter to Lily gently suggested that it was too much like a "polite comedy." He told her he didn't think she had made her points. His critique on March 15 came late, for the play opened on April 12. Recognizing this, he said it was in some ways the most interesting play she had done, with "swell stuff." He also added she was

a cutie. He wished her a "long and opulent run." They both
worried until the opening—unnecessarily. The reviews for *The
Searching Wind* were so admiring that it ran opulently for more
than three hundred performances.

Dash wrote to her at once. The news about the play was
marvelous. It was time she stopped being his pupil. "Let this
be a lesson to you, my fine buxom cutie. You are a big girl now
and you write your own plays the way you want them and you
do not necessarily give a damn for the opinions of Tom, Dick
and Dashie unless they happen to coincide with your own."[8]

During 1944, Dashiell's letters were his most affectionate.
Before the army, his love had seemed so changed that their
writer friend Jerome Weidman said publicly that Dash no longer loved Lily in the same way because she had outstripped
him as a writer. Some friends thought the army was Hammett's escape from that conflict. The war letters brought them
together.

Dash believed nothing essential had altered in their joint
lives. Nothing that could not be fixed. But in 1944, something changed. Lillian was invited on a cultural mission to the
Soviet Union. She arrived in Moscow after a dangerous two-
week journey across Siberia, was ensconced in Spaso House,
the residence of the American ambassador, Averell Harriman,
where she met a married foreign service officer, John Melby.

Dash encouraged Lily to go to Russia, but once she had
embarked he was at a loss. "From now on I'll be writing to you
in a kind of semi-vacuum," he moped, "not knowing whether
you're yet off to the other side of the world."[9] Her concealed
resentment showed in the fact that she had not given him a
return date, nor had she instructed her secretary to inform him
where to send his mail. On November 5, he wished he was with
her in Moscow, where she was doubtless flirting with handsome
colonels in stylish white uniforms. Lily was indeed flirting, but

mainly with the dour young second secretary to the embassy, who shared her dinner table at Spaso House on November 11.

Father of two sons in El Paso, Melby was thirty, nine years younger than Lily, with a scar on his partly paralyzed face so that only one side smiled. She found this sophisticated diplomat interesting, but Dash's recent postal wooing made her ambivalent. Deciding to let events and emotions take their course, she did not write to Hammett. But nor did she tell Melby of Dash's crucial importance in her life.

By the third week in November, Dash mourned: "This is a long dry spell my darling."[10]

Lily felt more positive about Melby. They walked the wintry Moscow streets, danced together, and trawled shops. By Christmas 1944, Melby had even offered to divorce his wife. Dash steadily kept up his one-sided correspondence!

Though Dash and Lily had not been lovers for a long time, their attachment ran bone deep, and she had grown wary, even weary, of affairs with married men, alert to the way physical attraction could displace judgment.

Melby, whose career took him constantly abroad, would expect her to follow or wait patiently for his return. This would not meet her needs as an independent, successful playwright. Nor would it take into account her unbreakable bond with Dash. Yet, still she did not write to Dash, nor did she mention Dash to Melby.

Hammett's letters from Alaska increased. Though he lacked everything he thought he valued—Lily, Jo, Mary, Jose, floozies, fame, smart society—he was entirely happy. He told Lily he had fallen in love with Adak's mountains, lakes, and austerity. Again, he was drawn to the isolation of islands, the feeling of not being trapped. As a writer, he regained some measure of self-esteem from editing *The Adakian*, the daily newspaper for the troops, and writing *The Battle of the Aleutians*, with coauthor Robert Colodny. Although he was able to write this kind of journalism, he was unable, drunk or sober, to dredge up even one fictional paragraph, despite constant efforts throughout his war service.

Writing had once given Hammett a defense against the inanity of meaninglessness, which his rational self knew was what everybody faced. Politics had been helpful to his problem over writing, but in the company of other activist writers, he felt shamed. He had returned the $5,000 advance for a new novel to Bennett Cerf, saying he was scared he would never write it.

In 1945, when Hellman returned to New York, she resumed writing. Hammett, who received two notes from her on March 15, sarcastically responded that it was "awful nice" being on her mailing list again.

On April 15, Melby returned, met Lillian, and they slept that night at her house. When he left, *they* restarted writing. Lily, corresponding with both men, told neither about the other. Dash told Lily *he* was restarting a book. It was about a man who came home from war and did not like his family. The tentative title was *The Valley Sheep Are Fatter*. When Melby came back to New York, Lillian took him to Hardscrabble, where he met the Kobers and Dash and Lily's circle. Melby wanted Lily to accompany him to China, but Dash had told her he would join a training unit at Fort Richardson in April for the final five and a half months. Then he would be home. He would want her to be there when he arrived.

In January 1945, MGM had released the movie *The Thin Man Goes Home*, and seven months later, on August 28, the Thin Man himself left Fort Richardson to go home. On September 6, 1945, Sergeant Sam Hammett was honorably discharged at Fort Dix Separation Center. Ironically, he gave Hardscrabble as his address.

In New York, he hastened to Lily's house. In the hallway, he spotted a man with a facial scar. The scarred man's books were strewn around. The scarred man's clothes took up Hammett's space. Dash had not been warned. Awkwardly, Lily asked Melby to move out to the Plaza for a few days. When Melby returned, confused, realizing he had not taken into account the importance of this thin man, this thin man had disappeared. The word "betrayal" hung in the air. First, Hammett checked into the Hotel Roosevelt, then he lived briefly at 15 East 66th Street before moving to 28 West 10th Street. He bought Jose a house in West Los Angeles with a primrose kitchen. She liked that. Hammett liked nothing about his old life. He did not much like Lillian either, anymore. Hammett would not acknowledge he felt rejected, but Lily's treatment of him precipitated a descent into an alcoholic binge.

In 1946, Hammett began teaching courses in mystery writing at the Jefferson School of Social Science, which was established in Lower Manhattan by the US Communist Party in 1944 to teach Marxism to the working classes. He also served on the school's Board of Trustees, which he continued to do until 1956.

In January 1946, an Oppish radio serial, *The Fat Man*, started and would run until 1950. On July 12, another radio serial, *The Adventures of Sam Spade*, began. This run would continue until 1951. Versions of his old work haunted him. Money rolled in and he wrote nothing.

In 1945, at fifty-one, Hammett the ex-soldier wanted to hole up at Hardscrabble. But Lily entertained visitors whom Hammett called "grotesques." Melby would not be at Hardscrabble long. Nor would he last much longer in Lily's life. But Dash was not yet sure about that. Dash had Lily's ring, but he was not sure he had Lily.

PART SIX
POLITICS, AUTUMN GARDEN, AND JAIL, 1946–1952

CHAPTER 14

Between 1945 and 1948, Dash's drinking grew wilder. There came a "lost, thoughtless quality," which Lily and their friends had not seen before. Dash was not at ease with anyone. Angry that Lily was finding her own way writing *Another Part of the Forest*. Angry that he could not see *his* way, could not write fiction at all, angry at his truncated homecoming, for which he blamed Lily. Dash suspected that, underneath, Lily had not entirely given up on him. But underneath was a complex country for which he had no passport.

Hellman broke through their mutual distrust by discussing with Dash her idea that, through *Forest*, a Southern father's struggle against unhealthy lust for his daughter, Regina (played by the beautiful Patricia Neal), Lily might now confront her crushing childhood. Hammett, pleased to be play consultant again, delighted in the *Forest* rehearsals. The couple was back on track. The cast noticed that, when Hammett arrived, Hellman flowered. Hammett, still depressed, remarked soberly he would commit suicide if it weren't for the trouble it would cause Lily. "Oh, don't let that stop you," she retaliated wittily.

"I've had troubles before!"[1] Cast members also noticed Dash couldn't take his eyes off Pat Neal, who treated him as an amusing, affectionate uncle.

As postwar anxiety about the threat of Communist subversion worsened, Hammett's pro-Communist participation increased. According to FBI records at the time, he was New York State president of the Civil Rights Congress, which was labeled as subversive by the attorney general. In that capacity, Hammett asked the New York City mayor to stop police brutalities toward blacks. He was named as a Communist in September 1946 by a State Department adjutant. In the same year, Hammett spoke at another organization, the New York State American Youth for Democracy Convention, which was also labeled subversive by the attorney general, as was the Tenth Anniversary Dinner of the Veterans of the Abraham Lincoln Brigade, at which Hammett spoke. On February 28, 1947, he signed a petition that appeared in the *Daily Worker*, condemning "the shameful persecution of German anti-Fascist refugee Gerhardt Eisler and calling for abolition of the Un-American House Committee." He was also named as a Communist by an anti-Communist group within Actors' Equity Association.[2]

This FBI record shows the extent of his influence among liberal groups. It also helps to explain his political reputation. Hammett's political standing with left-wing liberals was so high that he became an even more prominent target for those who would investigate him.

Like Hammett, other liberals and radicals were forced to choose between loyalty to the causes of labor and civil rights (Hammett's original partisanship) and loyalty to the Hollywood branch of the Communist Party, which had been formed by the Conference of Studio Unions, who cared little for the plight of American workers.

The "Un-American House Committee," better known as the House Un-American Activities Committee, or HUAC, was an investigative committee of the House of Representatives, created in 1938 to investigate alleged disloyalty or subversive activities by private citizens or public employees or any organizations suspected of having Communist ties. In 1945, it was made a permanent committee. About this time, HUAC decided to track down Karl Marx's footprints by investigating Hollywood. The committee saw subversive propaganda everywhere. The FBI believed that the hidden purpose of Lily's play, *Another Part of the Forest*, was to reveal Communist ideas. Hammett and Hellman came under greater surveillance.

Hammett stumbled through the start of a book about Helm, an artist who had been drunk since his discharge from the army. He gave up and began another about two men recently discharged, one of whom wanted his friend to marry his sister so that the two men could still hang out together. He thought a lot about men in groups, men in company, the company of men. He had felt at home with army fellows.

Max's wild tempers and paranoia, exacerbated by his dementia, finally led Lily to place him, against his will, in a mental sanatorium. When Max was lucid, he blamed her for jailing him as a punishment. Lily, desperate, needed Dash's advice. Did Dash also blame her? Before they could talk, Max died, on August 4, 1947. Lily immediately phoned Dash at his West 10th Street apartment so that together they could bury Max in the same cemetery as Julia. Dash managed to accompany Lily to Martha's Vineyard to help her recover.

Dash, the absentee father, was finally called upon to get help for his drug-addicted daughter, Mary, in 1946, for Jose was desperate over her "bad, bad state." Dash must take her away.

Jo had tried to help her sister.

But even as a toddler she caused terrible trouble. She went to a Catholic school and slugged a nun. She played truant. [Uncontrollable] she shoplifted. . . . By fourteen, she drank all the time. By sixteen, she was without doubt an alcoholic and she took . . . drugs. Mama couldn't bear it, and she wouldn't tell Papa the truth. Mama went on praying, Mary went right on drinking, and then there were the men. She got into sex at thirteen. We couldn't even talk about that. Papa got a glimpse when we went East to see him in summer 1941. I think he was frightened for her, or maybe for himself.

Dash went west immediately. He could get Mary good care in New York.

Jo said: "I don't think he wanted to take her. . . . I said her brain was twisted. She didn't think like other people, she never thought about other people. . . . No shrink, nothing could help her, but I wanted her to go. Mama needed space, peace, so did I. I wanted Papa to take her."

At sixteen, Mary had told Jo she had never had one happy day in her life. At twenty-four, she went with Dash back to New York, ostensibly to get orthodontic help. She slept with the orthodontist, became pregnant by another man, asked Dash to arrange an abortion, injected drugs, drank more than Dash, battled with him. He told Jo, "Your sister is a whore." Hammett's feelings for Mary were strange and violent. Because she seemed both frail and tough, he wanted to help her, but at times he almost wanted to kill her.[3] The tension escalated. Living together in Dash's small apartment, they lashed out in frightening intimacy and abused each other publicly.

When Dash brought Mary to Hardscrabble, she arrived with dark bruises around her eyes. Father and daughter fought, kissed, and hated each other, and it seemed to Lily and their friends that they were mutually attracted. Lily could not bear to contemplate a possible meaning of what she witnessed. She begged Dash to stop drinking in front of Mary, insisted he get Mary her own apartment. But still Mary ruled Dash's life. She liked Rose Evans, Hammett's black housekeeper, disliked Marge May, her father's secretary. Hammett fired Marge. Mary opened Hammett's mail, found a telegram from Aunt Reba saying Dash's father was dead. Was Dash going to the funeral? "No, I'm paying for it," he quipped, "let somebody else do the crying."[4] But he *had* been in touch with his father and bought him an artificial leg when his own was amputated. Aunt Reba, who came to visit, begged Mary to return with her, but Mary would not leave Dash. Later, psychiatrist Joseph Teicher said Mary was fixated on Hammett. Finally, they found a place in New York for Mary to live until 1951, but, sadly, she remained promiscuous.

On July 6, 1948, Dash and Mary went west to attend Jo's wedding to Loyd Marshall. Lillian sent Jo a blue cloisonné locket, but, diplomatically, Jo wore Jose's pearls. "Papa was cold stone sober when we walked down the aisle, but after our honeymoon, he was much worse."

Dash, constantly drunk, provoked Lily so much she wanted to sever all ties with him, but psychiatrist Zilboorg said Dash needed her. She would not abandon him, but as long as he drank, she kept an icy distance. She feared he would drink till he died.

But she was wrong.

Rose Evans saved him. Lillian had refused to see him. Dash stayed in bed drinking, mainly beer. Rose got very frightened when he could hardly make it to the bathroom, wouldn't stop drinking, and didn't move. She panicked. "Don't call Lillian," Dash said weakly. But Rose told Lily's secretary: "Please come down here and see to Mr. Hammett because I think he's going to die." Reluctantly, Lily headed for West 10th Street.

Hammett, shaking and screaming with DTs, could hardly lift his arms or legs, but by 3:00 a.m. he was in Lenox Hill Hospital, where he spent Christmas 1948. Dr. Abe Abeloff told him that if did not stop drinking he would be dead within six weeks. Hammett gave his word that he would stop.

To everyone's amazement, he stopped drinking completely. Six years later, Lily told Dash the doctors did not believe he would stay on the wagon. He looked puzzled. "But I gave my word that day," he said. [5]

In January 1949, he was allowed out of the hospital, broken but sober. Where should he convalesce?

Hardscrabble Farm, of course, Lily said briskly.

Hardscrabble Farm, of course, Hammett said calmly, is the place "where I belong." It is the place "where all sensible people are whenever possible." [6]

Sensible was a new word in his vocabulary. Dash knew the synonyms. Level-headed, sagacious, sane, shrewd, rational, reasonable, wise. He tried them out. He had not been known for those cautious epithets. What he *had* been known for—wildness, weakness, and drunken disorder—had not served him well. Resolutely, he began his physical and spiritual recovery. He and Lily had come through a shabby time. They needed serenity and peace. They needed to share it. No fights, no bickering. No drink. They settled into something resembling an idyll, even better than their previous time at Hardscrabble. For two years, a blue haze drifted over the farm, completing their dreams of companionship. Hammett grew fat, suntanned, and contented; together they bred poodles, even owned fifteen dogs. Hammett bought them a television. They watched old movies like a happy married couple.

They spent summers on Martha's Vineyard, where they helped Cathy Kober, whose mother, Maggie, was dying. "Dash," she said, "really knew what it was like to be a child, and I don't think Lillian quite got it."[7] Dash's comforting letters to Maggie were filled with his own excitement about the robins, insects, and flowers crowding their country life.

When Lily went fishing, Dash cleaned their house, mopped the floors, then sat in the sun reading theoretical physics and Stendhal's *The Green Huntsman*.

Their friends noticed how caring they were. Hammett had a new openness, a chaste, loving quality. Lily flourished on their passionate affection. Those were the best of times. Hammett attended meetings about a movie deal for *The Fat Man*; wrote a report for Bloomgarden on ways to stage Sean O'Casey's *Purple Dust*; and hired an attractive, red-haired assistant, Muriel Alexander. He *would* write.

Hammett knew the dangers of Hellman becoming a "known Red": trials, imprisonment, bankruptcy, censorship, loss of earnings, and more. Nevertheless, he encouraged her to help organize the Scientific and Cultural Conference for World Peace, along with leftists Shostakovich, Leonard Bernstein, Albert Einstein, Norman Mailer, Thomas Mann, and Arthur Miller. The conference was held at the Waldorf-Astoria Hotel in New York City in March 1949. Predictably, the California State Senate Committee on Un-American Activities labeled Hellman a Communist party-line disciple. National censorship followed fast. The Second Red Scare continued to whistle through America.[8]

Hellman was forced to sign a loyalty oath, which was required of all Dramatists League members. The American Legion categorized her as an Untouchable, one of 128 celebrities suspected of Communist leanings. Hammett, sober, not yet blacklisted, was briefly courted to write screenplays. But with Hellman increasingly blacklisted, their financial stability was rocked. They watched HUAC namings and blamings increase. Yet, despite economic danger, they felt unrealistically cocooned, even blessed, when Dash's first grandchild, Ann (after Annie Bond Hammett), was born May 24, 1950, on Jo's twenty-fourth birthday. Dash, almost fifty-six, visited two weeks later. "Papa was gaga about Ann . . . he held and looked at her as if she were the first baby he had ever seen."[9]

Dash took Jo to a lavish baby boutique in Beverly Hills, bought Ann luxury clothes. Then they lunched at the Beverly Wilshire. Lillian was as keen as Dash to bring Ann to Hardscrabble. The following spring, 1951, Dash flew east with Ann, cared for her for ten days, and Jo followed to stay a further week. Dash and Lil behaved like elderly married parents. It was as if their own aborted baby had been restored. Lily fell deeply in love with Ann and almost bored Dash with baby stories. She also softened her attitude about Dash's constant contact with Mary and Jose.

In June 1949, sobriety had allowed Hammett to start writing a new novel entitled *Man and Boy*. Sadly, his words dried up, but he began another titled *Look for Something to Look For*. His talent was now for titles, not follow-ups. Movie producers, however, were still on his side. In January 1950, Dash was employed as a screenwriter for Paramount to write Sidney Kingsley's *Detective Story*, directed by William Wyler. On arrival at the Beverly Wilshire in Hollywood, a loving letter from Lily awaited him. He hoped sobriety would make him write. Feeling claustrophobic, shut in with his typewriter, he told Lily he loved and missed her. His consolations were taking Jo to the Santa Anita races, seeing Lee Gershwin, which revived painful memories of George's death, and visiting Maggie Kober, who was struggling with the final stages of multiple sclerosis. Many evenings, he shared virtually silent suppers with Pat Neal. He gazed at her, made occasional witty remarks, and ended the evenings with a chaste kiss. Despite missing Lily, he spent much of his time in Jose's company at the house he had bought her in West LA. Jo believed that Jose was still devoted to him. Certainly, Dash found solace and quietude in her presence, even as he missed Lily's vivacity. He was glad Lily no longer felt threatened by Jose, but he carefully downplayed his times with her and with Pat.

After two months of working on *Detective Story*, Hammett felt that, realistically, there was no chance of completing the screenplay, so he returned the $10,000 advance. He left Hollywood for good in June 1950.

Dash worked on Lillian's next play, *The Autumn Garden*, which reflected their joint memories, hopes, and lost illusions. While he did so, Hammett tried to come to terms with what he had made or failed to make of his life. Lily's play echoed this precisely in portraying lodgers in a Southern boarding house confronting their illusions. Dilettante artist Nick Denery, the Hammett figure, had not finished a portrait in twelve years, the exact length of time Hammett had not written a novel. Hammett's verdict was that the play was the best written by any writer for years. But he believed one speech, delivered by a Major Griggs, whose life's failure needed correcting, was inadequate. Hellman's version was that Hammett alone rewrote the speech, so that it became the play's symbolic highpoint.

So at any given moment you're only the sum of your life up to then. There are no big moments you can reach unless you've a pile of smaller moments to stand on. That big hour of decision, the turning point in your life, the someday you've counted on when you'd suddenly wipe out your past mistakes, do the work you'd never done, think the way you'd never thought, have what you'd never had—it just doesn't come suddenly. You've trained yourself for it while you waited—or you've let it all run past you and frittered yourself away. I've frittered myself away . . .

Hellman made much of Hammett's brilliance in rewriting her mediocre speech. But I saw all Hellman's working drafts, which show that Hammett edited but did *not* write it. Hellman did. Hammett reworked one of her drafts. [10]

Hellman's generosity in publicly crediting Hammett with more than he merited and his acquiescence reveal the changed nature of their relationship. She dedicated "their" play "to Dash" for tirelessly preparing it for production. She made sure that he was financially well taken care of for doing so. On January 2, 1951, she confirmed their agreement that in return for his assistance he would receive for life 15 percent of her royalties, which were 10 percent of the weekly box office gross. Sometimes, Hellman generously paid him in advance.

The FBI were about to remove their golden time, which would never return. In July 1951, agents invaded Hardscrabble Farm, acting on information from a "confidential source" that four Communist fugitives who had jumped bail might be on the premises. [11] The agents interrogated Hammett. They found no fugitives. They saw no incriminating evidence. Finally they left.

Why did this happen?

The government's stance toward the American Communist Party had toughened. The Civil Rights Congress had come to the assistance of eleven Communists and sympathizers who had been convicted, under the repressive Smith Act, of criminal conspiracy to advocate the overthrow by violence of the government. The men were appealing their convictions, and the CRC had paid their bail, using $260,000 of a bail fund established several years earlier to aid defendants arrested for political reasons. Hammett was one of the five bail fund trustees and their chairman.

On July 2, 1951, when all appeals were exhausted, four of the eleven jumped bail. The New York Southern District Court declared the $80,000 bail fund posted for the four forfeited, but to arrest the fugitives they had to establish their whereabouts. The trustees were subpoenaed. They were expected to be asked the names of contributors to the CRC bail fund, on the theory that fund contributors might be sheltering the fugitives. But the contributors' names were considered privileged information by the CRC and the trustees.

The night before Hammett's court appearance, on Monday, July 9, Lillian asked him why he wouldn't simply testify that he didn't know the names. "I can't say that." Why? she asked. "I don't know why. I guess it has something to do with keeping my word, but I don't want to talk about that."

He assured her that nothing much would happen, though he thought he would go to jail for a while, but she was not to worry.

"I hate this damn kind of talk, but maybe I'd better tell you that if it were more than jail, if it were my life, I would give it for what I think democracy is, and I don't let cops or judges tell me what I think democracy is." [12]

Maybe he did say exactly those words. But he did not, in fact, go to jail for being heroic about democracy. He was imprisoned not so much for refusing to name the contributors, but because he refused to answer any questions except to identify himself. For that, he was found guilty of contempt of court.

The court proceedings, powerful in their consequences on Hammett's health, on the day were woefully humdrum. Hammett probably did *not* know the whereabouts of the four missing men. But Civil Rights Congress documents held by the court showed that as chairman of the trustees, he did have a role in formulating policy and therefore had greater responsibility to divulge information than other trustees. As evidence, the government had the Civil Rights Congress charter signed by Hammett; audits of the fund signed by Hammett; and bail fund meeting minutes initialed by Hammett. It was hardly surprising this celebrated writer was their star witness.

The trustees' attorneys, Mary M. Kaufman, who at only thirty-six had been a prosecutor at Nuremberg, and labor lawyer Victor Rabinowitz, argued that the court had no jurisdiction to inquire about the bail fund, that such questions were irrelevant to the fugitives' locations. They encouraged the trustees to take the Fifth when questioned about the Civil Rights Congress. All trustees at some point used the Fifth to remain silent, but Hammett took it to extremes. He knew the likely outcome, because millionaire Communist supporter Frederick Vanderbilt Field, another trustee, had already testified, relied on the Fifth, and been sentenced to six months' jail for contempt.

Hammett testified to his full name then stopped cooperating. When asked questions about the Civil Rights Congress, he took the Fifth. When asked questions about the bail fund, he took the Fifth. When asked to identify his initials or signature on documents, he refused to reply on the grounds that the answer might tend to incriminate him.

The court, faced with his total intransigence, judged him to be an uncooperative witness in criminal contempt. He was placed in the custody of a federal marshal until 7:30 p.m., when the court reconvened to sentence him. Judge Sylvester Ryan asked him if he had anything to say before being sentenced. "Not a thing," Hammett said. Judge Ryan sentenced him to prison for six months or until he purged himself of contempt.

Hammett was taken immediately to the Federal House of Detention, West Street, New York City. Judge Ryan denied Rabinowitz's request "for the contemnor to be released in reasonable bail." The judge's decision was based "upon the entire conduct of the witness throughout his entire examination," conduct described as "contumacious." Initially, the judge had been inclined to "impose a longer sentence upon him," because Hammett had seen what happened to cotrustee Field and because he was chairman. Ironically, Ryan said, "I feel that I have dealt with him extremely leniently."

Mary Kaufman asked the United States Court of Appeals for the Second Circuit to intervene. She argued that, pending appeal, Hammett's case should be treated as an application for habeas corpus.

On Thursday, July 12, 1951, Judge Learned Hand issued a temporary order for bail of $10,000. As efforts were made to raise that sum, Hammett learned that the Treasury Department had filed an income tax lien for $100,629.03 against him for failing to pay any taxes between 1942 and 1945.

Hellman gave a face-saving inaccurate account to Diane Johnson of how hard she tried and failed to raise Hammett's bail money. She even invented a fictitious note from Hammett: "Do not come into this courtroom. If you do I will say I do not know you. Get out of 82nd Street and Pleasantville. Take one of the trips to Europe that you love so much. You do not have to prove to me that you love me, at this late date. D. H."[13]

No evidence bears out Hellman's implausible tale of her money-raising efforts. Her 1951 diary shows she was not prepared to mortgage her 82nd Street house, and she took psychiatrist Zilboorg's advice not to put up any bail money herself.

What was true was she booked a passage to Europe.

Jerome Weidman, Hammett's friend, *did* offer to put up the $10,000, appalled that others were too scared to do so. Kober, Lily's ex-husband and Dash's close friend, told Jerome that he himself was steering clear of the situation and Lily was afraid to jeopardize her chance to write a *War and Peace* screenplay for Alexander Korda.

Muriel Alexander, Hammett's loyal secretary, went twice to the Federal Courthouse with $10,000 cash. A rich comrade had handed over the money but wished to remain anonymous. When Alexander was asked for the source, she said it was her own. When the court didn't believe her, she refused to divulge the donor's name. Fifty-six years later, she still refused. With no legal precedent, Judge Ryan ruled that money from the Civil Rights Congress was no longer acceptable. After Mary Kaufman's objections were overruled, Muriel withdrew the offer. On July 17, Judge Hand, petitioned by federal attorney Irving Saypol, revoked his order. Bail was no longer allowed Hammett throughout his long appeals process.

The shiftiest aspect of the case was the court's refusal to accept the bail money, which was partly at the request of the prosecutor, Irving Saypol, the nation's number one legal hunter of top Communists.

At the West Street detention center, Hammett worked in the library and was pleased to find that they owned a copy of *The Maltese Falcon*. He received regular visits from Muriel, with mail and messages from Lillian, who did not once visit him, but who immediately fired both Kaufman and Rabino-witz, neither of whom charged Hammett a fee. Next, Lillian hired thirty-four-year-old Charles Haydon to file a brief for the Appeals Court, then on August 3, she left America and fled to Claridges in London.

When prisoner number 8416AK was moved on September 28 from the West Street detention center to the Federal Correctional Institute near Ashland, Kentucky, he was allowed to send letters only to his family, and Jo was the main recipient of his correspondence. Hammett therefore asked Jo to ferry messages to Muriel and Lillian. "I could tell he was surprised and hurt [about Lillian]. But not angry," Jo said later. Dash told Jo that he'd heard Lillian was having a pretty good time despite her anxiety. "I didn't detect any . . . heavy-duty irony—only a kind of understanding wistfullness."

He stayed in Ashland until his release. He was sick, exhausted, and fainted in the food line. Recovery took weeks, and he did not write even to Jo until mid-October. "He had to nerve himself up to write me. Even when you know you've done the right thing, the only thing, it would be hard to write your child from prison."[14]

Jose and Mary wrote regularly, and initially Muriel but not Lily was on his submission list of correspondents. After three months, Dash asked for Lily's name to be added. The Bureau of Prisons director contacted the FBI for Hellman's suitability as a prisoner's correspondent. The FBI sent them a document filled with Hellman's pro-Communist affiliations. In October, permission was refused. Jo alone was a go-between.

The one message Jo found it hard to deliver was her father's instruction to tell Pat Neal "sometimes I've found it awfully easy to be in love with her in jail."[15] Jo admitted: "I felt sympathy for Lillian about Pat. He had never kept that attraction secret . . . it really hurt Lillian. . . . He shouldn't have sent Pat messages through me in the same paragraph as an inquiry about Lillian. It seemed disloyal to the woman I thought of as my father's wife."

Hammett's response to prison was more like that of young men talking about survival in a tough football game. When prison was behind him, Hammett said it had felt like going home. Jo said some post-jail romanticism enveloped her father.

"Maybe more like he was back in his Pinkerton days— locked up in a Butte jail cell with some Wobbly . . . rubbing shoulders with the same kind of rough guys the Anaconda miners had been—illiterate and stupid. . . . He didn't look down on them, but he was not one of them either."[16]

But in prison, Hammett found nothing romantic. It was claustrophobic and demeaning. Though few knew, he had suffered from lifetime claustrophobia. He was scared of elevators and small places. Jo hoped having prison bars to see through might help.

Outside, Lily had such troubles with the Internal Revenue Service that she knew she would have to sell their farm. In September, during a HUAC hearing, Martin Berkeley denounced Hellman as being present at an organizing meeting of the Hollywood Communist Party. Her professional career was now blacklisted totally. Things were made worse for them all by Maggie's death on May 16, and Dash and Lily, who could have used each other's support, were forced to grieve separately.

Hammett was released from prison on December 9, 1951, ten days before the United States District Court refused his second appeal to overthrow his conviction. He had served twenty-two weeks of his twenty-six-week sentence, gaining a reduction for good behavior. Having lost fifteen pounds in jail, Dash was very weak and needed to be escorted home from Kentucky. He had hoped, even expected, that Lillian would meet him; she had promised Jo she would fly to Ashland. Instead, Charles Haydon arrived holding two sets of clothes chosen by Rose Evans, with the news that Lily could not come on her lawyer's advice, she said.

Hammett reported to the warden's office, receiving a Greyhound ticket and $50. At Charleston, he met an ex-convict and gave him the fifty. Then he boarded the plane to New York. When it landed in a snowstorm, he staggered out, swept by waves of nausea, then rushed to the men's room to vomit. Lillian had arrived at La Guardia in a limousine. Dash said it must have been a bad hamburger. At 82nd Street, she had prepared oysters, quails, and sweetbreads, but he was too sick to eat.

He returned to his apartment to be greeted by Rose Evans. Living alone at West 10th Street, he suffered several weeks of acute illness, unable to restart his teaching in January at Jefferson. He looked forward to going to Pleasantville, counting on the farm to revive him. Then Lily broke the news. Her own tax difficulties, her unemployment, and Hammett's legal fees had left her severely in debt. She feared she would be called before HUAC and would have to finance more lawyers. She had been forced to sell Hardscrabble, which she advertised as "authentic Colonial lovingly remodeled," set in an "enchanted forest" where, among fertile fields and woodlands, the lucky buyer could "step into another world, another century." Dash and Lily believed every word of that advertisement.[17] This time they grieved together.

Then Dash submerged his sorrow, writing to Jo on April 10: "Lillian's been moving P'ville this week. . . . I haven't thought about it much except to know it's going to leave quite a hole in life."[18]

It left a huge hole. It had been their shared home for twelve years. Lily felt that saying their farewell to the place together would just make it worse, so Dash did not help with the move.

In 1952, except for the birth of Evan, his second grandchild, Dash had little comfort. He had absolutely no money, for his income was attached by the Internal Revenue Service in lieu of back taxes totaling $111,008.60. Hellman made a list of those who owed him money. Hammett wouldn't let her send any letters. "Forget it," he said abruptly.

The fierce blacklist in Hollywood excluded from employment all party members and fellow travelers except those who had recanted and "reformed." Hammett had done neither, so his major sources of income, the radio shows *The Adventures of The Thin Man*, *The Adventures of Sam Spade*, and *The Fat Man*, were canceled. None of his books were reprinted, posters advertising a movie of *The Maltese Falcon* were torn down. He was unable to send any money to Jose, who was forced to return to nursing in Santa Monica but understood better than anyone how hard prison had been for Dash.

He could no longer afford his rent. In October, his friends Sam and Helen Rosen offered him a four-room cottage near their weekend house in Katonah. Lily suggested he take the tiny payment of $75 from her safe each month, and the Rosens, who paid his telephone and electricity, agreed to tell the IRS Dash was staying rent-free.

The United States government had almost broken his spirit, while claustrophobia had emotionally destroyed him. He had left prison with health massacred by incarceration. He would never again be well, not even for a few weeks. Though he lived ten more years, at this point he started his slow painful death, to which he seemed indifferent. He did not encourage callers; he shrugged off friends.

Dash never talked or wrote about the fact that Lily had betrayed him. He appeared to accept it, as he accepted his sentence. Somewhere, Dash knew his life plot had one more twist. HUAC was not finished with him. On February 21, 1952, it attacked.

CHAPTER 15

Hammett's release from jail on December 9, 1951, allowed him ten weeks and four days without battles with HUAC. Then Hammett was faced with a new problem.

On February 21, Lily received a subpoena from HUAC to appear as a witness before a subcommittee investigating subversion in the entertainment industry. Dash told her she must not name names. For counsel, he approved of the world-renowned New Deal lawyer, Abe Fortas, from whom Lily initially sought advice. Fortas was enormously effective in defending witnesses against HUAC. He suggested informally that she should stake out a moral position and testify about herself but not about others. Dash, fearful that Lily would be jailed, rats would attack her, and she wouldn't survive, opposed this. Then Fortas found himself unable to represent Hellman, so he sent her to lawyer Joseph Rauh, founder and national chairman of the liberal Americans for Democratic Action, both anti-Communist and anti-McCarthy. Hammett approved the choice, for he admired Rauh's fierce belief in civil liberties.

Rauh decided Lily should take the Fifth Amendment's protection against self-incrimination, then give it up if HUAC agreed not to ask her about other people. She was to write a letter to the press, pointing out that she was standing up for her conscience, and let fireworks go off during the hearing. Dash hated this strategy. He felt she should simply take the Fifth. No tricks, he told her.

But the trick worked. Opposing counsel Frank S. Tavenner read out the now-famous letter, including the dramatic line, "I cannot and will not cut my conscience to fit this year's fashions," which made political history. Lillian was not sent to jail and instead became a national heroine, having won a rare battle against HUAC.

Hammett was less lucky.

On March 26, 1953, he was summoned to appear before Joseph McCarthy's Senate subcommittee, the Senate Permanent Subcommittee on Investigations, which asked him about two main areas of his alleged Communist interests. The first was whether he thought Communism was superior to the current American form of government. Hammett said he couldn't give a definite answer. Asked whether he favored adopting Communism in their country at the present time, Hammett said no. When questioned further, he said his negative answer had been because it would be impractical, as most people were against Communism.

The second area of investigation was of more interest to Hammett, as it was about books and writing. The committee was investigating the purchase of books written by Communists for State Department libraries abroad. They asked Hammett whether, if he were fighting Communism, he would allow books by Reds to be distributed internationally. Dash said he would not give people books at all!

Naturally, all Hammett's books were efficiently removed from State Department libraries.

Hammett, knowing that his time to write was growing short, had begun the year before to write *Tulip*, his final work of fiction. [1] It gave him his one satisfaction.

"I am looking on the book as something that might turn out to be very worth while," he wrote to Lily. Then on August 24, 1952: "I'm having a mess of trouble with my book, but it's the kind of trouble I suppose I ought to be having. . . . I'm having a hard time making it as nearly as good as I want it in the way I want it."[2]

Tulip, which Hammett wrote intermittently but never once gave up on, achieving twelve thousand five hundred words before his death, *was* a new departure: autobiographical, reflective, descriptive, with anecdotes replacing plot. He hoped it would be the book he had been waiting years to write.

Each fictional event mirrored a real one. His white-haired writer, Pop (Hammett's army nickname), a lunger from Tacoma hospital who has just been released from jail, having been attacked by the state and federal governments and sentenced for improper politics, tries to tell his friend, Tulip, who, like Hammett, has been stationed in the Aleutians, why he has stopped writing.

Tulip, who believes Pop, now on the wagon, is short of subjects, says, Write about me. Pop replies: "Organizing the material is the problem, not getting it."

Fourteen-year-old Tony, their host's son, joins them. "I suppose most of my talking was done to him and I think Tulip knew it. . . . I had always beaten Tulip by not talking, or, at least, by not talking about the things he wished to talk about."

Did Lily flinch when she read this?

Through Tony, Pop talks to his readers:

I've been in a couple of wars—or at least in the Army while they were going on—and in federal prisons and I had t.b. for seven years and have been married as often as I chose and have had children and grandchildren and except for one fairly nice but pointless brief short story about a lunger going . . . for an afternoon and evening holiday from his hospital . . . I've never written a word about any of these things. Why? All I can say is they're not for me. Maybe not yet, maybe not ever. I used to try now and then . . . but they never came out meaning very much to me.

Yet, Pop admits his one lunger story contains "more material than I got out of wars and prisons." Does personal experience benefit writers? Pop and Tulip, two warring sides of Hammett's nature, debate the question, then focus on the relationship between "the real" and "the written."

Pop contends that anything can become symbolic but admits "stuff of that sort" is not his literary style. Symbols are "devices of the old and tired." Hammett's last antihero suggests that, if you are tired, it is better to ease up. "You ought to rest, I think, and not try to fool yourself and your customers with colored bubbles."

These lines in the original manuscript occur on page fifty-one, where it appears that Hammett initially decides to end his story. Here the narration breaks off.

But tossed in with the fifty-one-page manuscript was one extra unnumbered page, which Hellman said later was Hammett's final page. Her apparent evidence for this was that Hammett had scrawled "last page" on that unnumbered sheet. Editor Joe Fox followed her instructions. In the published book, after the "colored bubbles" line, a paragraph in square brackets in the center of the page states: "*Tulip* was never completed and the manuscript ends here. But Hammett evidently wrote the very end of the book, and this is it, *L.H.*"

Then followed a page containing four paragraphs:

Two or three months later I heard Tulip was in a Minneapolis hospital, where he had a leg amputated. I went out to see him and showed him this.

"It's all right, I guess," he said when he had read it, "but you seem to have missed the point."

People nearly always think that.

"But I'll read it again if you want me to," he added. "I hurried through it this first time, but I'll read it again kind of carefully if you want me to." [3]

The line, "It's all right, I guess, but you seem to have missed the point," offers evidence for the view that Hammett was concerned with the relationship between reality and invention. Fiction might seem to miss the point for those concerned with reality, as Hammett had been all his life. [4]

Hellman's later view was that those four paragraphs were all written at the same time and that this was Hammett's decisive ending.

My evidence suggests Hellman might be wrong.

First, the fourth paragraph, "But I'll read it again . . . kind of carefully if you want me to," is in a different typeface, suggesting that it was added to the previous ending at paragraph three: "People always think that."

Second, the words "last page?" scrawled on the original manuscript are not in Hammett's handwriting but in Hellman's and have a question mark. [5]

It seems to be Hellman who designated *that* particular page as the last one. So, it is plausible that Hammett intended *Tulip* to end on the "colored bubbles" line. If the book ended that way, it was provisional and negative, like Hammett's characteristic philosophy. If the book ended on "people always think that," the tone was definite and ordered, like Hellman's philosophy, but negative because the narrator had missed the point. If the book ended with "kind of carefully if you want me to," the ending was provisional, like many Hammett conclusions, but hopeful and positive, a new Hammett slant.

If Hellman found the extra page and it did not contain Hammett's "last page" instruction, then her manipulative decision to make it the final page gave readers a Hammett, who, quite out of character, had an orderly goal.

Some biographers have said that Hammett stopped writing *Tulip* in 1953, but Jo Hammett told me he never stopped writing novels, especially *Tulip*; he merely stopped finishing them. Certainly, as his debilitating diseases of the lungs and liver progressed during the late fifties, he continued to reconstruct his experimental novel. Thirteen days before he died, Hammett still fretted about *Tulip*. On December 27 or 28, 1960, Lily wrote wearily: "[He] spoke of Tulip. Said he couldn't work, had never liked writers who didn't know what they were doing, and now he didn't know what he was doing . . . I am so torn with pity and love and hate and so bored by the struggle."[6]

On February 23, 1955, Hammett was again subpoenaed, this time to testify before the New York State Joint Legislature Committee investigating charitable organizations said to be Communist fronts. Under oath, Hammett said: "Communism to me is not a dirty word. When you're working for the advancement of mankind, it never occurs to you if the guy's a Communist or not."[7]

In 1955, Dash's strength failed dramatically. He could do nothing. Books were piled high on chairs. Unanswered mail crowded the desk. The typewriter remained untouched.

Lily bought a new house in Martha's Vineyard, which included a separate apartment, ideal for a sick guest, but

Dash didn't want to be her guest any more than he wanted to be sick. They argued. He was too ill to hold the pen. He admitted he had been falling down and agreed he couldn't live alone, but told her he would go into a VA hospital. Lily, appalled, would not hear of it. Dash visited her house. Then in August, he had a heart attack on Martha's Vineyard.

Heart disease, added to his lung and liver maladies, enabled him to claim total disability. He felt trapped by creeping disease and literary silence.

In March 1957, James Cooper of the *Washington Daily News*, who interviewed him, recognized how grim his situation was. When the FBI interviewed him, also in March 1957, they estimated that he owed $140,795.96 back taxes. Hammett claimed he was unemployed, had no income, had not received royalties for years, earned only $30 the previous year, had no stocks, shares, or insurance policies, and lived alone, rent-free, in a friend's cottage. He had no personal possessions apart from furniture and clothes. He had started a book called *Tulip* but now could hardly write. His debts included: $1,000 to accountants Bernard Reis Associates, $300 to Burrell's press clippings service, and $15,000 back taxes to New York State. He could see no possible future change in his financial status. Hammett told journalist Cooper: "All my royalties are blocked. I am living on money borrowed from friends."[8]

However, it was not merely finances that were grim.

Poignantly, Hammett told the journalist that he harbored three typewriters to remind himself he was once a novelist. He said he stopped writing because he was repeating himself. He had settled for style with its diminished artistic integrity. He was now learning to be a hypochondriac. Previous biographers have taken these words to be a literary explanation. I believe those lines to be deeply ironic, as was characteristic of Hammett's dealings with the press. What was accurate was that he was able to sit up only for short intervals while a single breath exhausted him.

Distressed at being beholden to Lily, Dash activated his VA pension so he would have some income. On April 29, 1959, he applied for compensation from the Veterans Administration on the grounds of respiratory illness, saying the most he expected to earn that year was $300. Without self-pity, he said he was almost entirely bedridden. In May, they granted him a pension of $131.10 a month.

Lily, who had moved him to her house in New York, gave him her room and dressing room, where he placed the manuscript of *Tulip* on his desk. Some days when Lily was away, she telephoned Dash. Lily's secretary, Selma, saw him rush to the phone, eager to talk to her. Yet, when Lily was at home, he never once showed his affection. They were a strange couple, Selma thought, all emotions deeply buried.

When Lily's highly original play *Toys in the Attic*, about the destructive nature of love, opened in New York in February 1960, Dash bought his first new dinner suit for decades. The indomitable Hammett had devised and helped her construct it, despite his debility. Though X-rays revealed that Dash had inoperable lung cancer, he struggled from bed to the theater to watch it with her. Later, as critics showered the play with awards, Hammett lay prone with *Tulip* on the counterpane.

In spring 1960, when Dash and Lily were at Martha's Vineyard, Loyd Marshall flew east with Jo and their children. Jo, heavily pregnant with Lynn, arrived at Lillian's Vineyard house with Ann, ten, Evan, eight, and Julie, three.

"Lillian was charming to the children," Jo said. Jo's father was lying down, almost asleep after his lung treatment. Dash was dressed casually in charcoal slacks, sports coat, and a paisley neck scarf, looking unbearably thin. Jo felt that it was almost as if he were not there inside the beautiful clothes.

She described his face as paper white and infinitely sad. She said, "I knew that he still loved us, but now it was in a muted, abstracted way. Part of him was already gone."

Hammett told Jo he still tried to use a typewriter but his fingers would not follow his brain's instructions. Jo felt stumped and confused. She said she reached into her "handy Catholic grab-bag" and pulled out a Catholic cliché: "I guess we all have our crosses to bear." The poor young woman felt embarrassed, but her father merely laughed. What he said was: "Boy, how right you are."

By December 31, back in New York City, Dash's stoicism deserted him. Lily's typed note said:

"Tough" and he cried with one tear.
"Tell me."
"No, I'm trying not to think about it."

That night Lily recorded: "This was the night the nurse called me—Dash was irrational."

The next day, January 1, 1961, Dash, unbearably reluctant to go, was taken to the hospital by ambulance. As bearers put him on the stretcher and Lily put on her coat, Dash opened his eyes wide with surprise. Are you coming? he asked. As if she would not, she thought. But Dash was preoccupied with death, not diplomacy.

The next Sunday, at 4:00 a.m. in Lenox Hill Hospital, the night nurse told Lillian to run to the bed and shout loudly in his ear. Lily yelled. Dash, disrupted from dying, opened his eyes, and in that moment she saw his profound terror. Then he fell back into a last coma.

The sixty-six-year-old writer had already left. But it took two more days before his body caught up.

On Tuesday, January 10, 1961, Lily made a stark note: "Dash died about 7:00 a.m. . . . . I arrived about 7:23 a.m."

The cause of death was lung cancer, complicated by emphysema and pneumonia, as well as diseases of the heart, kidneys, liver, spleen, and prostate gland.

Hammett died virtually penniless. For years, his sole income had been his veteran's pension: $131.10 monthly. On his death, there were liens against his estate, mostly for back taxes of more than $220,000. His only assets were his five novels, his many short stories, and the *Tulip* fragment.

On Thursday, January 12, at 4:00 p.m., there was a funeral and memorial. Funeral costs of $931.90 were divided between his estate, which paid $399.37, and the Veterans Administration, which paid $532.53. Dash was dressed in the tuxedo he wore for *Toys*. There were three hundred mourners, but not Jose, Jo, or Mary. Jose wanted to go. "I'm the wife," she said. Her children stopped her, because they could not imagine her sharing a car with Lillian. As Jose cried alone, Lillian's eulogy praised a man who believed in the right to dignity and never played anyone's game but his own. He did not always think well of the society he lived in, but when it punished him, he made no complaint.

On January 13, Dashiell Hammett, veteran of two wars, was buried, as he wished, at Arlington National Cemetery.

In her eulogy there, Hellman said those who leave good work behind would be blessed. Hammett did, and Hammett was. Suddenly, the sun came out. His fiction was reprinted in the United States and kept in print. *Tulip* (as far as he had written it) was between hard covers. Europe discovered Hammett. One hundred and eighty separate translations were published between his death and 1975. In 2013, all his works are in print.

In 1928, young Hammett told Blanche Knopf that his hope was to elevate the mystery genre to literary excellence.

International acclaim today suggests that his hope has been realized.

NOTES

The following abbreviations have been used in the notes:

AK	Arthur Kober
DH	Dashiell Hammett
DJ	Diane Johnson
HRHRC	Harry Ransom Humanities Research Center, University of Texas, Austin
JD	Josephine Dolan (Hammett)
JHM	Jo Hammett Marshall
LH	Lillian Hellman
PF	Peter Feibleman
SC	Sally Cline
SL	*Selected Letters of Dashiell Hammett 1921–1960*, ed. Richard Layman with Julie M. Rivett (Counterpoint, 2001)

Unless otherwise indicated, information about DH family history throughout this book is largely based on SC's interviews and conversations with JHM, 2004–6.

CHAPTER 1

1 See Marion Elizabeth Rodgers, *Mencken: The American Iconoclast* (Oxford: Oxford University Press, 2005), 190.

2 Rodgers, *Mencken*, 16–18.

3 Dashiell Family Records, Baltimore; also St. Mary's County Historical Society.

4 DH, *The Maltese Falcon*, in *The Four Great Novels* (London: Picador,1982), 429.

5 JHM, *Dashiell Hammett: A Daughter Remembers*, ed. Richard Layman with Julie M. Rivett (New York: Carroll & Graf, 2001), 101.

CHAPTER 2

1 Annie Bond Dashiell, born June 3, 1864, daughter of Anne R. Evans and John V. Dashiell; married May 18, 1892; died Baltimore August 3, 1922.

2 DH, "The Gutting of Couffignal," in *The Big Knockover*, ed. with intro. by LH (New York: Vintage, 1989), 33.

3 DH to editor, *Black Mask*, March 1, 1924, *SL*, 25.

4 DH to editor, *Black Mask*, November 1924, *SL*, 27.

CHAPTER 3

1 Cushman was US Public Health Hospital No 59. DH admitted November 6, 1920; transferred February 21, 1921, to Camp Kearney until May 15, 1921.

2 David Fechheimer to SC, 2005. He interviewed the Hammetts October 12, 1975.

3 Fechheimer to SC.

4 Fechheimer to SC; JHM to SC.

5 Richard Layman and Julie Rivett, the editors of *The Selected Letters of Dashiell Hammett*, wrote "February" in brackets because

they believed Hammett had written the wrong date when he wrote "Sept." Their evidence was that Hammett was transferred to Camp Kearney from Cushman Hospital on February 21. This letter obviously was written just after he arrived. Other bracketed dates have the same source.

6 DH to JD, September 27 [i.e., February] 1921; Friday [probably March 4, 1921]; March 9, 1921; March 13, 1921; March 21, 1921; Friday [March 1921]; SL, 8–15.

7 DH, "Seven Pages," unpublished MS, HRHRC.

8 Unpublished MS, HRHRC. JHM refuted the idea that this story was based on a detailed description of Jose, as her mother never used strong language.

9 DH, *Tulip*, in *The Big Knockover*, 333.

10 DH to JD, Friday [March 1921], SL, 15.

11 For the next eight years, he lived in seven different San Francisco apartments, which offered him material for fiction.

12 April 24, 1921, SL, 17. JD and DH were married by Father Maurice J. O'Keefe before two witnesses.

13 Joan Mellen is the sole biographer who suggests that Mary was not DH's daughter. There is *no* evidence from family, interviews, or documents that JD slept with another man.

14 The dates of DH's employment with Samuels are in doubt. DJ suggests he answered a Samuels newspaper advertisement in 1921, may have worked there part-time. SC's evidence from her HRHRC research shows DH worked part-time from 1923, with breaks for sickness, then full-time in 1926.

CHAPTER 4

1 William F. Nolan, *Hammett: A Life at the Edge* (London: Arthur Barker, 1983), 62–63.

2 DH to JD, October 4, 1926, SL, 30–32.

3 DH to JD, November? 1926, SL, 36.

CHAPTER 5

1 *The Thin Man's* context, however, is 1932.

2 SC is indebted to Sinda Gregory for this idea.

3 DH to Editorial Department, Alfred A. Knopf, February 11, 1928, HRHRC.

4 DJ, *Dashiell Hammett: A Life* (New York: Random House, 1983), 70.

5 Sinda Gregory, *Private Investigations: The Novels of Dashiell Hammett* (Carbondale & Edwardsville: Southern Illinois University Press, 1985), 33.

6 DH to Blanche Knopf, March 20, 1928, and April 9, 1928, HRHRC.

7 Richard Layman, *Dashiell Hammett*, Literary Masters, vol. 3 (Detroit: Gale Group, 2000), 26; André Gide, *Journals*, vol. 4: *1939–1949* (Urbana and Chicago: University of Illinois Press, 2000), 191.

8 Samuels revealed (interview with William Nolan, 1930) that DH borrowed several employees' names for his characters. Leggett was the switchboard operator. Employee David Riese became a fictional doctor, and even Mrs. Priestly in silverware appeared as a character.

9 DH, *The Dain Curse*, in *Four Great Novels*, 244.

CHAPTER 6

1 DH to Block, June 16, 1929, July 14, 1929, HRHRC.

2 DH quoted in Don Freeman, "Sam Spade's San Francisco (Seeing the City Through the Author's Eyes)," *Saturday Evening Post*, March 1, 1992.

3 DH, *Maltese Falcon*, in *Four Great Novels*, 401.

4 See Dennis Dooley, *Dashiell Hammett* (New York: Frederick Ungar, 1984).

5 DH, *Maltese Falcon*, in *Four Great Novels*, 404, 569.

6 In 1930, the population of the United States was 122,775,046 (Fifteenth United States Census, conducted April 1930).

7 Franklin Pierce Adams, *The Diary of Our Own Samuel Pepys*, vol. 2 (New York: Simon & Schuster, 1935), 961.

8 Blurb about *The Maltese Falcon* on dust jacket of *The Glass Key* (New York: Knopf, 1931).

9 DH to Herbert Asbury, February 6, 1930, HRHRC.

CHAPTER 7

1 *The Glass Key* was serialized in *Black Mask* in four parts: "The Glass Key," March 1930; "The Cyclone Shot," April 1930; "Dagger Point," May 1930; "The Shattered Key," June 1930.

2 DH to Knopfs, July 19, 1930, August 14, 1930, HRHRC.

3 Richard Layman, *Shadow Man: The Life of Dashiell Hammett* (New York: Harcourt Brace Jovanovitch, 1981), 133; *Dashiell Hammett*, 28.

4 DJ to SC.

CHAPTER 8

1 DH to LH, March 4, 1931, late April 1931, HRHRC.

2 LH, *An Unfinished Woman* (Harmondsworth: Penguin, 1972), 15–16.

3 Emily Hahn interviewed by Joan Mellen, 1993.

4 DJ to SC.

5 DH to LH, April 30, 1931, HRHRC.

6 PF to SC.

7 DH to Knopfs, April 17, 1931, HRHRC.

8 JD to Alfred A. Knopf [probably 1932], HRHRC.

9 AK to his mother, 1932, Wisconsin.

10 AK, "Having Terrible Time," unpublished autobiography, Wisconsin.

CHAPTER 9

1 JHM, *Dashiell Hammett*, 79–80.

2 LH, *An Unfinished Woman* (Boston: Little, Brown, 1969), 270.

3 DH, *The Thin Man* (New York: Knopf, 1934), 192; (Harmondsworth: Penguin, 1935), 188–90.

4 DH to JD, January 22, 1934, *SL*, 82.

CHAPTER 10

1 LH, Introduction, *Four Plays* (New York: Random House, 1942), xiii.

2 DH to LH, about September 17, 1935, HRHRC.

3 "Closed Doors; or The Great Drumsheugh Case," in William Roughead, *Bad Companions* (New York: Duffield & Green, 1931).

4 Quoted in T. Nagamani, *The Plays of Lillian Hellman: A Critical Study* (New Delhi: Prestige, 2001), 43.

5 Until now, no biographer has looked at the strong literary connections and the coincidental themes and patterns between Hellman's play and Hall's novel, but they merit attention, which I gave in my unpublished manuscript "Lillian Hellman and Dashiell Hammett: Memories or Myths," chapter 16: "The Lesbian Hour and Radclyffe Hall." I gave a full analysis of the themes and subject matter in both the play and the book.

Both *The Well* and *The Children's Hour* hold indisputable positions in the history of literary censorship. When the book was published and when the play opened, each was labeled by hostile critics as "melodramatic"; each was banned as obscene (the *Well* ban lasting from 1928 to 1948); yet each has a moral tone, a high-mindedness, and a sense of honor that make nonsense of such judgments. These trials and bans, however, had implications for the artistic merit of each work, which might otherwise have won literary prizes.

6 Irving Drutman, "Miss Hellman and Her First Screen Venture," 1941 clipping, HRHRC.

7 Marilyn Berger, "Profile: Lillian Hellman" (April 1981), in *Conversations with Lillian Hellman*, ed. Jackson R. Bryer (Jackson, Mississippi, and London: University Press of Mississippi, 1986), 240.

8 DH to LH, November 26, 1934, *SL*, 92; October 29, 1934, HRHRC.

9 LH, *Pentimento* (London: Macmillan,1974), 154, 156–7.

10 See DJ, *Dashiell Hammett*, 114–17.

11 DH to LH, 5 November 1934, HRHRC.

12 DH to Knopf, June 4, 1935, HRHRC.

13 DJ to SC.

14 DH to Knopf, September 24, 1935, October 28, 1935, HRHRC.

15 *New York Herald Tribune*, December 14, 1952.

16 Pauline Kael, *For Keeps: Thirty Years at the Movies* (New York: Dutton, 1994), 252.

CHAPTER 11

1 Ed Rosenberg and LH, both quoted in DJ, *Dashiell Hammett*, 125.

2 LH, *Pentimento*, 170–1.

3 DH to Mary Hammett, postmarked January 16?, 1936; to JHM, postmarked January 20, 1936, *SL*, 97.

CHAPTER 12

1 DH to LH, February 1937, *SL*, 116–17.

2 JHM confirmed Hammett went to Jose's house and talked privately to her in the kitchen.

3 DH to LH, September 7, 1937 (telegram); September 9, 1937; December 26, 1937; January 15, 1938; *SL*, 120–1, 127–8, 129.

4 Quoted in Mary Cantwell, "Comparative: Lillian Hellman, J. D. Salinger," *Vogue*, October 1998, 214.

5 Margaret Case Harriman, "Miss Lily of New Orleans," *New Yorker*, November 8, 1941.

6 Dotson Rader, *Cry of the Heart: An Intimate Memoir of Tennessee Williams* (New York: New American Library, 1985), 243.

7 Bennett Cerf, *At Random* (New York: Random House, 1977), 206.

8 Berger, "Profile: Lillian Hellman," 241.

9 DJ to SC; Barbara Sheppard to SC.

10 PF to SC.

11 DJ to SC recalling her conversation with LH.

CHAPTER 13

1 DH to LH, September 27, 1942, *SL*, 184.

2 DH to JD, September 28, 1942; to Mary Hammett, July 15, 1943; *SL*, 185, 209.

3 DH to LH, October 1, 1942; December 14, 1942; January 7, 1943; *SL*, 187–8, 191, 192–3.

4 DJ, *Dashiell Hammett*, 172–3.

5 DH to LH, January 23, 1943; May 9, 1943; July 17, 1943; *SL*, 198–9, 206, 209–10.

6 DH to LH, September 23, 1943; October 17, 1943; *SL*, 228, 242.

7 DH to LH, February 3, 1944; *SL*, 277.

8 DH to LH, March 13–15, 1944; April 17, 1944; *SL*, 301–2, 316.

9 DH to LH, October 26, 1944, HRHRC.

10 DH to LH, November 18, 1944, HRHRC.

CHAPTER 14

1 LH interview with Fred Gardner, in Bryer (ed.), *Conversations with Lillian Hellman*, 107–23.

2 This FBI record of DH's activities in the late 1940s comes from a twenty-page report dated January 17, 1950, submitted to Washington by a special agent in the New York FBI office.

3 DJ to SC.

4 DJ, *Dashiell Hammett*, 221.

5 LH, *Unfinished Woman*, Penguin, 1972, 210.

6 DH to JHM, February 2, 1951, HRHRC.

7 Carl Rollyson interview with Catherine Kober.

8 The label "Second Red Scare" refers to the hounding of left-wing thinkers and writers during the late forties and fifties by anti-Communist crusaders who feared America would be taken over by Communist principles.

9 JHM, *Dashiell Hammett*, 141.

10 Again, evidence found by SC at HRHRC contradicts reviewers' and biographers' suggestions that DH wrote this key speech. Some corrections to LH's early drafts are in DH's handwriting, but later drafts and the final version are undeniably in LH's. Her generosity in allowing it to be thought that DH wrote this speech contributed to the DH legend she was carefully developing.

11 Carl Rollyson, *Lillian Hellman: Her Legend and Her Legacy* (New York and San Jose: toExcel Press, 1999), 312.

12 LH, *Three: An Unfinished Woman, Pentimento, Scoundrel Time* (Boston: Little, Brown, 1979), 282–3.

13 DJ, *Dashiell Hammett*, 247.

14 JHM, *Dashiell Hammett*, 151, 148.

15 DH to JHM, October 18, 1951; *SL*, 564.

16 JHM, *Dashiell Hammett*, 156.

17 For Sale notice, *New York Times*, October 14, 1951.

18 DH to JHM, April 10, 1952; *SL*, 582.

CHAPTER 15

1 *Tulip* was published in 1966 in the collection *The Big Knockover*.

2 DH to LH, August 18, 1952; August 24, 1952; *SL*, 585, 588.

3 DH, *Tulip*, in *The Big Knockover*, 304, 331, 340, 347–8.

4 See Julian Symons, *Dashiell Hammett* (San Diego & New York: Harcourt Brace Jovanovich, 1985), 153.

5 Evidence for LH's handwriting: (a) looped letter *I* seen in LH's scribbled word *file* on letter from Leon Auerbach to Edward Twentyman, July 27, 1966; (b) Greek style *E* seen in LH's scribbled words on Cassell's blurb, May 10, 1966; (c) Greek style *E* seen on letter from Edward Twentyman at Cassell to Robbie Lantz, July 8, 1966; (d) small loopedvs is a constant in her handwriting.

6 LH's typed notes, loose page tucked into 1960 appointments book, HRHRC.

7 Quoted in Martin Duberman, *Paul Robeson: A Biography* (New York: Ballantine, 1989), 430.

8 DJ, *Dashiell Hammett*, 285.

SELECTED BIBLIOGRAPHY

Note: This bibliography is not a full record of works and sources consulted during the author's research, but it includes all those referred
to in the text.

ARCHIVES

Academy of Arts and Letters, New York.

Academy of Motion Picture Arts and Sciences, Margaret Herrick
Library, Los Angeles.

Arthur Kober Papers, Wisconsin Historical Society, Madison,
Wisconsin.

CIA Files, Lillian Hellman, New York.

City of New Orleans Official Archives.

Columbia University, Special Collections and Oral History Archives,

Dashiell Family Records, Baltimore, Maryland.

FBI Files, Hellman, Hammett.

Harry Ransom Humanities Research Center, Austin, Texas: Dashiell
Hammett Collection, Lillian Hellman Collection.

Library of Congress, Washington, DC.

National Archives and Records Administration, Washington, DC.

New York Public Library, Berg Collection.

Newcomb College Center for Research on Women, New Orleans.

Princeton University Library.

Stanford University: William Abrahams Collection.

State Department Library, Washington, DC.

Tulane University, New Orleans: Amistad Research Center; Sophie Newcomb Archives.

University of California, Los Angeles: Special Collections.

University of Southern California, Los Angeles: Special Collections.

University of Washington, Seattle: Letter Collections.

Warner Brothers and Theater Collections, Los Angeles.

William Wyler Southern Methodist University Oral History Project.

Yale University: Beinecke Library Manuscripts and Archives Collections.

WORKS BY DASHIELL HAMMETT

Novels

Red Harvest. New York & London: Knopf, 1929.

The Dain Curse. New York & London: Knopf, 1929; New York: Vintage, 1972.

The Maltese Falcon. New York & London: Knopf, 1930; London: Orion, 2002.

The Glass Key. New York & London: Knopf, 1931; London, Orion, 2002.

The Thin Man. New York: Knopf, 1934; London: Barker, 1934; Harmondsworth: Penguin, 1935.

Woman in the Dark. New York: Vintage, 1989.

The Four Great Novels: Red Harvest, The Dain Curse, The Maltese Falcon, The Glass Key. London: Picador, 1982.

STORY COLLECTIONS

Nightmare Town, ed. Ellery Queen. New York: Spivak, 1948.

The Big Knockover. Ed. with introduction by Lillian Hellman. New York: Random House, 1966; New York: Vintage, 1972. Includes "The Gutting of Couffignal," "Fly Paper," "The Scorched Face," "This King Business," "The Gatewood Caper," "Dead Yellow Women," "Corkscrew," *Tulip*, "The Big Knock-Over."

The Continental Op. Ed. Steven Marcus. New York: Random House, 1974.

OTHER BOOKS

Secret Agent X-9, Books One and Two. Philadelphia: David McKay, 1934. Hammett's comic strip.

(with Robert Colodny) *The Battle of the Aleutians*. Adak, Alaska: Alaska Intelligence Section, Field Force Headquarters, 1944.

Selected Letters of Dashiell Hammett 1921–1960. Ed. Richard Layman with Julie M. Rivett. Washington: Counterpoint, 2001.

MAGAZINE PUBLICATIONS

"The Parthian Shot." *Smart Set*, October 1922.

"From the Memoirs of a Private Detective." *Smart Set*, March 1923.

"Holiday." *New Pearson's*, July 1923.

"Arson Plus." *Black Mask*, October 1,1923.

"Laughing Masks." *Action Stories*, November 1923.

"Bodies Piled Up." *Black Mask*, December 1, 1923.

"The Tenth Clew." *Black Mask*, January 1, 1924.

"Zigzags of Treachery." *Black Mask*, March 1, 1924.

"The House in Turk Street." *Black Mask*, April 15, 1924.

"The Girl with the Silver Eyes." *Black Mask*, June 1924.

"Nightmare Town." *Argosy All-Story Weekly*, December 27, 1924.

"The Whosis Kid." *Black Mask*, March 1925.

"The Scorched Face." *Black Mask*, May 1925.

"Corkscrew." *Black Mask*, September 1925.

"Ruffian's Wife." *Sunset Magazine*, October 1925.

"The Gutting of Couffignal." *Black Mask*, December 1925.

"The Creeping Siamese." *Black Mask*, March 1926.

"The Big Knock-Over." *Black Mask*, February 1927.

"$106,000 Blood Money." *Black Mask*, May 1927.

Red Harvest. In four parts. *Black Mask*: "The Cleansing of Poison-ville" (November 1927); "Crime Wanted—Male or Female" (December 1927); "Dynamite" (January 1928); "The 19th Murder" (February 1928).

The Dain Curse. In four parts. *Black Mask*: "Black Lives" (November 1928); "The Hollow Temple" (December 1928); "Black Honey-moon" (January 1929); "Black Riddle" (February 1929).

"Fly Paper." *Black Mask*, August 1929.

The Maltese Falcon. In five parts. *Black Mask*: September 1929; Octo-ber 1929; November 1929; December 1929; January 1930.

The Glass Key. In four parts. *Black Mask*: "The Glass Key" (March 1930); "The Cyclone Shot" (April 1930); "Dagger Point" (May 1930); "The Shattered Key" (June 1930).

"Behind the Black Mask." *Black Mask*, June 1930.

"A Man Called Spade." *American Magazine*, July 1932.

"Woman in the Dark." In three parts. *Liberty*: April 8, 15, and 22, 1933.

"The Thin Man." *Redbook*, December 1933. Bowdlerized condensed version of the novel.

Secret Agent X-9. Syndicated by King Features Syndicate: daily, Jan-uary 29, 1934 to April 27, 1935.

"This Little Pig." *Collier's.* March 24, 1934.

"A Man Named Thin." *Ellery Queen's Mystery Magazine*, March 1961.

"The Thin Man." Fragment of unfinished novel. *City Magazine*, November 4, 1975.

MOVIE ADAPTATIONS OF HAMMETT'S NOVELS

Roadhouse Nights (1930), *Yojimbo* (1961), *A Fistful of Dollars* (1964) (based on *Red Harvest*).

The Dain Curse (1978).

The Glass Key (1935), *The Glass Key* (1942).

The Maltese Falcon (1931), *Satan Met a Lady* (1936), *The Maltese Falcon* (1941).

The Thin Man (1934), *After the Thin Man* (1936), *Another Thin Man* (1939), *Shadow of the Thin Man* (1941), *The Thin Man Goes Home* (1944), *The Song of the Thin Man* (1947).

Woman in the Dark (1934).

HAMMETT'S SCREENPLAYS

City Streets. Oliver H. P. Garrett from adaptation by Max Marcin. DH original story. Paramount, 1931.

Mister Dynamite. Doris Malloy and Harry Clork. DH original story. Universal, 1935.

Watch on the Rhine. DH. Edited with additional scenes LH. Warner Brothers, 1943.

WORKS BY LILLIAN HELLMAN

Plays and Adaptations

The Children's Hour. New York: Knopf, 1934.

Days to Come. New York: Knopf, 1936.

The Little Foxes. New York: Random House, 1939.

Watch on the Rhine. New York: Random House, 1941.

The Searching Wind. New York: Viking, 1944.

Another Part of the Forest. New York: Viking, 1947.

Montserrat. New York: Dramatists Play Service, 1949.

The Autumn Garden: A Play in Three Acts. Boston: Little, Brown, 1951.

The Lark. New York: Random House, 1956.

Candide, A Comic Operetta Based on Voltaire's Satire. Score by Leonard Bernstein. Lyrics by Richard Wilbur. Other lyrics by John Latouche and Dorothy Parker. New York: Random House, 1957.

Toys in the Attic. New York: Random House, 1960.

My Mother, My Father and Me. Based on Burt Blechman's novel *How Much?* New York: Random House, 1963.

Four Plays: The Children's Hour, Days to Come, The Little Foxes, Watch on the Rhine. Introduction by Lillian Hellman. New York: Random House, 1942.

MEMOIRS

An Unfinished Woman: A Memoir. Boston, New York & London: Little, Brown, 1969; Harmondsworth: Penguin, 1972.

Pentimento: A Book of Portraits. Boston, New York & London: Little, Brown, 1973; London & Basingstoke: Macmillan, 1974.

Scoundrel Time. Boston: Little, Brown, 1976; London & New York: Quartet, 1978.

Maybe: A Story. Boston: Little, Brown, 1980; London, Melbourne & New York: Quartet, 1981.

Three: An Unfinished Woman, Pentimento, Scoundrel Time. With new commentaries by the author. Boston: Little, Brown, 1979.

BOOKS ABOUT HAMMETT

Adams, Franklin Pierce. *The Diary of Our Own Samuel Pepys*, vol. 2. New York: Simon & Schuster, 1935.

Bruccoli, Matthew J. & Richard Layman, eds. *Dictionary of Literary Biography: Documentary Series*, vol. 6: *Hardboiled Mystery Writers Raymond Chandler, Dashiell Hammett, Ross MacDonald.* Detroit: Gale Research, 1989.

Dooley, Dennis. *Dashiell Hammett*. New York: Frederick Ungar, 1984.

Gores, Joe. *Hammett: A Novel*. New York: G. P. Putnam's Sons, 1975.

Gregory, Sinda. *Private Investigations: The Novels of Dashiell Hammett*. Carbondale & Edwardsville: Southern Illinois University Press, 1985.

Herron, Don. *The Dashiell Hammett Tour*. San Francisco: City Lights Books, 1991.

Johnson, Diane. *Dashiell Hammett: A Life*. New York: Random House, 1983.

Layman, Richard. *Dashiell Hammett: A Descriptive Bibliography*. Pittsburgh: Pittsburgh University Press, 1979.

———. *Shadow Man: The Life of Dashiell Hammett*. San Diego, New York, London: Harcourt Brace Jovanovich, 1981.

———. *Dashiell Hammett*. Literary Masters, vol. 3. Detroit: Gale, 2000.

Marling, William. *Dashiell Hammett*. New York: Twayne, 1983.

Marshall, Jo Hammett. *Dashiell Hammett: A Daughter Remembers*. Ed. Richard Layman and Julie M. Rivett. New York: Carroll & Graf, 2001.

Nolan, William F. *Dashiell Hammett: A Casebook*. Santa Barbara: McNally & Loftin, 1969.

———. *Hammett: A Life at the Edge*. New York: Congdon & Weed, 1983; London: Arthur Barker, 1983.

Symons, Julian. *Dashiell Hammett*. San Diego & New York: Harcourt Brace Jovanovich, 1985.

Wolfe, Peter. *Beams Falling: The Art of Dashiell Hammett*. Bowling Green, Ohio: Bowling Green University Popular Press, 1980.

BOOKS ABOUT HAMMETT, HELLMAN, AND THEIR CIRCLE

Bryer, Jackson R., ed. *Conversations with Lillian Hellman*. Jackson, Mississippi, and London: University Press of Mississippi, 1986.

Cerf, Bennett. *At Random.* New York: Random House, 1977.

Cline, Sally. *Radclyffe Hall: A Woman Called John. A Biography.* London: John Murray, 1997; New York: Overlook Press, 1998; paperback: John Murray, 1998.

———. "Lillian Hellman and Dashiell Hammett: Memories or Myths." Unpublished manuscript.

Duberman, Martin Bauml. *Paul Robeson: A Biography.* New York: Ballantine, 1989.

Ephron, Nora. *Imaginary Friends.* New York: Random House, 2002.

Feibleman, Peter. *Lilly: Reminiscences of Lillian Hellman.* London: Chatto & Windus, 1989.

Gide, André. *Journals*, vol. 4: *1939–1949.* Urbana and Chicago: University of Illinois Press, 2000.

Griffin, Alice and Geraldine Thorsten. *Understanding Lillian Hellman.* Columbia: South Carolina University Press, 1999.

Hall, Radclyffe. *The Well of Loneliness.* London: Virago, 1983.

Kael, Pauline. *For Keeps: Thirty Years at the Movies.* New York: Dutton, 1994.

Kessler-Harris, Alice. *A Difficult Woman: The Challenging Life and Times of Lillian Hellman.* New York: Bloomsbury Press, 2012.

Kober, Arthur. "Having Terrible Time." Unpublished autobiography. Madison, Wisconsin: Wisconsin Historical Society Archives.

Martinson, Deborah. *Lillian Hellman: A Life with Foxes and Scoundrels.* New York: Counterpoint, 2005.

Mellen, Joan. *Hellman and Hammett: The Legendary Passion of Lillian Hellman and Dashiell Hammett.* New York: HarperCollins, 1996; New York: HarperPerennial, 1997.

Nagamani, Tenneti. *The Plays of Lillian Hellman: A Critical Study.* New Delhi: Prestige, 2001.

Rader, Dotson. *Cry of the Heart: An Intimate Memoir of Tennessee Williams.* New York: New American Library, 1985.

Rodgers, Marion Elizabeth. *Mencken: The American Iconoclast.* Oxford: Oxford University Press, 2005.

Rollyson, Carl. *Lillian Hellman: Her Legend and Her Legacy.* New York: St. Martin's Press, 1988; San Jose, New York: toExcel, 1999.

Weidman, Jerome. *The Sound of Bow Bells.* New York: Random House, 1962.

ARTICLES ABOUT HAMMETT AND HELLMAN

Atwood, Margaret. "Mystery Writer." *Guardian Saturday Review*, February 16, 2002.

Berger, Marilyn. "Profile: Lillian Hellman" (1979). In Jackson R. Bryer, ed. *Conversations with Lillian Hellman*, 232–73. Jackson, Mississippi, and London: University Press of Mississippi. 1986.

Cantwell, Mary. "Comparative: Lillian Hellman, J.D. Salinger." *Vogue*, October 1998.

Chandler, Raymond. "The Simple Art of Murder." *Atlantic Monthly*, December 1944.

Cline, Sally. "Lillian Hellman and Dashiell Hammett: Treasures in the Archives." *Harry Ransom Humanities Research Center Newsletter*, fall 2007.

Fechheimer, David, ed. *City of San Francisco Magazine*, November 4, 1975.

Freeman, D. "Sam Spade's San Francisco (Seeing the City Through the Author's Eyes)." *Saturday Evening Post*, March 1, 1992.

Gardner, Fred. "An Interview with Lillian Hellman." In Jackson R. Bryer, ed. *Conversations with Lillian Hellman*, 107–23. Jackson, Mississippi, and London: University Press of Mississippi, 1986.

Harriman, Margaret Case. "Miss Lily of New Orleans." *New Yorker*, November 8, 1941.

Johnson, Diane. "Obsession." *Vanity Fair*, January 1985.

Parker, Dorothy. "Oh, Look—Two Good Books!" *New Yorker*, April 25, 1931.

Rae, B. "New Mystery Writers." *The New York Times*, May 3, 1931.

Rivett, Julie M. "On Finding My Grandfather's Love Letters" (unpublished essay), 2001.

Symons, Julian. "Why the Writing Had to Stop." *The New York Times*, May 8, 1983.

INDEX